Prue Carmichael was born in Brighton. She has lived in Spain, Paris and Nepal, and she has led an extensive and varied career in film-making. She writes full time, currently hopping between Notting Hill Gate and Morocco. *Sand* is her second novel.

Also by Prue Carmichael

THE WINDFALL

Sand

PRUE CARMICHAEL

WARNER BOOKS

To Judith and Lahassan

A *Warner* Book

First published in Great Britain in 1998
by Warner Books

Copyright © Prue Carmichael 1998

The moral right of the author has been asserted.

A CIP catalogue record for this book
is available from the British Library.

ISBN 0 7515 2278 3

Typeset by Hewer Text Ltd, Edinburgh
Printed and bound in Great Britain by
Clays Ltd, St Ives plc

Warner Books
A Division of
Little, Brown and Company (UK)
Brettenham House
Lancaster Place
London WC2E 7EN

PROLOGUE

O N A DARK, December afternoon, Flo Lucas
stood motionless outside Marks & Spencer in
Kensington High Street; the pavement deep with
shoppers, held back by the police. At first she thought it
was a bomb scare but if it was, the crowd would not be
laughing. A woman, standing near, hoisted up a small
child to see above the heads. Flo stood on tiptoe but
there was no need. In front of her, led by keepers in
white robes, serenely unperturbed by Christmas lights
and buses, five white camels stalked in an elegant single
file. A man started to whistle, 'We Three Kings'; someone
said they were for the Ryad Exhibition at Olympia and
someone else guessed they were for a pantomime. The
camels passed at their own pace. The buses started to
move slowly, the police stepped aside, the crowd thinned
out, strangers agreeing with each other that it was a most
amazing sight. Flo didn't move; her stomach was tight
with shock, her eyes full of tears. On the whole, she
didn't believe in signs and suchlike, but recently she'd
been aware of coincidences, more and more of them, little
prods, dazzling with significance. And now five white
camels had ambled past her along High Street Ken.

*   *   *

Three days later her Christmas shopping was done. The gifts, mostly for her four-year-old granddaughter, who reminded her severely that she was actually four and a half, were wrapped and delivered. Her cards were written and stamped, the flat was clean and tidy and she'd written little notes for those who needed them. Then she made three appointments for the same day. First, her solicitor, to make her will. He told her she was doing the right thing, that it was most unwise to be intestate. It could lead to complications. She said she quite agreed, intestate sounded horrible, like mangled innards. He was not amused. Then her doctor. She'd known him most of her adult life and was very fond of him because he was the only doctor in the world who still smoked and never scolded her for doing so as well. He offered her a cigarette from a silver box on his desk, told her she was remarkably fit, apart from her little problem of not sleeping well, and renewed her prescription.

It was quicker to walk than take a taxi from Montagu Square to Regent Street. Her collar turned up and hands deep in her pockets, she strode fast, nipping and dodging round the faceless crowds milling past the gilt and glitter of shop windows. There were even more people in Regent Street, shuffling beneath the lights, tinsel stars and reindeer bobbing up and down above them in the cold wind. She missed the lights and stood marooned on an island in the middle of the road, searching the empty faces for one alive and smiling. Just one, it didn't matter who. But they blundered on, grey and pinched and anxious. The rain started as the lights turned green and she swarmed with the others to the far side of the road and hurried

2

on until she reached a heavy plate glass door and pushed it open.

Inside, the heat was almost tropical. Three dark girls strained over their computers. At the far end of the room an older woman sat at a desk, talking on the phone. Flo recognised her. She was a little plumper and a little grey now, but then so was she. Flo sat down on a blue leather chair and waited until eventually the woman finished her call, hung up and looked at her.

'Mrs Lucas?' The woman recognised her too, smiled and handed her an envelope, saying it had been a long time. Flo nodded, took the envelope, wished her a happy Christmas and left before her courage failed. Outside the rain had turned to sleet but, despite high heels, she beat an American couple laden with bags from Liberty's and hopped into a taxi, rightly theirs. The cabbie was on her side, speeded off and made a sharp left before their stupefaction had time to turn to outrage.

'Home,' she told him as they joined the tail end of the traffic, at a standstill in the hissing rain.

PART ONE

'WHAT ARE YOU doing for Christmas?' As there was no reply to this bleak question Alex assumed Flo must be in the garden, still having trouble believing that her cordless phone worked out of doors.

'Flo? Flo? Are you there?'

'Yes,' replied Flo, who was examining a weeping nozomi. The year before she'd lost one: overnight the leaves had all curled up and the tiny pink flowers turned crisp and brown. In her hand she held a can of something that promised instant death to greenfly, mould, spider mite, thrips, leaf-hoppers and a lot of other nasty-sounding things.

'Flo?'

'Yes, I'm still here.'

'I said,' repeated Alex from her mother's cordless phone in Maida Vale, 'what are you doing about Christmas? It's in the papers already.'

'Christmas?' What on earth could anyone do about Christmas? 'Dunno. I haven't thought about it yet.' But she had, once or twice, since the days had started getting noticeably shorter. 'It's only August.'

August Bank Holiday and for two days whistles

shrilled, steel bands clanged and beer cans clattered in the gutter as the Carnival thumped through the last Monday of another muggy London summer. Flo closed the shutters of her front windows and retreated from the crowds invading Notting Hill, ignored the revellers and shunned the wriggling, prancing dancers.

'It's not what it used to be,' was her tepid excuse for being a killjoy. 'And if you can't join it, beat it!' Usually she did, to friends in France, but more often to Alex in Spain. This year, somehow, it hadn't happened. Alex, tired of life in the sun – 'It's not what it used to be' – cited water shortages, polluted beaches and a new Fascist mayor as her reasons for putting her little villa on the market and stretching out her annual visit to her mother.

'What are the girls doing? For Christmas, that is?' Even as she asked, Alex knew the answer. Flo's girls hadn't been home for three years.

'Do you know there's been an earthquake in Cuba?' Flo fended her off with the only thing she could remember from her own Sunday papers. 'A big one . . . a very big one.' It worked. Alex stopped talking about Christmas. For a while they gossiped, and discussed Alex's chances of selling up in the dreadful financial climate, the chaos of the suffering world, their despair over politicians and all the other crooks and imbeciles in charge and the futility of trying to do anything about it. When world events ran out Flo asked, 'So what else have you been up to?'

Alex spent her time in London using it the way it should be used, she said. Which meant speeding from galleries to cinemas, fringe theatres, concerts and spending more money than she could afford stocking up at Boots and bookshops. Her social life, less hectic

these days, was spent in cheerful tête-à-tête reunions
with ex-lovers, usually available for an auld-lang-syne
encounter or two, depending on their marital status
and the state of that status.

'I had lunch with Roger. You remember him? Just
lunch. His new wife's only twenty-four. Can you imag-
ine? Went to that new thing at the Curzon . . . terribly
depressing. I was going to stay with Chris in Suffolk
but something came up. Got my new contact lenses . . .
and that's about it. Oh, I hate August, such a cul-de-sac
of a month. Everyone's away!' Flo wasn't. Neither were
the hordes bouncing around in Notting Hill.

'What's Millie doing? And your mum? For Christmas,
that is?' Absurd and infuriating, 'Away in a Manger' had
started up in Flo's head.

'Mum's going on another cruise, Madeira or somewhere, and Millie . . .' There was a slight pause. 'Millie's
going to her boyfriend's parents in Dundee.'

So that was it. Millie's first independent Christmas.
For Alex, who usually free-wheeled nonchalantly from
one week to the next, it had seemed unusual that
she should be focusing on something months away
but Millie Had Made Plans. It was three years now
since Flo's girls Had Made Plans, or rather, decided
not to. They both had good jobs, they were making
it, or so she was led to believe by their frequent,
if brief, transatlantic calls from New York and Los
Angeles. Times were tough, good jobs hard to come
by and in America, they explained, you had to cling
on like a limpet or there was someone else at your
desk overnight and you were out on your butt.

'Bum,' Flo suggested, as she did whenever they
said elevator instead of lift and sidewalk instead of
pavement.

'Christmas is no big deal here, Mum. Just one day.' Sweet reason told Flo it was ridiculous for them to spend a fortune on fares only to rush back after Boxing Day.

'You're right,' she told them. 'It is only another *day*.' But the Day itself, she remembered as being one of the longest of her life.

'He's a sweet young man and absolutely crazy about her. Should be lovely, Scotland in the snow.' Alex was still prattling on about Millie's new boyfriend. But to Flo, who was quick about such things, it came over a bit flat.

'Come to supper,' she suggested on an impulse.

'But what about the Carnival? Will I get through?' A daft question as Alex could have picked her way daintily through the Charge of the Light Brigade.

'You'll be OK. They pack up early these days.' Flo took the phone away from her ear. The din had died down and the crowds, shepherded by mounted police, had started kicking their beer cans back to the main road.

She clicked off the phone, gave the little rose tree a final squirt and walked slowly towards the house, dead-heading as she went. Only a few streets from where she grew up, she'd lived on the rambling ground floor flat of the double-fronted villa since the tall house in Chester Street became too tall when the girls left for America. It was a relief to Flo to quit the sterile, silent streets of Belgravia and return to the raffish familiarity of the Portobello Road, even though it was not nostalgia that drew her back but the garden. Paved with York stone and guarded either side by mature horse-chestnut trees it was, for London, an impressive space. The estate agent had claimed the trees as a feature even though they were actually in the neighbouring gardens either

7

side. Reluctantly, he had admitted that her prospective garden was in need of attention.

'You're right,' she had said, looking at the leathery, labour-saving shrubs, stuck uncomfortably in the grey soil.

'And that could go.' He had pointed at a green wooden water butt with a hole where the water seeped out.

'Oh, I don't know.' She liked it and decided to let it stay.

'I expect you've got green fingers.' The estate agent had pushed on, talking about wisteria and magnolia. She didn't know if she had green fingers or not, never having dealt with anything more challenging than bunches of flowers from Pulbooke and Gould, a few expensive pot plants and an avocado stone in a jam-jar on the kitchen windowsill. But she said yes, she'd take it.

She learned about topsoil, compost, mulch, bonemeal and backache. She learned that hostas double their size every year but were prone to slugs. She learned that slugs could be vanquished to a beery death with little saucers of Special Brew, that clematis and vines should be pruned back hard and, if one was lucky, plumbago could survive an English winter. And that, no matter how hard one tried, August came and the garden began to flag. Everything seemed to have already started to retreat into the earth for winter. The delphinium spires were grey, the creamy foxgloves, set against the dark camellia leaves, were naked spikes, and the roses, which had been so good at midsummer, competing with the smell of huge, white Casablanca lilies, were definitely past their best. Mourning the loss of colour, she dragged the hose and sprinkler towards a puny second flowering of the Gloire de Dijon rambler and turned on the tap. Of course, there were still the geraniums to be thankful for, so generous and undemanding in the big pots she'd lugged back from Spain. They'd gone on right into November the year before. November, with the consolation of catalogues, decisions as to what could stay and what must go and experiments to consider with things marked 'rare, difficult to raise, but worthwhile'. Backed by an unexpected rainbow from the spray, she caught sight of her reflection in the French windows. Her hair was sticking to her head, her hands were filthy and her ugly, flowered blouse was buttoned up all wrong. A blouse Alex wouldn't be caught dead in. Tight as money was, Alex believed that one should always look one's best, even clearing out a drain. 'Not for other people . . . for oneself!' she protested if Flo teased her.

Tearing off the awful Liberty mistake, she hurried indoors to find something light for supper, wishing she could have her roots done and lose about eight pounds before Alex arrived.

'We should have gone, you know,' Alex called out from the sitting room as the news was finishing on a token up-beat note. The Carnival committee and the police agreed that it had all gone off very well. Only one stabbing, forty arrests for outrageously blatant drug-pushing, twenty-three cases of heatstroke and a small fire at a food stall on the corner of Colville Terrace which caused momentary panic but no injuries. Minor crimes such as theft, drunken harassment and the temporary loss of small children were not mentioned, all being part of the fun. Alex finished the last flake of her smoked trout, dropped her untouched roll back into the breadbasket and stretched out prettily on Flo's big sofa. She liked Flo's home, the sense of ease, the golden pools of light here and there, creams, corals, turquoise, strong furniture in dark woods and thick, white curtains framing the last blue light of the garden. In her opinion, the only things the room lacked were a few decent pictures. Alex worked in an art gallery in Marbella discovering local talent, organising exhibitions and selling on commission. Once in a while she found a bargain in a back street of Seville or Granada but these were rare and sold off at Sotheby's for herself. In the past she'd offered one or two to Flo at a very good price, but Flo was adamant, hanging only faded textiles on her walls.

'Nobody signs them,' was the odd reason for her preference.

'Anything worth watching?' Flo came back from the kitchen with the coffee and another bottle of wine as Alex flicked through all five channels.

'Nothing. Where's the TV guide?' But she'd thrown it out with the rest of her half-read Sunday papers.

'I don't know why you bother to buy them.'

'Nor do I.' Flo refilled their glasses. 'They're so contaminating. Habit, I suppose.'

'This is nice.' Alex sipped her wine and looked at the label on the bottle.

'It's one of John's,' Flo told her.

'John? How's he doing these days?'

Fate had thrown Flo and Alex together on the steps of the law courts, both having got divorced half an hour beforehand, both diving for the same taxi in the rain and both feeling strangely unencumbered. They had compared remarkably cheerful notes and had had a drink at the Savoy. Since then, out of a sense of continuity rather than genuine interest, they sometimes asked about the milestone men in each other's lives. Like John and Donnie, ex-husbands and fathers of their children. Not that Flo really needed to ask about Donnie, who was still a megastar, the nearest thing America would ever have to Sasha Distel, who these days was forever declaring publicly and most embarrassingly the joys of his sobriety to the media. When Flo was starting on her second batch of nappies and giving meaningless little dinner parties in Belgravia, Alex was doing what every self-respecting Flower Child would do: leaving home and Maida Vale at sixteen, going on the road with a band and marrying the lead singer. He was called Reg then, but soon changed his name to Donnie, developed a passable mid-Atlantic drawl and wrote a song that shot to number one. In the early days he used to dedicate his songs to his new bride. Not that she ever had one featuring her name, such as Layla or Suzanne, probably due to the difficulty of finding anything to rhyme with Alex, but she'd blush when he sang them and hide from his fans in his blacked-out six-door Cadillac. They were heady times. Then Millie was born and Alex stopped going on the road and became a stay-at-home wife in Weybridge. Although Millie was her pride and her delight, Weybridge could be pretty boring. Alex had a philosophy about life and men unchanged by the passage of time.

'Pain or pleasure . . . a ratio of one to ten.' Donnie's ratings dropped to less than zero when uppers, downers and under-age fans took over. It was time for all concerned to move on and move out. But even in those days he was famous in the music world for what was politely called his business acumen.

'For which,' remarked Alex in the light of time, 'read chronic anal retention.' Their lawyers battled it out for two long years but hers was no match for his and apparently had never heard of community property, even though they were married in Las Vegas. He managed a minimal income for her and Millie and the house in Weybridge. Then he had the nerve to send her a bill so large she had to sell the house to pay it. Donnie married a few more times (years he now described as 'being in the wilderness') and finally shacked up with his therapist, who lured him from destructive substances and Southern Comfort and encouraged him to go into real estate in La Hoya as a sideline. Due to his frequent quoting of the Bible, it was suspected that he'd been Born Again but this had yet to be confirmed.

'John?' Flo frowned, as if trying to remember who Alex could mean. 'Oh, John. He's doing very well, I think.' She held her glass up to her eye and looked at the quiet room through the red glow. *The cattle were lowing* . . . Strange what things one forgot and what ridiculous things one remembered. Like that last horrible Christmas in Chester Street. The year the turkey leaped for freedom out of its pan and slithered in a sizzling lump across the kitchen floor. The year John had met his Frenchwoman at a commodities conference in Singapore. Was it tin? Or was it coffee? Or was it Hong Kong? Not that it mattered now or even then. They'd entertained anyway, 'for the sake of the children'. And the parents (his, since hers, even in their seventies, were beavering away at some archaeological dig in Tasmania). Once she looked up entertaining in the dictionary. It said, 'Entertain: Amuse, occupy agreeably, receive with hospitality, welcome, cherish.' There'd been an awful lot of receiving with hospitality

12

in Chester Street. Like seventeen for Christmas lunch. But that other word, cherish, had caused her eyes to fill with sudden tears. But the welcome had gone without a hitch. No one was any the wiser about the turkey, once she'd skewered it, slapped it on to a platter and shoved its stuffing back inside. The table had been exquisite, a shimmer of green and gold and the meal perfect, right down to the last, silly walnut.

'Guess!' John had challenged the male guests from his end of the table. The wine game. They played it every year. It was already poured, garnet red in crystal glasses, the bottles swaddled in white napkins. The idea was for the men to guess the name of the vineyard, the vintage, the grape and, as far as Flo could make out, the name of the man who made the ruddy barrel. After much sipping and thoughtful frowns, the men were still flummoxed.

'B . . . C . . .' John had given them a heavy hint.

'Really, darling?' Uninvited and out of sheer wilfulness, Flo had chipped in from her end of the table. 'It's kept terribly well.' It wasn't very funny and the guests thought it best to ignore such flippancy but the girls, who were at that age, had convulsed with giggles. The muscle in his cheek throbbing, John had glared at them and looked as if he was going to send them to their rooms. For two pins, Flo would have gone with them.

'Beychevell,' he had pronounced, ignoring his wife with the contempt she merited. There were murmurs of appreciation all round for such a seriously respected claret. Flo had left the table before the crackers. On Boxing Day, John had moved into his club. He was generous, due to jute. Or was it coffee? Flo got the girls, the house in Chester Street and an adequate settlement for, as John put it, services rendered. He had married his Frenchwoman, bought a château near Bordeaux with a defunct vineyard, which under his supervision had no option but to flourish. Every so often he sent Flo and the girls a case of wine to prove it.

Alex roused herself and prowled along the bookshelf that ran the length of the room, glad to note that the heavies, Camus, Sartre and all those gloomy Russians Flo had had a go at, had been relegated to the top shelf. The next shelf was filled with boxfiles, each numbered but every one marked miscellaneous. There were plenty of new gardening books and a good selection of novels. All the *How To Get Your Life Right in a Week* books were gone, probably to Oxfam for other wretched women to find marked-down magical solutions to their lives. Like Flo, most of Alex's friends had got married young, had children and stopped dead. Then, in those swiftly liberating times, got divorced but, ill-equipped for brilliant careers, stopped dead again. Those who didn't repeat the same marital mistake out of fear, loneliness and redundancy, opted for therapy. Some were now dishing it out themselves. Alex didn't believe in all that. Neither did Flo. And from a certain amount of reading and observation came to the conclusion that analysis, be it Jungian, Freudian, Transactional, Holistic or Humanistic (whatever that was), came down to tearing the layers of life away from the beginning to the present and, like peeling an onion, one cried a lot.

'But why?' she asked those who did. 'Whatever for? It doesn't seem to change anything.' With infuriating condescension or smug understanding they told her that it wasn't meant to *change* anything.

'Then why do you do it? It takes for ever, costs a fortune and you end up with an onion in bits!' They told her she was in denial.

'It's *what* happens, not *why*. There isn't time for why.'

Alex quite agreed. Flo's means of finding out what rather than why took her to an occasional visit to a clairvoyant. Fairground psychology, she called it, convinced it was as effective as, and certainly more fun than, harrowing visits to a shrink. The Tarot, the crystal balls and palm prints, all agreed that she was going to make astounding changes in her middle years. But the middle years were here and so far, apart from switching courses at the City Lit from time to time and having a few highlights in her tawny hair, she hadn't noticed anything spectacular.

'Got any videos?'

'Nothing new.' Flo searched for her glasses under the sofa cushions and through the junk mail on her desk, before finding them in the pocket of her housecoat where they'd been since she read the sell-by date on the coleslaw. Her New York daughter used to scold her for fumbling.

'It's so ageing, Mum.' But for Flo, lighters, cigarettes, lipsticks, keys and lists were never where they were before.

'I've fumbled all my life.' But now she was aware of it and tried not to.

'Of course,' remarked Alex, still at the bookshelf and leafing through an atlas, 'we could always go somewhere.'

'When?'

'Christmas.'

'Why do you keep saying that?' *The Little Lord Jesus no crying He makes.*

'What do you want me to call it? Yuletide? The Festive Season?'

'It doesn't matter what you call it.'

'Well, we could, couldn't we?'

'Could what?'

'Oh, Flo. Go somewhere!'

'Like where?'

'I don't know, anywhere.' Alex slipped the atlas back.

'Not a cruise!' Flo was horrified.

'Of course not, we'd be the youngest by twenty years, maybe thirty.'

It occurred to Flo that perhaps that mightn't be a bad idea for a change. Recently she'd felt old, if that was what it meant to wake every morning feeling that her fingers were being gently prised away from hope. Hope that the next day might be different as she rushed through it, as though trying to cheat time by getting there first then waiting in a vacuum for it to catch up with her. Only when sliding into sleep did she feel the relief of escaping the next minute and the next and her own relentless expectation of a future that never seemed to arrive. Adult education and the City Lit left her better informed but all the duller for it. Work was supposed to be the antidote, but there again, the research she sometimes did for Halliday and Ross she could do in her sleep. It was, she'd decided, a natural and uncomfortable consequence of getting older. If she'd admitted this to Alex, she'd have got short shrift.

Alex didn't believe in age. She lived life as she felt it, which swung from twenty-four to thirty-five which Flo put down to natural optimism, a happy childhood and vitamins. Of course they were both too sensible to talk in dates and numbers, or use that silly thirty-something, forty-something dodge. Things sank, things spread. Lines appeared from nowhere on horrible video screens in banks and supermarkets and especially in the broad backs of glassed-off taxi drivers. It was inevitable but as unnecessary to fear, flaunt or even discuss as one's bowel movements. Natural or not, it didn't mean giving up on maintenance which Flo, of late, seemed to have done. A pity, Alex thought, since she had a trump card of which she seemed totally unaware. She had good legs, amber eyes, high cheekbones which age could never destroy, tawny hair, but there was that inexplicable magic in her genes that made it possible for her to look no more than twenty-eight. Even, surprisingly, when she was very happy or very sad. Like now, barefoot, searching for a video and looking a little like a nicer-natured Louise Brooks.

'What about *Zorba*?' Flo asked from the depths of the cupboard.

'Seen it.'

'*Streetcar*?'

'Too hot.'

'*Carmen*?'

Flo was running out of ideas. Everything she'd got Alex had seen a thousand times in English and several times in Spanish.

'Aha!' she cried, sitting back on her heels. 'Bet you haven't seen this.'

The Garden of Allah was one of her earliest memories. When her archaeologist parents were off digging up things in climates deemed unsuitable for a very young child, Flo was cared for by her grandmother who had a thing about George Raft and a very low tolerance level with nannies. No sooner had she arrived at the house in Lansdowne Road, in an astrakhan coat and galoshes and carrying a wind-up gramophone, the hapless woman in charge was dismissed within forty-eight hours, as being unsuitable.

'Too much starch, no style,' was the usual reason given, which gained Flo's parents a terrible reputation with every domestic agency in London, who had given up bothering to find a replacement until their return and then only after profuse apologies from her mother. Today Flo would be called an abandoned child, the social workers banging on the door, but in those days there was no such thing as bonding. You were dealt a hand at birth and got on with it. She got plenty of postcards of pyramids and squat earth goddesses and was only too happy to stay up until all hours listening to Benjamino Gigli singing 'Over there' to the troops in the First World War.

'A collector's item, my child,' declared her grandmother, winding away and replacing the little gold needle in the gramophone head. 'As indeed, is this,' which was usually Grace Moore singing 'One Night of Love'. Her grandmother's passion for romantic music was matched only by her addiction to the cinema. Flo often thought it was a pity she hadn't lived to see the miracle of video. But then, perhaps it wouldn't have been the same as the plush red and gold glories of the cinemas in Leicester Square and the Haymarket. From the age of three, after peering down from the dress circle to see where the man playing the organ had gone, she was exposed to the tantrums of Bette Davis, the murderous inclinations of Joan Crawford and the velvety brooding of James Mason. God alone knew how her grandmother had smuggled her in past the box office. But *The Garden of Allah* was no problem. It was made in 1936 and when her grandmother discovered it having a re-run at the Electric Cinema in Portobello Road she was as exultant as her parents probably were, falling upon a shard or a bit of flint.

'One of the greatest films of all time. It's a bit of a fleapit so you'd better go to the lavatory first.' Flo was swooped into the night, given an ice cream in a tub with a little wooden spoon and they sat through it twice. She remembered it best because it was in colour. And because the walk home was so endless that her grandmother had to carry her for the last part.

'What is it?'

'I'm not going to tell you.'

Flo slipped the cassette into the video and settled herself down next to Alex who was curled up like an elegant cat. She lit a cigarette. Alex slid the ashtray up to her end of the low table.

'I hope it's funny.'

'Not exactly,' admitted Flo as the opening credits rolled to the swoop and swell of music reaching one unbearably romantic climax after another. 'Here we go! Oh, wait!' She leaped up and rushed into the kitchen for some chocolate mints.

'Oh, sit down and relax.'

Flo returned just as Marlene Dietrich, in a convent of no known denomination, was asking the Mother Superior if she could become a nun. The Mother Superior, wise woman, suggested that this was not an ideal vocation for Marlene. Marlene, with tears in her eyes, whispered, 'What shall I do, Reverend Mother? What shall I do?'

After a reflective pause, the amiable nun replied that life was full of interesting things.

'Perhaps the desert, my child,' she said, becoming more specific.

'The desert?' Marlene's eyebrows arched even higher before she asked breathlessly what she would find there.

'Perhaps yourself,' replied the Reverend Mother, a trifle ambiguously.

'She finds Charles Boyer.' Flo couldn't resist.

'Shhh,' said Alex.

The next scene found Marlene beside a stack of luggage looking elegantly bewildered in a railway station somewhere in North Africa. She was wearing an uncreased travelling suit in beige and a hat with brown chiffon looped under her exquisite chin.

'Edith Head,' said Alex knowledgeably and in her excitement forgot herself and ate a tiny bit of chocolate.

'Ernst Dryden,' corrected Flo without taking her eyes off the screen. Marlene's adventures then took her to a hotel (Hôtel des Dunes) where now, draped in pale grey chiffon, she gazed down from her balcony at the hubbub of camels, donkeys, street vendors, going about their business among the palm trees. Her next stop was a seedy night club with a belly dancer where she ran into Charles Boyer, whom she had already spotted in a bit of a state on the train. Kismet! But before marrying him and setting out for some unspecified reason to the desert, she was warned by a soothsayer, with rolling eyes and shaking hands, that doom lay ahead. But she didn't listen. In each scene, her impeccable clothes became more diaphanous and clinging as she, languid and distant, paced up and down the sand dunes looking for Charles Boyer, who had gone missing. Unbeknown to her, although not to the audience, he was a monk who had jumped over the wall, taking the precious secret of his monastery's liqueur with him. The end was sad. Marlene's charms were not enough to hold him, and with tarnished vows he went back to his monastery to the accompaniment of a thousand violins. Flo had finished the chocolate and Alex the wine as the video started to rewind.

'I expect she went back to her convent,' said Flo, after a moment.

'Nah,' said Alex, stretching. 'He'd be back.'

Flo lifted the curtain and looked out on to the street. It was quiet now, with only a few staggering stragglers. A floorboard creaked overhead, which meant her upstairs neighbour was back from his weekend and tomorrow would be normal. Still looking out, she remarked, 'They peed behind the hedge last year.'

'How revolting.' Alex was combing her hair, a sure sign she was on the move.

'Do you want a cab?' Flo dialled for one. It came in moments. 'She'll be right out,' she answered the intercom and opened the front door.

'I enjoyed that,' Alex said as they pecked each other on the cheek and gave each other little pats on the arm.

'So did I.'

'You know something?' She paused in the hallway and looked back at Flo.

'What?'

'We could always go to Morocco.' As they did so often, they said it at the same time.

'I'll call you first thing,' promised Alex.

* * *

Overnight the weather changed; a few leaves chased each other round the garden and a couple blew in through the open French windows. It was definitely cooler. Flo shut the windows, admitting that the sharp little stab on her top gum really was toothache. Not the throbbing, wincing sort but it was definitely there. Her dentist, a hearty young Australian with a year-round tan, had grim plans up ahead for what he called a bridge.

'This won't take a moment,' he'd lied during her last full-scale session with probes, drills and injections. His sense of passage of time was very different to hers. When he'd suggested that she come into the office for a little chat about the proposed bridge, she'd protested. But he, ignoring any possible emotional turmoil over losing four front teeth and its implications, had assured her that she'd realise a bridge was the best thing that could happen in her life. With grave doubts about the deep divide of their way of looking at things she had fled. Reluctantly, she now looked up his number and reached for the phone. It rang. She half expected it to be Alex, but it was a bit early for her. It was Halliday and Ross, from whom she hadn't heard for nearly eight months.

'Everybody Loves a Winner!' A new young man who introduced himself as Damian pronounced the theme of their next conference.

'Where?' She picked up a pencil.

'Venue,' corrected Damian, 'Scarborough.'

'Scarborough?' Before, it was Bangkok, Rome or Washington.

'Everyone's cutting back. We're lucky to get this one,' he told her indiscreetly. But she already knew that. Big companies no longer spent thousands, even millions, on week-long jamborees for their sales reps. Sales reps were thankful to have a job, without being wooed with prizes and expensive trips to faraway places.

'What are you looking for?'

Damian told her they wanted winners. 'High Achievers.' For example, someone who had sailed round the world single-handed, preferably a woman. 'Blind?' he suggested hopefully. Perhaps she could find Olympic Gold medalists (British), an Oscar winner, a Nobel prizewinner and someone who had climbed Everest.

'What about the man who skied down it?'

'Good girl!' exclaimed Damian. Considering he was probably no more than twenty-three, Flo thought she took this rather well.

'When?'

'A week.' They always said that but the conference wasn't until January.

'I'll try.'

She put down the phone and ran her tongue behind her tooth. Winners. She pulled several of the boxfiles down from the shelf, blew off the dust and spread them on the floor. The LA daughter was appalled by her boxes.

'Those lists, Mum, they're Neanderthal. Why don't you get a computer?'

'What for?' Flo was baffled. She worked from home, making phone calls paid for by Halliday and Ross, securing the presence of, as it happened this time, high achievers. She also had to find them witty after-dinner speakers. Usually they wanted Billy Connolly but more often than not it would be Dennis Norden. The after-dinner speaker was paid a fat fee and five-star expenses for self (and partner) to say a few nice things about refrigerators, computers or pharmaceuticals and hand out prizes to the Rep of the Year.

'Your work,' insisted the LA daughter.

'My work is talking to people, being persuasive.'

'Well, other things.' Like what? Bills? The gas, electricity, community charge, water rates, credit cards. At most ten which could just as easily be shoved into a dressing-gown pocket then boxfiled before eventually being paid.

'No, darling, I think not.' For Flo the world of technology was denied, other than the video, and that had taken all the imaginative skills of the young man who sold it to her for her grasp. But she tried. She enrolled at the City Lit for a course of computer literacy. After the third week, her brains had stuck together like boiled sweets in a bag and her tutor agreed that perhaps it was best to call it a day. His name was Duncan. He had a long, black ponytail and was writing a book on Virtual Reality. He'd explained the principles again and again, as simply as he could, assuring her that a child of three would get it in a flash, then was unnerved to see a grown woman so near to tears.

'I'll see if I can get you a refund,' he said kindly. 'I've never had a genuine technophobe before.' She cheered up when told there was a name for it and rang the LA daughter that night to tell her.

'Bullshit, Mum, a child of three could get it.' Who were these three-year-old children? Flo stuck to her lists and boxes and came up with the goods. Halliday and Ross were never aware of her machineless status, but if she could get Felicity Kendal to go to Prague and say a few nice things to reps who sold freezer units to Bird's Eye, it was all right with them. Prague was one thing, but Scarborough? The first person to call was the cheery, beery editor of *Sports Magazine* who knew everybody and their agents and always called her Petal. She opened her first file, the one with the old phone books. The red one fell open at R. R for Robert.

In the first flurry of freedom after the divorce, she'd had a few propositions, mostly from friends of John who professed they'd always fancied her. This was unexpected and sometimes flattering, but she shied off. Although among their friends and most of their acquaintances it was commonplace for husbands and wives to change partners, move to another house streets away from the first one, acquire each other's children and continue going to the same dinner parties, to Flo it felt incestuous. She wanted not someone new, but a life that was different. All the magazines said it was vital for an independent woman to have at least twenty orgasms a week (multiple). If one didn't, one was doing something wrong. Or he was. All her friends did, protesting too loudly and too laughingly how wonderful freedom was. But she noticed that it was the transience of these wonderful affairs which pitched most of them into their therapies.

Eventually she met Gerard. He was a sleek and cultured Frenchman who told her she was a golden coin in a room full of tarnished pennies. He commuted between Paris and London, buying and selling objets d'art so rare, they usually landed up in museums or with anonymous Belgian collectors. He was a wonderful cook and raconteur. In fact he never stopped talking. Although she never dared to cook for him she boned up on Camus, Sartre and de Beauvoir, to whom he referred as if they were old friends he'd been dining with the night before. But it didn't last long. He was French and she didn't expect it to. Then there was Frederic, an archaeologist and fervent admirer of her father. Like her father, he was always going away. Later came a journalist, who never went away and wanted to move in with her after the first few days. She had to stretch her mind now to remember his name. From none of these relationships did she come away either dazed or disenchanted. Robert was different. A milestone man.

She met him in a lift, going up. It was, she realised, the first time she'd met anyone without being introduced.

'You mean he picked you up,' said Alex.

'No!' protested Flo. 'We just happened to meet in a lift.' She was on her way to Halliday and Ross, pleased with the research she'd turned up and having got Bertolucci and Sophia Loren for a conference in Rome. She'd had her hair done and was humming the first few bars of 'Travellin' Light'. Robert got in the lift and stood beside her looking at the ceiling. She thought she caught a slight scene of lemons. As she got out, he stood aside for her then in a low whistle picked up the melody of 'Travellin' Light', pitch perfect. She turned and smiled at him. He was going to Halliday and Ross too. But only for a moment. He asked her out to lunch and swore he'd never done anything like that in his life before. When she got to know him better she knew that he was telling the truth. Also that he'd had his hair cut that morning too. A few days later he asked her out to dinner. He was married. He had two very expensive teenage children and a mortgage on a large house in Greenwich that was devouring him.

'And his wife?' asked Alex, when Flo finally admitted how it was she'd lost nearly a stone and spent a fortune on clothes.

'He doesn't get on with her very well.'

'Oh, please,' groaned Alex.

'But it's true,' Flo insisted.

It lasted nearly two years. Two years when she looked forward to the day ahead, and laughing, even at his funny cryptic messages on her answerphone when he had to cancel. But time was an enemy and Greenwich a hell of a place to get back to at night and there was a limit on how many times he could use the excuse of a bomb scare on the Underground.

They managed one weekend away, but only one. After endless uncertainty on his part, they flew to Paris in time for lunch, hired a car and drove to Fontainebleau. Their room overlooked the gardens of the palace. They stayed in bed all morning and most of the afternoon. Giggling, Flo told him that she wouldn't mind filling in a questionnaire for *Cosmopolitan*. They got up and went to the Django Reinhardt concert on a little island further up the river. They listened to gentle jazz, ate roast chicken and drank red wine. Monday morning at the airport, Air France announced that due to Air Traffic Control, there was a considerable delay. Robert read the *Independent* and looked as if he were waiting for tumbril. They took off hours late, sat in silence on the plane and made their separate ways at Heathrow. Later on, in August, he went to Brittany on the family holiday and broke his leg shrimping in a rock pool.

'What do you mean, shrimping? I thought your kids were past all that.'

'They are.'

'Then what the hell were you doing shrimping?' He told her that his wife had gone antique hunting and both the children had been sleeping off a late night at a disco.

'I was bored. I think I missed you,' he admitted sheepishly. 'So I broke my leg.' She put his reasoning down to painkillers but brittle secrets break too and for Robert this was a sign. She kept the rules and never rang to see if he was getting better. When at last he threw away his crutch, he asked her out to lunch. 'Somewhere really nice.' She thought it was because they hadn't seen each other for weeks and bought a pretty cream suit and a pair of Manolo Blanick shoes. Underneath she wore a pair of stay-up stockings. He took her hands, both of them, across the table and told her it was over.

'Is there someone else?' she asked, as women do. 'Apart from your wife, that is?'

'No. It's just that I can't bear the lies.' Strange that truth should be her undoing. It was because he was so honest and so funny – making out his guilt to be a sad affliction such as dandruff – that she loved him. Just to make sure she realised it was nothing personal, he told her that his firm was sending him to Canada for five years.

'Maybe longer, if it works out.' He told her that his wife was over the moon about it. 'She's got a sister in Toronto.'

'How nice,' said Flo miserably.

'Chin up,' he said, his floppy hair falling over his eyes.

'You need another haircut,' she told him, to stop herself from crying at the Ritz.

'Huh!' was all Alex had to say about it. Flo bought her last book from the Women's section at Waterstones, called *All the Best Ones Are Married*. Which, after the event, didn't help very much. Not long after that she had to admit that she needed glasses for reading. Then her dentist started up about that horrid bridge. It was inevitable and since then she never even looked at another man and, eventually, never even thought about it. She called it facing up. Alex called it giving up.

The doorbell rang. It was Alex, neat, pretty and excited with two guide books and a map of Morocco. Flo slipped the red phone book back into the file.

'I hope you don't mind but I gave Sotheby's your number.' Alex put the books down on Flo's desk.

'Sotheby's?'

'The sale,' Alex reminded her. 'Those etchings. If they don't fetch their reserve it won't be much of a holiday.'

'Fingers crossed.'

Flo remembered what hopes were pinned on the auction, then said, 'Holiday?'

Alex sat down at the desk and pushed the guide books aside.

'It's not as if we'll need them but they're useful for phone numbers and things.' She dialled directory enquiries and asked for the number of Royal Air Maroc.

'What are you doing?' The blank expression of Flo's face told Alex she'd been pondering, which, with her, came perilously close to brooding. A very bad habit, that.

'Well, we are going, aren't we?'

'I suppose so.' Flo picked up the map of Morocco, pushed the box files to one side and spread it out on the floor. Alex hung on for her number. Flo looked round for her glasses.

'They're on your head,' Alex pointed out.

She started at the top of the map. Tangier? She'd been there once before with John. A brief visit. They'd stayed at the Minzah, but even with those exquisite five-star walls he managed to get food poisoning on the first day. Probably psychosomatic, as it was she who'd persuaded him to break from his golfing holiday at Sotto Grande.

'Only to see it. Not for long.' Unable to move more than a few feet from the lavatory, he had stayed in their room. Flo had sat in the courtyard reading Patricia Highsmith. The fountains played, splashing gently into mosaic pools with glints of gold, the sun shone through carved screens making patterns on the tiled floors, and waiters in white robes bordered with gold thread, brought her mint tea in silver pots which they poured from a great height into little, octagonal glasses. Then they glided off and it was very quiet. John had told her most emphatically not to leave the hotel and venture into the teeming streets as she'd only get ripped off and probably have her bag stolen. She closed the door of her mind on Tangier, not even thinking, 'perhaps another time,' as she watched the pretty shadows. After a while, for lack of anything else to do, she bought a silver bracelet at the hotel boutique.

'Don't let's bother with Tangier,' Alex agreed, never having thought much of William Burroughs. 'Let's get as far south as soon as we can. What's Agadir like?' They both reached for a guide book and read. There'd been an earthquake there in the sixties; it was almost totally modern with no hotel less than five hundred rooms and very popular with the Germans.

'No thanks.' Alex said she wasn't having anything to do with Agadir. 'Marrakesh? Casablanca?' She continued talking prices to Royal Air Maroc.

'There's a place called Taroudant nearby. It sounds all right.'

The book said it had a heat-hazed backdrop of the

High Atlas, orange groves, ramparts, rose red in the sun, a souk with spices, hand-made carpets woven by Berbers and ingenious leather crafts. Ingenious leather crafts!

Alex made a neat line under RAM's prices and was about to ring British Airways when the phone beat her to it.

'Yes, this is Mrs King. Yes, Lot 751?' She put her hand over the mouthpiece. 'It's Sotheby's,' she hissed. 'Pray!' Then she turned pink. 'Thank you, thank you.' She hung up and slumped over the desk. 'Three times the reserve!' Flo jumped up and ran across the map to the kitchen for champagne.

Alex rang Millie to tell her she could get that cashmere coat she'd had her eye on. As she fiddled with the wire of the cork in the kitchen, Flo could hear Millie's excited squeaks and youthful chatter and Alex saying, 'Yes . . . Yes . . . He *didn't*.' Then, after a pause, 'Well, what do you expect?' Flo came back with the champagne which fizzed all over the map.

'Poor kid.' Alex had finished her call. 'She asked her father for just a tiny little extra for her allowance. D'you know what he said?' She closed her eyes in exasperation. 'He said, and I quote, "Behold the lilies of the field!" Can you believe it? Oh, sod him!' She rang Millie back and told her to get some boots as well. 'Lovely ones, darling.' Then she started looking up the best hotels in Marrakesh. 'Not that we'll need to book. We could meet in Gibraltar, get the boat to Tangier, fly to Marrakesh and see what happens.' The pressure off, she was back to let's see what happens next.

'It might be a good idea to know where we're staying, just on the first night.'

'True.'

Flo crawled over the map. 'There are some pink things

here at Ouarzazate called ergs. Do you think that means desert, real desert?'

'It says here,' Alex poured some more champagne, ' "camel trips under the stars". What do you think one wears on a camel?'

'Jodhpurs?' Flo pushed Marlene and bias-cut satin out of her mind. For a while they discussed which would be the most fetching, white jodhpurs on a black camel, or black jodhpurs on a white camel.

Towards the middle of November, Flo rang the LA daughter and mentioned, quite casually:

'I'm going to Morocco for Christmas.'

'You're *what*?'

'Going to Morocco.'

'Whatever for?'

'Just for a change.'

'Should be great.'

'Yes, I'm looking forward to it.'

'I say, Mum, you know something? I bought a Moroccan carpet out in Venice. Only a small one. Wish I'd got a bigger one. If I send you a Polaroid, do you think you could get me another, something like it but bigger?'

'Of course, darling, I'll try.'

'Look, Mum, I must fly, I'm wanted on my mobile. Or do you want to hold?'

'No, it's all right. We'll talk before I go. Goodbye, darling, don't work too hard. Take care of yourself.'

Within a few hours the New York daughter phoned.

'Hi, Mum, h'ya doing?'

'Fine.'

'What's all this I hear about you going to Morocco?'

'Simple. I'm going to Morocco for Christmas with Alex.'

'Great. Whereabouts in Morocco?'

'Not sure yet. Just going to see what happens.'

'When do you leave?'

'The nineteenth of December.'

'But that's your birthday.'

'Yes, I know.'

'Isn't it your fiftieth or something?'

'Forty-eight,' said Flo.

There was hardly any wind and the sea was flat. On the Moroccan coast, Jebel Moussa rose from the water like a giant iguana and they reckoned it wouldn't be long before they saw Tangier.

'That's the beginning of Africa,' Flo kept telling herself. 'From there it goes right on down to Cape Town.' But it was too much to believe.

'They used to have dolphins following the boat nearly all the way.' Alex pushed the hair out of her eyes and stared down as the ferry cut deep, green slices in the water. As she spoke, a cry rose from the other side: 'It's the dolphins!'

Backpackers of all nations with cameras at the ready and a few Moroccan families rushed to the rail. There were only two joyous leaping shapes but a sigh went up from the passengers as if only for a moment, a little insight into what a better place the world could be had been achieved.

'That was something, wasn't it?' A handsome young Australian asked no one in particular.

'I'm sure it must be lucky.' Alex started to chat him up. Flo strolled to the front of the boat and watched the dolphins until the ferry changed course. They vanished

'Wait!' cried Alex. 'More luggage! *Plus de baggage.*' The guide tucked two of her bags under his arms, Flo's round his neck on a leather strap and managed the third in his hand.

'Hotel, very good, very clean, very cheap.'

'Airport.'

He led them towards a row of battered taxis and stopped by one whose driver was a deaf mute.

Alex took charge. 'You have to haggle for everything.'

Flo wondered how you could haggle with a deaf mute but he was astonishingly articulate with his hands and fingers.

'How much?' Alex found her calculator. The guide translated for the driver three hundred and fifty dirham.

'Oh my God, that's twenty-seven pounds!' She argued both of them down to two hundred which Flo tried to work out in her head.

'Oh, it doesn't matter.' Having achieved a point of honour Alex got into the taxi and Flo got in beside her. The driver turned on the ignition.

'A moment, a moment,' shouted the guide. 'Airport, airport.' He hustled two Spanish girls towards the taxi. The girls smiled and nodded. The guide started to haggle on behalf of the driver again. Flo looked at her watch. Finally Alex motioned the girls into the taxi and in very good, very rapid Spanish told them it would be two hundred dirham. Each. The girls were horrified but capitulated.

But they didn't want to go to the airport. They wanted to go to a hotel in the centre of Tangier called the Hôtel Suisse. Alex told them to find another cab. The driver, nodding wildly, took both his hands off the wheel and waved them about. Flo explained to everyone in French that they'd miss their plane. Alex told them all in Spanish. The girls didn't look as if they cared. The driver took no notice of any of them as he headed into the centre of Tangier and pulled up outside a shabby building called the Hôtel Sahara.

'Hôtel Suisse, Hôtel Suisse,' screamed the Spanish girls, waving their guide books at him. There were now only forty-five minutes to get to the airport and catch the plane. It took ten minutes to resolve the problems of the Spanish girls, their fare and luggage.

'Drive on,' ordered Alex, which the driver did as soon as the girls had parted with their money and left them standing on the pavement outside the Hôtel Sahara, waving their fists.

'But, madame, there is no such plane to Marrakesh,' said the young man at the Royal Air Maroc desk. 'And even if there was, it would have gone by now.'

'But I booked it, I phoned from London,' insisted Alex. 'They said I couldn't book internal flights from there, I had to do it here. I phoned. Someone said I could pick up the tickets just before the flight and pay for them then.'

'Who?' asked the young man. He shrugged when she said she'd no idea.

'I always thought that sounded a bit odd.' Alex smiled at him several times but he remained adamant that there was no such plane.

'Now what do we do? When's the next one?'

'To Marrakesh, madame?'

'To anywhere,' replied Flo, who couldn't remember why they were going to Marrakesh anyway.

'There is a flight to Agadir at nine o'clock.'

'We'll take it.'

'But it's fully booked, madame. It will not be certain that there are two seats until forty-five minutes before take-off.'

'Now what?' They looked at each other. Most of the ground floor was in the process of being boarded up with a great deal of banging and dust. There was no sign of a bar except for a small arrow pointing up a steep flight of steps and a sign which said 'Restaurant'.

'You'd think they'd have some trolleys.'

'We'd never get them up there. Come on.'

The restaurant was a flyblown bar with puddles on the tables, empty polystyrene cups and three large Moroccans with unidentifiable uniforms staring at the tarmac, who then stared at them as they ordered coffee at the bar, paid for it and found a table. It was undrinkable. Alex took out her Walkman, fixed in her earplugs and closed her eyes. Flo stared at a limp wind-sock. *Happy Birthday, dear Flo, Happy Birthday to you.* She went to look for the ladies. It appeared to be unisex and it was flooded. She stayed as little time as possible.

'Are you sure you booked these tickets?' Flo asked when she got back.

'Of course I'm sure.'

'We should have flown straight there.' She stopped herself from reminding Alex that it was for her benefit and to save her both time and money that she'd agreed to start from Gibraltar.

'I'll go and see what's happening. You mind the bags.' Alex, still wearing her Walkman, glided off. The three Moroccans started at her then back at Flo, who wondered if they came there every day just to gape at tourists.

Alex returned in a few minutes. 'No one there. Looks as if we might have to spend the night here.'

'Here?' Flo edged away from a dripping coffee cup.

'Tangier.' Alex started to look it up in the guide book.

An hour later, Flo tried. The hall was empty and the young man now had nothing better to do than be of service to her. Half an hour later they were on the plane to Agadir.

'Where shall we stay?' They braked their trolleys in the Agadir arrival hall.

'Taroudant?'

'Might as well.' It was only about sixty kilometres. Flo felt the glow of someone who knows they are on the right course.

'If I can be of any assistance?' A Moroccan business-man in an Armani suit approached them. 'If you are going to Taroudant, you will need a taxi. There are no buses now. But you will have to go into Agadir first.'

'Why?' Alex allowed him to steer her trolley towards the first taxi in the rank, relieved to see the driver had all his faculties.

'Taroudant is beyond the driver's region. He has to get permission. We can share a taxi.'

The driver confirmed this in reasonable French. Flo wanted to ask if there was a war on or something but thought better of it. Alex feigned sleep against the businessman's chatter, which didn't stop until they reached an official-looking building on the outskirts of Agadir. He slithered out of the cab and retrieved a suitcase from the boot and advised them to stay at the Rhiad Salaam in Taroudant.

'Mention my name. They will give you a special price.' He handed them his card.

'What a nerve!' cried Flo, who'd only just realised he'd cadged a lift.

* * *

38

There was a big white moon, almost full. Sixty kilometres dropped to fifty, then thirty and they were almost there. Flo wound down the window. The air was sweet as they passed what looked like orchards on either side of the road. She thought it was orange blossom. But it couldn't be. Orange blossom shouldn't happen until spring. But if the seasons had all changed places that year, it was all right with her.

'Look.' She nudged Alex. Serene and strong in the moonlight they could just make out the ramparts surrounding the small town. Almost immediately the driver made a sharp right turn through an arch and headed up a deserted street.

'Which hotel, mesdames?'

'The Hôtel Taroudant.' They'd picked it at random from the more modestly priced. He stopped just short of what looked like a main square full of empty cafés and sleeping buses. Tucked away on the south side was an anonymous-looking building with a wooden door and the name Hôtel Français.

'No, no. The Hôtel Taroudant.' The taxi driver assured them that the Hôtel Français and the Hôtel Taroudant were one and the same. As he was already unloading their luggage and it was past midnight there was little point in arguing. The bags landed just short of the heads of two hooded figures sleeping on the pavement but, oblivious to the thudding bags, they slumbered on. Flo paid off the driver and turned to see Alex surrounded by a group of young men who had appeared from the shadows. She was chatting up their leader.

'Thank you,' she said graciously as he heaved her bags about eighteen inches towards the closed door. There was no sign of light or life. No bell. No knocker.

One of the boys took off his shoe and banged on the thick wood. The others joined in. It was a game they obviously enjoyed. Eventually it opened a fraction and the suspicious creased face of a night-watchman peered out through the small space. The leader of the boys shouted something at him in Arabic. It sounded very rude. The watchman made to close the door but Flo was too quick for him. She pushed past and beckoned Alex to follow. The young men threw the bags in after them.

'Jacoub!' shouted the leader, pointing at his skinny chest. 'Jacoub *à vôtre service*, mesdames. Very good carpets tomorrow, inshallah.' He was silenced by the door slamming and the bolts being set.

In the light of the flickering torch, the night-watchman told them that there were no rooms without reservations. He seemed pleased with the word.

'But,' said Alex, with great presence of mind and producing a nasty letter from her bank from the bottom of her bag, 'we have reservations!'

'We have?' Flo's eyes opened wide.

'Bet he can't read.' She was right. He couldn't. Which didn't stop him studying the letter from Lloyds upside down.

Flo, who was more used to being wafted to a gilded lift, if not by the manager, certainly by an under-manager, was ready to grovel at the feet of this disagreeable old man for somewhere to lay her head. Eventually he opened a cupboard door and took out a key, then led them down a short passage and out into a courtyard where tall palms stretched up to a starry haze and the air still smelled of oranges. He stopped outside a door and opened it onto a dormitory. In the dull light of a naked bulb they could just make out six beds, a curtainless cubicle with a shower and a hole-in-the-floor lavatory. They started to protest but he had gone.

Flo kicked off her shoes and sat down on the nearest bed. The rough cotton sheet was slightly damp and smelled of manure. There was a folded blanket in heavy, synthetic wool which, when shaken open, revealed a huge lion snarling at her.

Alex turned on the tap of the washbasin. Nothing. She tried the shower with the same negative result. 'Oh, shit.'

'You're not going to wash your hair now?' But with Alex it was possible. She hadn't washed it since the morning. Flo spread her grey shawl over the lumpy pillow, looked down at the bedside mat and quickly put her shoes on again.

'Tomorrow', said Alex in a tone of someone who really meant it, 'we are going to change rooms.'

'At least we've got it to ourselves.'

'So far.' They undressed quickly. Flo threw on a nightie and crawled under the bad-tempered lion. If they were going to share with God knows who, she'd rather be asleep. Alex took her time, creaming her face and wiping it carefully with Kleenex. Flo sighed. She'd have given anything for a cup of tea but settled for a cigarette.

'I hope you don't mind,' Alex kept her words light, 'but if we've got to share I'd rather you didn't smoke.' She rinsed her mouth out with neat Lysol and shrugged into a snow-white bathrobe that took up half of one of her bags. Flo looked round for an ashtray but there wasn't one. She got out of bed, put on her shoes and popped the cigarette down the lavatory hole, aware that this sharing business might get tricky. Alex had chosen her bed and lay with her Walkman plugged in, her hands folded on her breast, looking peacefully dead or waiting in full confidence for the arrival of her lover.

And she slept well, never stirring except to give a small whimper of distress when Flo surreptitiously attempted another cigarette. Even the desolate braying of a donkey somewhere quite close didn't disturb her. Flo listened to it as it sobbed for several hours until it was soothed by the muezzin. This call to prayer Flo at first took to be a siren. Almost at once, cocks began to crow at every point of the compass, followed by the racket of the waking town. Bicycle bells, rattling handcarts, small vans with sharp hooters, all raced along the street beyond the wall behind her head. Alex slept on, one hand draped gracefully over her hip. Flo wriggled out from under the lion, dressed hurriedly in yesterday's clothes and opened the door on to the courtyard. In daylight the rectangle of stars had changed to pure blue. Swathes of purple bougainvillaea and honeysuckle fell over a low wall bordering a miniature forest of banana palms. A Berber woman in scarlet, with a yellow scarf tied round her head in a complicated triangle, swept the mosaic-tiled path as if she had the rest of her life to do it.

'*Bonjour.*' She smiled at Flo, surprising her with brilliant green eyes, lined with kohl.

'*Bonjour. Petit déjeuner*?'

The Berber woman nodded towards the passage that led back to the hotel entrance.

The dining room was empty. There were twenty tables with white cloths, some bland watercolours of Normandy and a photograph of the king, but no sign of any service despite the smell of fresh coffee.

'Madame?' A man in a linen suit finished a phone

call at the bar in the lobby. He introduced himself as *le patron.*

'Is it possible to have breakfast in the courtyard?'

'Of course, madame, this is *comme chez vous.*'

The front door was open on to the street. The sleepers had gone but Jacoub was still there, sitting on the pavement, tossing a pebble in his hand. She wondered if he'd been there all night, then noticed he'd changed into a blue nylon shirt.

'*Comme chez vous.*' The *patron* led her back into the courtyard, waved her into a recess banked with damask cushions and shouted for a boy. Something moved beneath the brass table. It was a tortoise contemplating a cabbage leaf. By the time the boy arrived with fresh coffee in a glass and apricot jam and butter in a stone pot, the tortoise had made quite an inroad into his cabbage leaf. As Flo finished her first cigarette of the day Alex appeared, fresh and rested in a pretty voile dress, suede boots and carrying a linen solar topee.

'Can we change rooms?'

Without a word about reservations, the *patron* sent the breakfast boy to show them two rooms on the third floor reached by a stone staircase and still overlooking the courtyard. Each room had a shower.

'It's hot! The water's hot!' Alex flew back to her own room to fix the adaptor on her hairdryer.

There was plenty of time to unpack, have a shower and possibly finish the Ruth Rendell Flo had been reading on the plane. Of the sorry garments in her bag, she chose a white, crêpe-de-chine skirt and an Italian cotton blouse she'd bought in the Portobello Road that never seemed quite right in London. It still didn't look quite right. Originally it was destined to team with some harem pants which for some mysterious reason had stretched a size instead of shrinking every time she'd washed them. The skirt was crumpled but she reckoned it would drop out eventually, and even if it didn't, she thought, giving it a shake, at least it was comfortable.

'Shopping?' suggested Flo hopefully as they stepped through the big door into the sunlight. Jacoub tossed away his pebble.

'*Bonjour*, mesdames. You slept well?'

'Wonderfully.'

'French?' he enquired, falling into step with them as they headed for the square. 'Spanish? German?'

'Certainly not,' replied Alex who, although Jewish but never normally went on about it, sometimes got a bit prickly.

'English.' Flo put him straight.

'England? Where England?'

'London.' She spoke for both of them. Jacoub responded to this information as if they were domiciled in heaven as he guided them towards the café of his choice. They ordered coffee and invited him to join them. He refused bashfully. Then he started his assessment. Where had they come from? Was it their first time in Morocco? Where were they going next? The answer to the last question was unrewardingly vague as neither of them had the slightest idea. Such lack of purpose prompted Jacoub to make a quick but detailed itinerary for them, most of which centred on shopping for carpets.

A beggar hobbled past their table, a grimy hand extended and a well-worn mutter issuing from his toothless mouth. Jacoub waved him off but Flo noticed he slipped the man a small coin. The beggar continued his round of the café, filled mostly with men in djellabas and a few in European clothes. Like the men in the airport bar, they too were starers. They stared at Alex in her voile dress, at the solar topee she hadn't yet dared to wear and at Flo in her crêpe-de-chine and sandals. Alex took no notice and started up an exchange of family information with Jacoub. How many sisters? How many brothers? How many children?

'I am not married,' he told them, his brown eyes full of regret. 'But I would like to be married, to a Swedish lady. Or English,' he corrected himself.

The snow-topped Atlas gleamed in the distance: The slopes of orange trees grew up as far as the little town that scarcely spilled beyond its ramparts. Inside the walls, the towers of the mosques watched over the maze of flat-topped houses. Jacoub led them from the square, down a narrow street and into a bamboo-covered market, where they dawdled past stalls of fruit and herbs, mountains of camomile, rose petals, paprika and sacks of saffron. Since Alex and Jacoub were obviously delighted by each other's company, Flo wandered ahead, peering into doorways and on to courtyards of the secret houses with windows no more than slits in the wall, then glanced up at shrouded women on flat roofs, washing on lines and children staring down on the crowded alley life below. Alex and Jacoub caught up with her at a stall of unidentifiable roots, bits of animal skin and bone and tubs of black-looking jelly.

'Your skirt's a bit see-through,' whispered Alex.

'Oh, shit!' She clutched it round her legs as two young women, graceful in grey kaftans looked at her over their veils. It was impossible to say if their eyes held scorn or laughter.

'Only if you stand with your back to the light,' Alex assured her.

45

'But there's light everywhere!' They were standing in a patch of a sun glancing off carrots, tomatoes, oranges and onions. As she tried to manoeuvre herself to the wall, she bumped into a shocking pink, plastic tailor's dummy and knocked over a pile of brooms.

'It doesn't matter!'

'It does. They're Muslims.' And they both knew that Muslims had very strong ideas about the modesty of dress. A flock of Germans was driven past by their official guide, the women in sleeveless T-shirts, stout arms raw and peeling from too much sun and their fat bottoms squeezed into knee-length Lycra shorts.

'You see,' Alex soothed her. 'It doesn't matter if you're not Moroccan.'

'It *does* matter. How can they do it?' Flo demanded of the departing Germans. 'They'd never walk about like that in Frankfurt.'

'This is for the washing of the hair,' Jacoub interrupted, picking up a pot of black stuff. Alex looked at it.

'And this is for the lips,' he said as he wooed them towards some pots of carmine grease. A Moroccan woman, swathed in black, bought some of the shampoo with a swift exchange of coins.

'How much?' Alex asked the stall keeper, who told her it was the equivalent of one pound fifty.

'Bet she didn't pay that much.' She stared at the retreating figure of the lady in black. 'Flo . . . wait . . .' Flo had started down a narrow street hung with carpets, rugs and kaftans, like banners; orange, red, green, blue, purple, some with violent flowers or stripes and all bordered with inches of nylon braid. Jacoub darted from one to another.

'Better kaftans here,' he advised Flo who was dodging

bikes and donkeys in an attempt to keep in the shade. 'The shop of my cousin.'

She had the feeling that 'my cousin' was one of the boys he'd been hanging around with the night before.

'German? America? French?' The cousin entreated them to sit on a carpet-covered bench.

'We don't want to buy anything, we've only just arrived,' Alex announced firmly.

'*Bien sûr. C'est juste pour le plaisir des yeaux.*' Even though it was only for the pleasure of looking, almost immediately a small boy arrived with mint tea on a plastic tray with Michael Jackson prancing across it. Then, for the pleasure of their eyes alone, Jacoub's cousin, starting them off gently, loaded them with silver bracelets, suspect amber necklaces and earrings with brilliant glass stones. Flo fingered one of the kaftans.

'Polyester. Do you have any in cotton? Real cotton? If I had a couple of kaftans I could wear them all the time.'

'You are not wandering around Morocco looking like a hippie.' Alex was adamant.

'Well, I was a hippie,' Flo replied, holding a cream, nearly cotton garment up against herself. 'Almost.'

'That was some time ago,' Alex reminded her. At the word hippie, Jacoub's cousin fished down a heavy, black burnoose with a long pole with a hook on the end.

'I don't think so,' said Flo.

'Henna!' Alex remembered. 'That's what I need . . . henna!'

'Very good Moroccan henna!' Jacoub declared and rushed her out of the shop and back to the spice stall.

Left alone with Flo, Jacoub's cousin got serious, producing things like a conjuror from chests, the back room and even his pockets.

47

'I wonder . . .' she said, searching for the Polaroid and finding it at the bottom of her bag, tucked into Ruth Rendell. 'I wonder . . .' Jacoub's cousin merely glanced at the photograph from LA and in a suspiciously short time unrolled a carpet almost identical, declaring it to be very, very old. She haggled long (and she thought quite honourably) and capitulated with about a third off the original price suggested.

When the deed was done Jacoub's cousin said, without mercy, 'She has very good taste, your daughter.' He handed her a felt-tipped pen and watched her write the California address until she finished with the zip code, still worrying about the certain aspects of pink thread which were undoubtedly synthetic.

'Very good taste,' she was assured again as he propped the long paper tube in the corner. 'Very good taste.'

'Well, it's done now.' But he hadn't finished with her.

'And now, for yourself.' He guided her attention to another pile of thick rugs in coarse wool.

'No . . .' Flo backed away. 'No, thank you.' She shook her head and was just short of wringing her hands.

'But you must. If you buy for your daughter you must buy for yourself.' He made it sound like a Moroccan custom. Flo assured him that she really, truly didn't want a carpet. Christmas or no Christmas. Daughter or no daughter. He gave her a look of deep reproach when she added that she couldn't afford one anyway.

'I will take credit.'

'Give credit, you mean.'

'Yes, give credit,' he said, unrolling a rug with a series of orange and black zig-zags.

Flo shuddered. 'Stop!' Jacoub's cousin was astonished.

48

'You see,' she said wildly, 'it's . . . it's against my religion to have carpets on the floor!' He had heard it all before but at last, to this, he had no reply.

'What have you done!' shrieked Alex, when she and Jacoub returned, having lingered to get to know each other better over a glass of fresh orange juice and having bought a black scarf covered in silver sequins at another cousin's shop. Flo was standing among a pile of plastic bags and wrapped-up packages.

'I don't exactly know.' She sounded dazed and wondered if he'd put something that affected reason in the mint tea. 'But he said he took American Express.' Two enormous fringed leather bags which postmen were supposed to use, which she knew the girls would shunt off to the nearest thrift shop, eight pairs of leather slippers in assorted sizes as 'presents', three large polished soapstone eggs, four quartz (he said) ashtrays, a box made of bone and copper, another inlaid with abalone, a large brass kettle and two silver bracelets which she was wearing.

'He did give me this as a present.' She showed Alex a tinny little Hand of Fatima. 'As a present.'

'Very big of him. At least you had the sense not to get a c-a-r-p-e-t.' Then she spotted the large brown paper tube.

'Flo!'

'I was asked to get one.'

'Carpet!' exclaimed Jacoub's cousin, having worked out the spelling.

'Absolutely not.' Alex stalled him with a look. 'Heaven knows how we're going to move around with all that stuff. We'll need a car.'

'Car?' cried Jacoub, deftly slipping his fingers under

the string of the parcels and giving them a smile that lit up the gloom of the shop. 'Car? No problem.'

There was nothing much to choose among the sad horses between the shafts of the carriages lined up for trips around the outer walls of the town. The one they chose looked near to death, haunches sticking up from its dull coat and flies buzzing round its eyes. Jacoub helped them and the parcels into a carriage with a red tasselled canopy. The bells on the horse's harness tinkled prettily and it livened up surprisingly as it trotted along the road. The tassels swung and the small town glowed deep ochre in the afternoon light. Alex asked Jacoub about its history but, other than repeating that it was very old, he didn't seem to know much about it. Flo, keeping away from facts, waved back at some pretty children playing under a datura tree then at an old man in a yellow straw hat riding on a donkey.

'Stop it,' said Alex. 'You look like royalty.'

'I feel like royalty.' She'd cheered up about the ridiculous rubbish she'd bought and turned her face to the sun, her eyes closed. Then opened them again in case she missed anything. Alex and Jacoub discussed the practicalities of cars. It appeared there were none for hire in Taroudant and they were unlikely to find one at Hertz or Avis in Agadir as it was the high season. Nevertheless, inshallah, Jacoub had a friend in Agadir who might be able to help. But they'd have to go there.

'Why? Can't they bring it here?' Flo didn't fancy another taxi ride in a backwards direction. Whatever the taxi would cost would surely cover the cost for someone to bring the car to them.

'You can buy whisky in Agadir.'

'But we don't want any whisky.' Jacoub's face fell but

he took it manfully and promised to get a car for them the following day. Alex linked her arm through his and asked him what those white birds flying south were.

'How far is Ouarzazate?'

'Ouarzazate? I have a brother lives in Ouarzazate.'

They dined in the bleak dining room, watched by the king and served by the breakfast boy who now had dark circles under his eyes. By the time they'd finished their couscous they'd made a rough plan to push on south to Ouarzazate.

'Or wherever those erg things are,' Alex said. They carried their coffee to the courtyard. There was an Arabic commotion going on by the front door. One voice was Jacoub, the other the *patron*.

'Madame Alex.' Jacoub had caught sight of her. 'Madame Alex!' he cried again, his voice charged with appeal.

'What's the problem?' she wanted to know.

'He say you invited him, madame,' accused the *patron*.

'And so I did. For a . . .' She remembered in time Muslims weren't supposed to drink. 'For a coffee.' The *patron*, dark with disapproval, glared as she wafted Jacoub off to one of the alcoves.

'The *faux guides* are not permitted in the hotel,' The *patron* told Flo.

'*Faux guides*?'

'False guides, street boys,' he snapped and sat down at his desk. Flo joined the now cosy couple in the courtyard and transmitted this information to Alex.

'Oh, sod him.' She turned back to Jacoub, whose arm was round her shoulder, and asked him about his mother. Flo sipped her coffee, feeling awkward and embarrassed. A bit the way she had when she'd seen the German tourists.

The new room was comfortable, the bed had a top sheet and didn't smell of anything and this time the blanket was an amiable-looking panda. There was an ashtray, a bedside lamp and Ruth Rendell waiting for her but she was asleep in twenty minutes. After the donkey, but before the crowing cocks, Alex tapped on the door.

'Can I come in?' Flo sat up.

'Look.' Alex approached her bed and sat down, covering her feet with the panda blanket. 'It's Jacoub. I had a bit of a problem with him. I made a bit of a mistake.'

'Oh Lord, what?' Flo lit a cigarette, felt guilty then remembered it was her own room and she was free to do as she wished. 'What happened?' When she'd left them it looked as if it might be a long night, but not necessarily a difficult one.

'He wants to come with us to Ouarzazate.' Alex was unsure whether to look woebegone or defiant and managed both. 'To visit his brother.'

'Yes?' Flo inhaled.

'Well, he's very sweet and all that but we don't really want to be lumbered with him, do we?'

'Did you, er . . .' Flo asked delicately.

'Of course I didn't. He did get a bit pushy so I said to him, "What about Aids?" They call it SEDA here. He said he wouldn't have anything to do with anyone with SEDA. I told him you never know if someone's got it. He said he would. Anyway,' she rushed on, 'I told him that this Ouarzazate business was up to you.'

'*Me!*'

'I know. I'm awfully sorry, but I told him that as we were sharing the car, if you said yes it was OK but if you said no there was nothing I could do about it.' Flo was speechless. 'You will tell him he can't come, won't you?'

'You want *me* to tell him?'

'It'll sound better coming from you. Easier.'

'I bet it will. Serve you right if I said yes.'

Jacoub was brazening it out on one of the barstools, and talking to the car hire man. He had a small travelling bag at his feet. When Flo approached, without Alex or any sign of a smile, his eyes widened with disappointment. To gather her wits, she decided to deal with the car man first, filled in the papers, produced her licence and named Alex as the co-driver. He took her outside to look at it. It was a Peugeot 105. It looked all right. The car man gave her the keys and headed off to the square as she went back into the hotel and, to delay matters further, asked the *patron* for their bill. Jacoub was looking at the floor. He knew what was coming and he knew she knew he knew but he wasn't going to make it easy.

'Jacoub,' she started gently enough, 'it's like this.' He interrupted her tactful rejection, declaring wildly that she didn't understand, that he loved Alex, he wanted to marry her and come to England.

'But she lives in Spain,' she pointed out as Alex obviously hadn't. This didn't bother Jacoub, whose wonderful brown eyes were now brimming with tears.

'She could change my life!' he declared.

'I know she could, Jacoub, but she isn't going to.'

'Is she married?'

'No, but that's not the point.' Jacoub's French, other

53

than 'Where do you come from?' small talk was limited so it took time to get this across. She feared that at any moment he might come up with the argument that Muslims were allowed four wives.

'How old are you, Jacoub?'

'Twenty-one,' he lied. She took his hand in hers and explained firmly but without disloyalty to Alex that she was considerably older than him.

'But that is not important. In Morocco these things are not important.'

'They are where we come from.'

'I could be her joy boy,' he suggested.

'Toy boy,' she corrected him without thinking. 'Oh, Jacoub, be sensible. What would your mother say?' He was about to tell her that his mother would think it a splendid idea but she outstared him and the tears spilled down his young face.

'I'm sorry, Jacoub.' And by this time she was. And furious with Alex for having got her into this. The *patron* stalked past, looked at the tragic little scene with satisfaction and gave Flo the bill. She glanced at it and Jacoub tried to read it upside down. She paid in cash and caught sight of Alex peering out from behind a pillar in the courtyard, making get-rid-of-him faces. She shook hands with Jacoub, assured him it was all for the best and gave him a hundred dirham. He accepted with a deep sigh, shouldered his little travelling bag and without another word headed back into the street.

'Let's get out of here.' Alex pulled her solar topee down as far as it would go and put on her large dark glasses. 'I'll drive, you navigate.' Which was fine with Flo, who had only limited experience of driving on the wrong side of the road and was terrified of all those unpredictable donkeys, trucks and scooters. Pointedly ignored by Jacoub and his friends, they piled their luggage and Flo's parcels into the boot themselves.

'How did he take it?' asked Alex, adjusting the driving mirror.

'It was very embarrassing. He was terribly upset but he'll probably get over it.'

'I bet he will. Look!' As Alex manoevred the car out of its parking space she caught sight of Jacoub in the mirror. He was shaking hands with the car hire man, having come to an agreement satisfactory with both of them. He turned away as the bus from Agadir drew up, opened his arms wide and with his wonderful smile greeted three Scandinavian girls in Lycra shorts.

Flo traced her finger down the map. Taroudant, Talouine, Tinzouline, Tamgroute, so many places beginning with T.

'Ah, Zagora. Let's head to Zagora.'

'Why?'

'Begins with a z. End of the road.'

Alex laughed and put on an Miles Davis tape. 'Can we make it in a day?'

Flo considered the distance. 'Should do if we don't stop. It's pretty straight except for some wiggly bits, but there aren't many.'

'Wiggly bits mean mountain roads, dear.' Alex snapped on her seat belt, moved into fourth and sped through the orcharded outskirts of Taroudant, dodging overloaded lorries, old men wobbling on bikes and younger ones going too fast on scooters.

'Stop!' commanded Flo, who had noticed a small shop.

'Why? What for?'

'Water. We must have water. We're going into the desert and that's the first rule.'

Reluctantly Alex pulled up outside a shack with a donkey tethered to a pile of ripped tyres outside the door.

'There'll be cafés up ahead,' she grumbled but Flo, who couldn't recall having seen any convenient cafés around in *Lawrence of Arabia*, had vanished into the shop. She came back with bread, oranges, dates, Vache Qui Rit cheese and two bottles of mineral water.

'OK. Let's go.' Alex started up again then suddenly there were no more emerald patches of field or pearl-green olive groves, just yellow earth with a few brave attempts at ploughing and a lone argan tree with white goats clambering nimbly among its spiky branches.

'Oh my God. Tree-climbing goats.' Flo let the guide book and the map slither to the floor as Eric Clapton now sang them on towards the south.

They began to climb up into the bleak, savage hills with a sheer drop on one side and walls of stone on the other. The few buses, lorries and cars they saw seemed either directly above or below as the road snaked back on itself. Every few hundred yards road signs warned them of the possibility of suicidal goats leaping in front of them, avalanches of large boulders crashing down on them and cars with a mad tendency to hurtle off into the ravines. These warnings were interspersed with more signs, exclamation marks, leaving other dangers to their imagination. At one point they passed a double exclamation point. They learned fast that buses were the worst hazard, obviously having the total right of the road. The only course was to cringe as far away as possible, preferably on

the mountain rather than the precipice side. Flo lit
a cigarette.

'Please,' said Alex, 'not in the car. We'll have a pit
stop in a minute.' At the start of the next steep climb,
she pulled over. They both got out to have a pee behind
a rock then became aware of several barefoot children
watching them with silent interest. Alex straightened
herself out, glanced up and pointed to a very large bus
winding down from above.

'Let's wait until it's passed.' Flo lit her cigarette, a
signal for a small boy to spring from nowhere and
offer them a large lump of amethyst. Alex explained
in several languages and a lot of hand talk that they
didn't want any amethyst. He stood his ground looking
wistful then hungry, until he was replaced by another
child holding a goat kid in his arms.

'Does he was us to *buy* it?' After more confused
exchanges, they finally understood he wanted to have
his photograph taken with the animal. Twenty dirham.
And the goat wanted ten. When no cameras appeared
his scale of optimism dropped rapidly to the pleading
whine, '*Un stylo, un dirham, une cigarette.*' Alex let Flo
deal with him as she looked up to see where the bus
had got to, but there was no sign of it. They waited for
ten minutes. The silent children stared at them. Nothing
passed, no truck, no car, no bus.

'Where's it gone?'

'Perhaps it stopped.'

'Not up there.'

'Maybe it was going the other way.' Alex looked at
her watch and Flo looked at the sun. A running latecomer
approached with a small, furry animal dangling by its
neck on a piece of string.

'What's that?'

57

'It doesn't matter. Let's go.' Flo stubbed out her cigarette which was pounced on by the goat boy.

Deaf to the cries of the child with the wriggling thing they started up the steep incline, anticipating the rush of the bus round every bend. Alex kept her eyes on the road and Flo scanned the upper and lower slopes until they reached the top of the pass. No bus. Not a sign of it. But there was a sign informing them that this was a *panoramique*. Obediently they pulled up in the lay-by and got out. Across the plain below they could see for fifty, sixty, maybe a hundred kilometers. Alex fished out a neat pair of binoculars from her bag and gazed down at the road ahead ribboning into infinity. No sign of the bus.

'It couldn't have been ahead of us or we'd be able to see it down there, even with a ten-minute start.'

'You don't suppose . . . ?' Flo hesitated before daring to suggest it might have gone over the edge. Alex swung her line of vision down into the deep shade of the valley.

'But we'd have heard the crash.'

'Perhaps it was a mirage?' Eric Clapton quiet now, they stood in silence. The wind blew softly on their faces as they looked at each other wondering if one could have joint mirages. Alex took in the vastness with one last sweep.

'Nothing here. Look.' She handed over the binoculars but Flo had lost interest and was gazing at the horizon with an expression of awe usually seen only on the faces of the truly devout. Waves of hills, grey, purple, grit-ash, black and ochre, scored with horizontal lines, rose and dipped for ever. She'd never been particularly religious. God was someone she seldom thought about, but if there was a God perhaps he was there. Perhaps this *was* God.

'This is a very strange place,' said Alex unnecessarily.

But it wasn't over. As they descended, their swiftly moving car was no more than an impudent intrusion, tolerated by the massive mounds, risen through heat, shock and heaving activity and totally indifferent to their tiny presence. Pocked with caves, mutilated by craters, dead as the craters of Calisto, those mountains watched and if one stayed very still, Flo thought, perhaps one could catch them breathing.

'It can't get any more . . . can it?' she murmured, not expecting an answer.

'More what?'

'More . . . more . . .' To prove her wrong, Jebel Kissane rose out of a faint mist ahead, the oddest mountain ever seen outside a children's book. It appeared tip-tilted, as if shaken from a giant, dented jelly mould and left to harden into a mass of spikes and purple fissures. Flo knew, if she stared long enough, hard enough, a secret entrance might reveal itself to the hidden world inside.

'I don't believe all this,' announced Alex as they started towards the palmeries of the Draa Valley. But Flo did.

Pushed by an unspoken urgency to reach Zagora before the light failed, they stopped briefly for petrol at Agdz and ate the oranges and cheese as the garage filled up the car. As they moved on, Flo turned in her seat, straining for a last look at Jebel Kissane turning lilac in the late sun.

The earth was now rich, red and fertile, willows on the banks of the river, tamarisks and almond trees with black, bare branches waiting for pink blossoms, and an endless forest of date palms. Villages of the same red mud rose either side of the road, giant sandcastles with crenellated turrets, slits of windows and bright blue doors. Children played in the dust, old men sat in silent rows outside the mosques and the women, dressed in black bordered with silver sequins, carried great sheaves of dried palm leaves on their heads, their babies on their backs and plastic shopping bags in their hands.

'It must be going-home-time.'

A woman shoved an overladen donkey down a slope and then disappeared into the deep green of the palmerie.

'What the hell!' Alex stamped on the brake as a man in a turban and a striped burnoose held up his hand like a biblical traffic cop. He beckoned, then shouted to a tiny old woman bent double under the weight of a large, red, studded trunk. As she hobbled in front of the car he prodded her to keep her on course. It took a long time for her to reach the far side of the road and safety where she too headed down the slope into the palmerie. The man waved them on with thanks and a collusive smirk.

'Of course,' remarked Alex, shifting up into third, 'he could have carried it for her.'

A road sign bade them 'Welcome to Zagora' in several languages. Others entreated them to stay at various hotels boasting different numbers of stars.

'La Fibule?' La Fibule said it had a pool, a restaurant, a *jolie jardin*, tranquillity and folkloric.

'What's folkloric?' Flo asked nervously having developed an irrational fear of anything that smacked of crafts, ethnic, antique or typique.

'Something to do with carpets, I expect,' Alex teased, as they drove into the town along an uninspiring main street with a few cafés, two electrician shops, a bank, a garage, a pharmacy, a shoe shop and a lot of holes in the wall selling plastic buckets. Here and there were untended boutiques with carousels of postcards, carpets, kaftans and long strips of woven fabric. At the far end of the town they reached a roundabout with more signs pointing south, informing them that La Fibule was only one kilometre on and that Timbuktu was fifty-two days by camel. Beyond the roundabout was a wide river and two small mountains that looked imported, one hummock shaped, the other rising into a sharp point.

'D'you think they'll have rooms, it being Christmas?' Alex was tired after her long night with Jacoub and a long day of driving. 'I'm dying for a bath.'

'What Christmas?' There hadn't been a sign of a snowflake, robin or deer. Not a carol or a jingle bell. Flo put on Bonnie Rait, loud.

'That's it!' A large black wooden door with metal studs stood open on to a garden of roses and white tents piled with brocade cushions. Under the tallest palms they'd yet seen linked with delicate points of light that had nothing to do with Christmas, they caught sight of a busy-looking bar.

'Oh God, I hope they've got rooms.' They pulled up in the car park. Alex slumped over the wheel for a moment then pulled herself together and brushed her hair. They got out and with the tentative, slow steps of weary travellers approached the entrance. A plump man appeared in front of them, his arms folded in the manner of a Grand Vizier. He wore a blue robe and a turban of twisted green and black. As he looked them up and down there was a loud shriek from behind him.

'*Ola!*' It was the two Spanish girls they'd left on the pavement in Tangier, who fell on them with cries of delight, obviously having either forgotten or forgiven being dumped outside the wrong hotel. The Grand Vizier opened his arms in welcome as he smiled, revealing a row of surprisingly childish teeth.

'Are there any rooms?' Flo asked. The Grand Vizier introduced himself as Ali, '*comme Ali Baba*' and assured them there was always room for his *gazelles*.

'Gazelles?' Flo and Alex looked at each other with raised eyebrows.

'Why not?'

They followed him into the tiled hallway of the hotel where Ali Baba started a quick exchange in Arabic with the man at the desk. It seemed there was only one room available, a double, with a bathroom. Or two small rooms on the top floor with a shared shower on the landing.

'We'll take the double,' Flo capitulated first, deciding to forgo smoking in favour of a hot bath.

'For how long, mesdames?' They looked at each other for the answer. 'You see, it is the Season,' he prompted them.

'A week,' Alex decided, which seemed to satisfy him, and then he started to explain to Flo that there was a supplement for New Year's Eve. Alex strolled towards the garden and noted a remarkably handsome European man, tanned and lean, standing by the bar.

'Foreign Legion,' Flo guessed as he lit a cigarette and the smell of Gauloise reached her. The receptionist gave her the key to the room and a boy staggered up the stairs with their luggage and her horrible parcels.

'Are you coming up?'

'Why don't we have a drink first?' Alex suggested, giving her hair a quick check in a mirror bordered with bits of coloured glass and, without waiting for an answer, glided into the garden towards the bar.

By the time Flo had checked their luggage into the room, chosen her bed, ascertained that the water was hot, done repairs to her unwashed face and descended to the bar, Alex was sitting next to the handsome man. They had joined a group of people in one of the tents and she appeared to have a drink already. Flo ordered a vodka and tonic for herself and joined them.

'*Eh voilà!*' cried Ali Baba and introduced her to the Spanish girls, (*mes gazelles*) who they already knew, a tired elegant woman called Cecille, who turned out to be Belgian, and her Moroccan husband, a melancholy man with a neat beard, a pristine silk shirt and beautifully manicured hands.

'And this is Claude. He flies aeroplanes, little ones.' As Flo suspected, he turned out to be French. He rose, shook her hand and sat down again, this time a little nearer to Alex, who made no attempt to move. It turned out he was on stand-by for spraying locusts which might, at any moment, swarm up from Mauretania.

'It must be terribly dangerous, flying so low.' The high excitement of the newly met and their traveller's tales flew around the tent. The Spanish girls, both talking at the same time and interrupting each other, told Flo how they'd hitch-hiked all the way from Tangier in two lifts. Which explained how they'd got there so quickly.

'With a lot of sheep in a truck.'

Flo told them they'd arrived by car but left out the bit about Jacoub. The Spanish girls seemed to think that two women driving over the mountains was an incredible feat.

'*Intrépido. Intrépido.*' Flo told them they were pretty *intrépido* themselves, hitch-hiking with a flock of sheep. Then she told them about the vanishing bus, which they didn't quite understand. But Cecille's Moroccan husband nodded as if it was quite normal for buses to vanish in such a manner. His wife cut across him to tell Flo that they were building a hotel in the desert.

'With my brother. It has four stars,' she added in pedantic English. The Moroccan husband nursed his whisky as Cecille started a tirade about the sharp practices and inefficiency of Moroccan workmen.

'It sounds much like builders anywhere.' Flo drained her vodka, suddenly exhausted by the impact of the mountains, mysterious palmeries and villages with origins as lost as Gothic Thebes. Cecille ran out of mileage on plumbers and noticed her looking up at the evening star, just visible between the giant palms.

'That is Venus,' she informed her. 'It is a planet so it doesn't twinkle. In the desert, we have many stars,' she added. Flo took it she meant other than her own particular four.

'You have daughters, madame?' asked the Moroccan husband unexpectedly. Flo replied that she had.

'Are they beautiful?'

'Exceptionally,' she replied with total confidence. He congratulated her and told her that women with beautiful daughters were very special. Flo made a mental note to pass this on to Alex, who was still enraptured by the habits of locusts.

'We will all dine together?' suggested Claude as the waiter appeared bearing menus. Everyone except Cecille agreed that would be delightful.

'We have a long drive. And plumbers,' she explained, rising. Her husband finished his drink; they shook hands all round.

'You must come and visit us in the desert,' she told Flo.

'Real desert?' asked Flo, remembering the ergs.

It was Christmas Day. It was raining. Claude had been summoned to deal with locusts and flown off in his little plane. Alex stood in the doorway of a heavily tiled salon at La Fibule and stared at the rain splashing down on to the rose garden.

'I wonder how long it takes to finish off a cloud of locusts.'

'Never mind. Something else will turn up.' It was small consolation, but with Alex, something or someone always did.

'How can it be raining in the Sahara?'

'Tomorrow, the sun will shine, inshallah!' promised Ali Baba, arriving with a large umbrella and the two Spanish girls, who both carried small rolls which could only be carpets.

'Look! Look!' they cried, delighted by their purchases of a couple of rugs no bigger than bathmats from Ali Baba's shop.

'At least he gave me his phone number,' Alex consoled herself after a perfunctory glance at what the girls had bought. The girls laid their little carpets on the floor and put on a flamenco tape. Ali Baba produced two long strips of blue cheesecloth from a plastic bag. The girls grabbed one each and tried to tie them into turbans.

'Not turban, *shesh. Comme ça.*' Ali Baba wound the cotton round their heads, twisting and knotting and finally drawing a left-over end across their faces and tucking it in.

'*Ole!*' cried the girls, prancing in front of a mirror and swearing they'd never take them off.

'All colours. Black, white, blue, all colours.' Ali Baba looked hopefully at Alex who was still staring at the little red rivers flowing along the paths of the garden.

'*Ça marche.*' A waiter who had been fiddling with a video at the far end of the room had got it to work. Ali Baba had borrowed it from a neighbour because he wanted to entertain his gazelles with *The Sheltering Sky* (borrowed from a cousin in Ouarzazate). It was in black and white with Arabic sub-titles. They'd all seen it before but it was Christmas Day and it was raining.

'Tomorrow sun,' he promised them.

He did indeed magic the sun for them the following day. The girls, still wearing a *shesh* apiece, greeted him with joy when he arrived in the dining room at breakfast.

'What can I do to entertain my gazelles today?' he asked with a great beam that included Flo and Alex. 'We go to see a kasbah?'

'He could be a Redcoat,' Alex muttered, putting down her coffee and looking round the dining room at the French families, very much *en famille*, and a few German couples eating a large, silent breakfast. Enough was enough.

'Let's go for a drive by ourselves.' She was so intent on escaping Ali Baba and the Spanish girls she didn't notice when Flo lit up her after-breakfast cigarette.

'Good idea.' Flo was a bit sick of being called a gazelle herself, having worked out that far from being the compliment they'd first assumed, it was just the Moroccan equivalent of 'birds'.

'Quick.' They left the dining room, hoping to give Ali Baba the slip. But as Alex reversed out of her parking space, he was standing by the gate all smiles, then minus the smile when he realised they were going off alone. Before he could ask where, Alex nipped neatly on to the road and turned right.

'Oh dear. Do you think we've offended him?'

'Probably.' Alex remembered Jacoub. 'For thirty seconds.'

'Let's drive on to Mehemide.'

After Zagora the valley opened out into a ten-kilometre stretch of stone and scrub on either side of the road, bordered in the distance by the comforting bulk of flat-topped mountains. Here and there patches of white glistened like ice and the few pools of water trapped by the rain were drying out fast.

'I wish I knew more about how it got like this. Do you think that white stuff is salt?'

'Could be. Do you want to stop and taste it?' Alex was in her go go go mood. Flo shook her head. But if it was salt it meant they could be driving over a long-vanished inland sea.

'Look, it's changing again!' The valley narrowed into a pass of rocks scorched on top, like burned cakes breathed on by some fiery breath, their undersides still uncooked and pink.

'No sand yet.' Ali Baba had promised he would show them real sand, arrange real camel rides, but Alex, after a closer look at the camels at the hotel, wasn't having any.

'No, thank you.'

'Oh, come on,' Flo had begged, remembering Marlene.

'No way.' She wasn't going anywhere near those agile necks and enormous teeth and anyway, they were very much taller than she'd expected.

'I prefer horses,' she had told Ali Baba grandly, which Flo knew to be a black lie as she'd never been near a horse other than the milk float in Maida Vale. But she was in luck. It seemed the only thing that Ali Baba couldn't magic up was a horse.

'It's hotter here.' Flo put her hand out of the window as they passed through Tagounite and headed on towards the border town of Mehemide.

'Oh my God!'

'What?'

'We forgot water!'

'Let's stop there.' Alex had spotted a building set back from the road a few hundred yards on. 'I told you there'd be cafés and things.'

'Look!' shrieked Flo. 'An erg!'

The Hôtel des Dunes stood foursquare as a child's fort, a turret at each corner and battlements painted white. Beyond it, about half a kilometre down a stony track, rose sand dunes with corrugated slopes. They drew up at the side entrance, which had another couple of turrets, but a tree in the middle making it impossible to drive inside.

'The Hôtel des Dunes,' said Flo, which Alex didn't find very significant, obviously having forgotten all about Marlene. Beside the turreted entrance was a well and round it a group of camels dozing in the hot sun. Alex was glad to note that they were all hobbled. They got out of the car and Flo walked towards them, shielding her eyes despite her sun-glasses. Beside the dunes were more camels, men in blue lounging beside them.

'Come on.' Alex, having combed her hair, started towards the entrance. A young man, very tall, very black, his *shesh* would round his head in a manner that accentuated high cheekbones and arched eyebrows, approached them. Unironed, his desert blue robe was torn in places, and his large feet bare and dusty, his big hands work-worn. He smiled, shy but straightforward and quite unlike any Moroccan they'd yet encountered.

'*Bienvenue.*'

'Can we get coffee? Lunch?' Alex asked him, hoping to get Flo away from those awful camels. He replied that all was possible. They followed him through a sun-baked garden with some struggling young palm trees protected by old car tyres painted in bright colours. There were a few green-tiled tables and a dark brown tent strewn with dusty carpets. An arched cloister ran round the courtyard of the main building, the centre part filled with pale clay pots leaning up against each other and a few, sad rose bushes. Primitive paintings of forceful half faces with many eyes stared at them from the mud walls and a few thin tabbies dozed on the tiles.

'Do you think he's a Tuareg?' whispered Alex as the tall young man showed them to a table in the shade. Flo shook her head. He asked what they would like to eat and although he implied everything was possible, the reality of choice boiled down to tagine and Coca-Cola.

'Tagine and Coca-Cola!' He grinned, delighted by their selection, scooped up a skinny cat and vanished without a sound.

Flo and Alex got up and walked slowly round the courtyard looking at the paintings, strings of amber beads slung artfully around mirrors framed with painted glass and a loom with a half-woven carpet. The cushions on the banquette seats were splitting open, the tables' legs scored by scratching cats and nearby one of the tables was still scattered with crumbs from someone's breakfast.

'Where do you think everyone is?' At this, a willing but absent-minded boy with a timid moustache, arrived with their tagine.

'A fork?' suggested Flo as he set it down. Deeply embarrassed, he ran back to the kitchen, his flip-flops slapping softly on the tiles and came back with six forks, wiping them on a tea-towel.

'What's your name?' she asked as he spread them round the table.

'Joseph,' he replied, blushing.

'Thank you, Joseph,' she said and didn't have the heart to ask him for a spoon.

When they finished eating they stretched their pale legs in the sun. Joseph came to clear the table and gathered up his courage to ask if they'd like to see the view from the terrace. By which he meant the roof.

'Do you want to drive on to Mehemide?' Alex asked.

'No, perhaps not. The girls did say it was a bit of a dump.' Alex looked relieved. Joseph showed them the way to the roof, up a dark staircase with shallow earthen steps.

'They are proper dunes.' Flo leaned on the parapet and gazed towards the hills of sand. Alex tried the wooden door of one of the turrets, which opened on to a simple bedroom with a slit window.

'What do you think that is?' Flo pointed to the right of the dunes to a large walled-off square. 'Do you think it's where the Foreign Legion train their horses?'

'Oh, you and your Foreign Legion.'

'It's exactly what it looks like.' They walked slowly round the terrace, looking down at the cats and pots in the courtyard below. The young man in blue passed underneath, smoking a joint.

'He's not Tuareg,' decided Flo. 'Too Afro. Tuaregs have got thin faces like Ethiopians. Oh, look, those must be the rooms.' On the shady side of the fort was a long, flat-topped building with a covered passageway. Each door had a name painted on it and was guarded by a squat, earth mother statue holding a bowl filled with sand which served as a giant ashtray. Behind the row of rooms lay another dusty garden with some scratching hens and a large cistern with dark green water and a diving board. Beyond the cistern was what appeared to be a cemetery for broken cars, where a chicken had just laid an egg in half a Renault.

'I like it here,' said Flo. Alex was alarmed.

'We're not moving out here. I don't want to be stuck in the middle of nowhere without a soul in sight.' But Flo was staring at the horizon again, looking as if she were about to go into a slight coma. Alex left her to it and went to have another look at the paintings in case she had fallen on undiscovered genius. Flo gazed on at the dunes, the unmoving men in blue beside them. The sense of rightness and recognition was so strong, for a moment she was startled, then she fell still. Being there was natural. The way it always should be.

But the peace was temporary, broken by the loud arrival of a battered Mercedes which drew up beside the dozing camels by the well. Flo watched from the terrace as a man leaped out of the car. He too was in desert blue, with a white *shesh* piled on top of his head in a haphazard fashion. He kicked off his sandals and strode into the courtyard shouting names.

'Joseph! Ali! Adi! Jalil!' There was the sound of hurrying footsteps, figures appearing through unexpected doors down below. A plump woman dressed in reds and yellows, with crochet in her hands, approached the newcomer and stretched out her apron to receive two videos. A thin, monkey-faced man in a white skull cap opened a door, peeped out and shut it again.

'Omar, c'est Omar!' Everyone had a question for him. A yellow dog barked and chased a turkey past his legs and Alex emerged from the shade of the cloister, smiling.

'There she goes.' Flo watched with interest and awe as Omar and Alex made their first encounter. There was an exchange of names, a boy was sent to find glasses and a corkscrew and a bottle of wine was withdrawn from a brown paper bag. It was amazing how she did it. And how instinctively, within seconds. Suddenly Flo realised that she wanted to stay. When Alex, appalled, had vetoed the embryonic idea, 'to be stuck out here in the middle of nowhere', she'd been content to let the moment gather itself into just a pleasant memory, one of those moments in life that could be recalled with pleasure. But now, with Alex obviously happy to be deep in conversation with Omar, perhaps it wasn't necessary to move away. Maybe they would stay. Omar poured the wine for Alex. Alex began to talk to him about the paintings. Flo turned back to the shadows and the sand dunes.

'Omar wants us to meet his camels,' Alex told her when Flo finally came down from the terrace. 'This is Omar, the patron.' Close to, he was older than from above,

72

with a moustache, a little beard, a big smile and his eyes hidden by blue-lensed glasses she could see her face in.

'I like the English,' he proclaimed, calling for another glass. 'They are intelligent.' It was a statement of approval without the hollow flattery they'd grown used to. 'They are wise.' It was an unlikely assessment of their national characteristic but before Flo could reply he leaped to his feet.

'Jalil? Where is Jalil?' The monkey-faced man opened his door, looked out, shook his head and shut it again.

'My uncle Ahmed,' Omar explained briefly. 'Where is Jalil?' Joseph, who was struggling past with a crate of Fanta, jerked his head towards the desert.

'Ah yes.' Omar remembered something and sat down again. 'Wine? More wine?' he asked. 'You must drink with me. You are not tourists, you are friends. I can always tell and I never drink with tourists.'

Within an hour, Alex had undergone an astounding change in her attitude to camels, managing to become quite enthusiastic as Omar introduced them one by one.

'This is Laassell, the oldest, the wisest, the best camel in Morocco. He is *chef de la troupe*.' He ran his hand down the long leg of one of the beasts, over a knee which looked as if it was made of crumpled leather. Its feet were the size of soup plates surrounded by a ring of curly hair and its hooves were cleft with what they took to be toes ending in almost human-looking toenails.

'The best camel in the world.' He patted Laassell's neck. Laassell managed a slight flicker of acknowledgement from under his long eyelashes then pretended he was shaking flies away. Omar finished another thumping pat, his hand coming to rest on Alex's shoulder for a moment. They walked towards the car, explaining they were returning to La Fibule to pick up their luggage.

'I have some other English staying. We are going into the desert. You will like that.' Flo said she'd love to. Amazingly, Alex agreed.

'On camels?'

'On camels.' They got into the car and Omar motioned them out on to the road.

'How old do you think he is?' Alex mouthed, looking in the wing mirror.

'Laassell?'

'No, stupid, Omar.'

'Dunno. Thirty? Thirty-five? It's difficult to tell with those *shesh* things. But he's a bit like Zorba, isn't he?'

Alex didn't think so. Omar leaned in through the driver's window to say goodbye again. The light was fading and the shadows stretching out on the dunes. A camel, silhouetted against the sky, approached at a half trot. The young man in blue sat on it easily, his arms around a small boy perched in front.

'*Voilà!* Jalil.'

'And?' asked Alex, wondering who the small boy might be.

'My nephew, the son of my uncle, Ahmed, and my aunt. They have many children. Jalil is bringing him home from school.' Home from school, on a large camel, across a golden desert to an enchanted, shabby fortress. Flo shook her head in wonder.

'Coming home from school,' she murmured as the sun slipped further down.

*   *   *

74

Without a qualm or prick of conscience, Alex told La Fibule that they were checking out the next day. Nobody seemed too bothered and by lunchtime they were on the road back to the desert.

The Hôtel des Dunes didn't have any official stars and was so reasonable there was no question of sharing. Flo was given a little red mud room with a rose on the door. Alex was in the adjoining one with a kitten. There was a washbasin, surprisingly clean and normal with two taps that gave a strong gush of salty water, but the waste pipe didn't seem to go very far and the water flowed straight out on to the rush matting, adding to a large water stain, others obviously having made the same mistake. With a room of her own, Flo could read all night and smoke to her heart's content but, as she also discovered, the generator packed up at about nine o'clock. With a couple of candles in the niche behind her head there was quite an adequate light if she tipped her book towards it. She read until the candles burned out and the unfamiliar noises gradually died away. Then there was the murmur of voices coming from one of the tower rooms, where Omar and the boys gathered and talked late into the night before the boys dropped where they were, rolled up in a blanket on the seats, in the tent, some on the stone floor of the path outside the guest rooms. Later she heard a shuffling, the toothless old night-watchman doing his rounds in the moonlight and then the sound of desert dogs, howling in the silver light.

'Joseph! Ali! Adi! *Agi*! *Agi*!' The desert. Yes, that was it. They were going into the desert, the real desert and they were going to sleep out there. She opened her little wooden door on to the garden. The boys scurried back and forth with piles of blankets, sacks and large, yellow plastic bottles. As she made her way to the shower room she could see the camels, all sitting, as the boys piled stuff on to each one. Jalil was tying things on with what looked like very complicated knots and checking either side of the saddles to see if the weight was evenly distributed.

Omar appeared beside Flo.

'*Bonjour*, Fatima. Did you sleep well?'

'Fatima?'

'Yes, you are Fatima. And your friend . . .' he searched for Alex's name without success. 'Your friend is Ayesha. I give you all Moroccan names, English names are impossible to remember. John, Jim, Joe, Sharon, Elizabeth!' He had trouble pronouncing that one. Flo laughed.

'Fatima?' It was a bit comical, but one up on being called a gazelle.

'*La bess*?' The plump lady ('the wife of my uncle Ahmed') waddled past working her crochet. Taking this to mean 'Did you sleep well?' Flo nodded.

'*La bess*?' The plump lady said it again as another wooden door creaked open and a tall young man, with very pale, almost girlish skin and a long, silky black ponytail, peered out on to the day and blinked. He looked at Flo and blinked again. Flo did a double take.

'Duncan? Duncan?' He gave her an 'I know I know you but I haven't the faintest idea who you are' look.

'The City Lit,' she prompted him.

'My technophobe!' he said, recognising his only failure.

'What on earth are you doing here?'

Before either of them could reply to this uninspired

76

question Omar said, 'You know each other? That is good, very good. Ali! Joseph! *Agi! Agi!*'

'You wouldn't happen to have a bacon sandwich on you?' Duncan asked wistfully when, showered and salty, they waited for their breakfast.

'Oh, don't be so daft.' They were joined by a young woman with prematurely white hair framing her pale Celtic skin, green eyes and delicately arched eyebrows. Duncan introduced her somewhat absently as Keltie as his eyes searched beyond the camels to the horizon, possibly for a bacon sandwich.

'He's been on about bacon ever since we got here. But he never touches it at home.' Keltie sat down and heaved a large camera bag on to the tiled table.

'Have you been here before?' They compared travel notes and told each other carpet stories.

'Must be some sort of initiation,' they agreed, then Keltie told her that they, too, came from Notting Hill. Just down the road, in fact. They crowed with surprise.

Jalil, walking by with a length of rope asked, 'You come from the same village?'

'You could put it like that.'

'That is good.'

'Ah.' Duncan stopped searching heaven for a bacon sandwich and settled for coffee, apricot jam, bread and butter and a small greasy omelette.

'I wonder . . .' he began.

'If you say bacon sandwich once more, a pig will fall on your head,' Keltie threatened him then took a close-up of his omelette. Duncan drained his coffee in one. So did Flo.

'Joseph!' They both called him at the same time. '*Encore du café.*' Joseph smiled nicely and forgot about it the next moment. Keltie zoomed in after him.

'Coffee?' Flo pleaded to another boy who didn't look a day over nine. She thought his name was Adi or Agi. 'Coffee, Adi.' Although willing, he didn't understand either English or French.

'Coffee?' Jalil reappeared from behind the big tent. He'd taken off his blue robe and was wearing baggy cotton pants in a startling tartan, a T-shirt with Bob Marley stencilled on the front, turquoise beads round his neck and a Walkman tucked into a wide leather belt.

'Wow!' Keltie snapped him as he gave her a wide, almost professional smile. She clicked again.

'Coffee?' Duncan was desperate.

'And for me,' said a bright, light voice as Alex appeared from her room. 'Good morning, everybody.' In black stretch jodhpurs, black boots, a white shirt and with the black spangled scarf she'd bought in Taroudant swathed round her face, she obviously hadn't forgotten about Marlene at all. Flo introduced her.

'Duncan . . .'

'Currently know as Mohammed.'

'Alex . . . and I think I'm called Ayesha.'

'Keltie.'

'What do they call you?'

'Can't remember,' Keltie replied vaguely as she checked her focus and Flo explained to Alex about the City Lit and Notting Hill. Keltie pointed her camera. Alex tilted her chin a fraction. Flo remembered she was still in her dressing-gown and jumped up.

'Remember to take something warm,' Alex called after her. 'They said it gets cold in the desert at night.'

The camels waited, saddled, loaded and ready to be mounted. Omar fondled Laassell's thick, woolly coat as Flo approached with a lump of sugar which the camel accepted as his due.

'Can I ride him?' she asked, as he had a wise, large head and didn't look as if he was going to do anything fast or dangerous. Omar looked dubious.

'He is very big, Fatima.' It was Jalil who spoke. Fatima it was obviously going to be.

'It doesn't matter,' she insisted, having established a tenuous link with a lump of sugar.

'Why not?' Omar agreed as Jalil tied a sack on one side and a tin of biscuits and a kettle on the other.

'Quick!' Jalil whirled round and shouted at Duncan who was about to mount the camel he'd selected for himself. 'Quick! That one, he moves!' He was too late. As Duncan put one long leg over the beast it did an amazing three-point movement and was on its feet before Duncan's other leg had left the ground and the camel was looking down at him, all but laughing.

'Do they all do that?' asked Alex in a faint voice as Jalil pulled the camel's neck, forcing it back on to its knees.

'Ouch, ouch . . .' it roared and gurgled, making a great show of not wanting to do the same thing over again. Jalil slapped its nose.

'Quick!' He held it down as Duncan leaped on to the blanket-covered space behind the hump and grabbed the thin rope Jalil handed to him while Keltie danced around taking pictures from all angles.

'It's great up here.' Duncan looked down at Alex, who had a little overnight bag clamped to her chest. Jalil knelt and examined the underside of the camel's plate-sized foot.

'Did you ever see feet like that?' Keltie moved in for a close-up.

'It's not its feet I'm worried about,' said Alex, making little furrows in the sand with her boot.

'Don't worry, Ayesha. For you I have a very special camel and I will lead you all the way.' Omar guided her towards a creamy, neatly made animal with large, dark eyes and long eyelashes. Perfect, with her black and white outfit. Alex allowed herself to be heaved on and clung to anything she could reach.

'I will lead you,' promised Omar. There was a small shriek from Keltie as her camel lurched to its feet and she nearly let go of her camera bag. Flo, the last to mount, walked towards Laassell who, now that she was closer, really did look big.

'One moment.' Lahassan, a little *chamellier* with a pointed beard, bright eyes and broken leather shoes, rushed up with a violin case and started to tie it on to Laassell's saddle. When it was secure he held out his hand to help her mount. With a one, two, three, hop, she sprang and landed more or less in the right place.

'Coffee?' asked Jalil, again appearing from nowhere and handing a glass up to her.

'*Yalla!*' shouted Omar. 'We go! Pull to the right to go right. Pull to the left to go left.'

'Omar,' Alex interrupted but Omar was training a small pair of binoculars (hers) at a large bus approaching along the road.

'*Vite! Les fourmis!*' He told them to rein in for a moment.

With the exception of Lahassan and Adi, all the boys rushed into one of the tower rooms and out again, struggling into blue robes mostly too large for them. The bus passed and turned on to the track to the dunes, the blank faces of Japanese tourists staring out at them. The boys ran full tilt after the bus. Jalil leaped on to a remaining camel and, kneeling behind its hump, shouted it into a gallop as he pulled his robes over the Bob Marley T-shirt.

'Will you look at that!' said Keltie. 'No hands!' She trained her camera on the vanishing camel. The bus arrived at the dunes and unloaded its passengers, who within minutes were scrambling around, black dots on the yellow sand.

Omar pointed. 'You see? *Fourmis*, ants.' They took pictures of each other and the boys who either stood around looking picturesque, or tried to persuade them to have a quick turn on a camel themselves. Two at a time. The cameras snapped furiously.

'Oh, *les Japonais*. Clack, clack, *merci* Kodak. Not you,' he added to Keltie. 'You are a professional. I can tell.'

'What's that place?' she asked, looking at the Foreign Legion building.

'It is nothing.' Omar dismissed it. '*Yalla*, now we go.'

'Is Jalil coming with us?' said Keltie, who knew a good photo opportunity when she saw one.

'He must stay. My uncle Ahmed is not accustomed to making guests happy. Jalil is wise, my best *chamellier*, but he must look after the hotel while I'm away. *Yalla*!' They wheeled the camels round.

'Omar!' cried Alex, looking wonderful but holding on for dear life. 'How do you make it stop?'

The silence of the desert was a myth, they discovered, as the camels plodded softly on their big feet out into the wide, empty space behind the dunes. Lahassan sang as he shuffled along, the soles of his shoes flapping as he walked; Adi ran ahead in flip-flops, letting out sharp little cries and throwing stones in a haphazard way at the sky.

'Hiya, hiya, hiya.' Omar shouted at the camels to speed up or slow down, none of them changing the rhythm. It was, Flo realised after about twenty minutes, almost impossible to fall off, even with her legs spread at an impossible angle over Laassell's broad back and all the baggage he'd been loaded with.

'*Ça va*, Fatima?'

'Fine.' She pushed the spout of the kettle from under her thigh, damned if she was going to complain.

'*Ça va*, Mohammed?' Omar tore a branch from a scrubby tree and whacked Duncan's camel on its skinny rump.

'Oh, please,' gasped Alex, 'no faster.'

'Will you look at Duncan?' shouted Keltie from behind as Duncan's camel managed to work up a tentative trot and started to vie with Laassell for the lead. Without apparent haste or effort, Laassell kept a nose in front.

'You see?' Omar was delighted. 'He is the leader of the troupe. *Ça va*, Fatima?'

'Fine,' said Flo again, shifting off the violin that was banging on her leg.

'Like this.' They stopped for lunch and Omar showed them how to tuck the ropes under a stone or tie them loosely round one to secure the camels and stop them wandering off. But had any of them taken it into their heads to move away, a string under a stone didn't seem likely to stop them.

'Yes,' Omar agreed, 'but they won't. Look.' The ropes were attached to a ring through the left nostril of each camel. 'The nose is very sensitive, if they pull the rope it hurts them. So they don't. Now, whisky Berber.' Lahassan had perched the kettle in its rightful place on the fire.

'I will never, ever move from here again.' Duncan threw himself down on a blanket Adi had spread in the shade of a palm.

'You need some sun block,' Alex reminded Flo, 'or your nose will peel.'

'It's my bum that's sore.' Flo rubbed the area of her coccyx.

'Don't talk about it.' Duncan groaned, shifted, then rose unsteadily to his feet, unashamed by the difficulty he was having in the area of his crotch. He moved off to a large rock, leaned against it and started talking softly into a little tape recorder. Lahassan and Adi stared in disbelief.

'He is talking to himself?'

'It's inspiration,' Keltie explained through Omar. 'He's writing a book.'

'Ah, a poet.' This apparently explained everything and from then on they regarded him with deep respect.

'It isn't quiet in the desert,' Flo remarked to Omar, thinking about the singing and the shouting.

'You have to make a noise,' he told her. 'In the desert you must break the silence or it will drive you mad. Now we eat.'

Duncan stood to eat his brochettes, fresh bread Lahassan had conjured from Laassell's sacks.

'If it's all the same to you, I think I'll walk for a bit,' he announced when it was time to remount.

'*Bien sûr*, my friend,' Omar sympathised. 'It is difficult for men. *Yalla*.' Duncan led his camel, talking to it and apparently getting answers from it with every snort and snuffle as they moved off into the hot afternoon.

'Thank God we've stopped.' Alex combed her hair and smoothed cream on her hands and face. 'It's cold.' She shivered plaintively. The camp site was a sheltered dip with a lone palm that the sun no longer touched.

'Here.' Omar wrapped her in his black burnoose. She posed for a moment against the dying light as Keltie took pictures. Flo sat on the ridge watching the boys as they hobbled the camels and sent them off to find whatever prickly nourishment they could. Lahassan had put up a tent, in reality a bit of brown sacking tied to a gnarled pole. A tagine was bubbling on the fire in the big, black pot that had been digging into the small of her back all day and the saddles and blankets were pulled up into a circle round the glowing wood. Omar produced two bottles of wine. Flo wished she'd had the sense to have worn boots. Or at least another pair of socks. She drew the grey shawl round her shoulders.

'Here, come to the fire.' Omar poured the wine into glasses that Adi had rinsed after they'd finished their tea.

'To the English.' Omar toasted them. Their faces were glowing with sun and clean air. Duncan was asleep. 'Welcome to the hotel of a thousand stars.' The moon rose and Lahassan, his little hands coated with sand and flour, began to play his violin.

Later, lit by the moon, Flo went off to look for a private place to pee. Having accomplished what was vital, she lit a cigarette and looked down at the camp. Lahassan was damping the fire. Keltie and Duncan were rolled up in their sleeping bags. When Lahassan had finished, he found a blanket, rolled himself into it and lay down beside Adi, who was already asleep in his woollen tube. She could just make out the camels, moving with a hopping motion in the distance. Alex, her face glowing, sat close to Omar who was rolling a joint in the light of a candle. They seemed to have no intention of turning in.

'For you, Fatima, the tent,' Omar told her as she slithered down from the ridge. She crawled in under the brown sacking.

'Sleep well.' It was Alex, who sounded as if she was just off to a party. Flo kicked off her sandals, lay one blanket on the sand, settled herself on it and tried to pull the other over herself. There was a gap between her socks and her trousers and her feet were very, very cold.

In less than an hour she realised that not only was the sand she lay on hard, less than eight inches down it was damp. She rubbed her feet and wrapped the grey shawl round them. It was quiet now, no wind, no sound of camels, no voices. She sat up. There was no sign of Alex. Or Omar. Her elbow dug into the sand. It was definitely wet. She lit a cigarette; the click of her lighter almost made her jump in the stillness. She inhaled deeply and looked up at the sky. There was a star directly above her but there shouldn't have been. There should have been brown sacking but Lahassan had pitched the tent on a slope and little by little she had slipped forward by about four feet. She knelt then dragged a pile of sand to make a bunker at foot level, making crazy sandcastles in the moonlight. Someone giggled. A very distinctive giggle. Only Alex could giggle like that and only if she had company. She peered towards the fire. Lahassan and Adi sleeping neatly, Keltie and Duncan in their rounded humps and a third mound of blankets now heaving back and forth. Alex was having it off with Omar. For a moment she felt turned to stone and then came the first, flashing reaction.

Alex, how could you? With Omar? Not that she had

anything against Omar, but they'd only known him for a day, a day and a half, not counting that first encouter. Shock boomeranged back on her and she was horrified with herself for being shocked.

'You prissy cow,' she muttered out loud. 'You judgemental prissy cow.' She pulled the shawl over her head and lay back on the rumpled, sandy blankets. Her feet would just have to fend for themselves. But no sleep came. For a long time she sat, a wakeful guardian of the camp, as the power of the night rolled over her, pulling at her to acknowledge feelings that she'd never permitted a foothold in the past. Sadness and regret that she had wasted so much time in her life. Loneliness. For a moment she tried to focus on Robert, an indulgence she'd allowed only fleetingly in the past. But that was ridiculous. Robert, whose idea of heaven was a civilised café in Provence, a pastis at his elbow and a re-read of Raymond Chandler. The mighty silence and the endless pinpoints of light above her pushed on without mercy, all senses exaggerated, the air clear, the sand colder, the wool around her shoulders softer, every second gaining in intensity. Looking down at her sleeping companions, she felt a love and warmth for them flood through her as she waited humbly for the dawn.

Like Joseph leading Mary, Omar led Alex as the little caravan headed back towards the hotel. Alex, alight with early sun and afterglow now held the saddle bar lightly with one hand. At breakfast she'd chosen to say nothing about her night of lust. Flo, slightly aggrieved, said nothing either, just remarking, 'It was cold last night.'

'So, Fatima, how was your first night in the desert?' Omar asked, without missing a beat.

'Fine.' She was damned if she was going to grumble, admit to cold, lack of sleep and anguished soul-searching. 'Fine. I'm sorry it's over,' she told Duncan who was sitting side-saddle on his camel, still trying to convey the relentless beauty of the desert to his tape recorder.

'Some people feel like that,' Omar told her. 'It is your heart speaking.'

'My heart may be sad it's over but my backside is delighted.' She shifted off Lahassan's violin. Omar laughed so much the boys wanted to know what the joke was. He told them in Arabic. Lahassan let out a shrieking giggle.

'*Eh voilà!*' The hotel was in sight in the far distance. They were approaching from the south, which meant they had gone round in a big circle.

'Couldn't we stay just one more night?' Despite her aches Flo was just getting the hang of it, ready to start again. Alex swivelled round and shot her a look of anguish. Omar lifted up the binoculars.

'Look!' He pointed. 'Nomads.' Far away, tucked under the cliff of the mountain behind the hotel, they could just make out two dark shapes, brown tents and minute dots that could have been camels or mules.

'That is rare, they seldom travel so far from the deep desert.'

Keltie held out her hand for the binoculars. 'Couldn't we go and see?' She fiddled in her camera bag for a new roll of film.

'Another time. Tonight, many people, a big party. New Year's Eve.'

'New Year's Eve?' she echoed having, like the others, lost track of time.

Jalil and the other boys greeted them as if they had

been away on a dangerous mission for several months. The camels knelt for the last time beside two parked buses and a van. Slowly and stiffly they dismounted.

'You ride well, Fatima,' Omar told her as she patted Laassell's neck. 'You may ride him any time. No charge.' Flo glowed under such praise and such an offer.

'What's going on?' demanded Alex. There were people everywhere, young Spanish climbing in and out of the two buses, chattering in the garden beside the well and at all the tiled tables.

'The Spanish. They come every year.' Omar broke off for a brief handshake with Ahmed who was turning over a pile of dusty carpets pitched from the van with his foot which he appeared to be buying by the kilo. The boys dragged them from the van and into the garden then attempted to lay them at odd angles between the crowded tables.

'Coffee, Fatima?' Jalil was at her side with two small glasses.

'Both?' she asked.

'Both,' he assured her.

'It's full of strangers.' Alex, already in her bathrobe, stormed out of the shower room. 'There's a queue a mile long and the lavatories are unspeakable. Joseph!' She collared him in a swift movement. 'Bring me a kettle of hot water, no, make it two and a bucket.' She made him repeat it and went back to the Kitten room. Keltie and Flo flopped down at a table with a tubby little man in a turquoise anorak, a black *shesh*, corduroy trousers and stout boots, who didn't seem to have any connection with the Spanish.

'You wish to sit here?' He rose and introduced himself as Bernard, from Alsace.

88

'Have you been here long?' Bernard gave Flo no definite answer.

'Is it your first visit?' Again, Keltie got an evasive response.

'This', he said, 'is very interesting.' He pulled a plastic bottle with no label out of his pocket. 'I have it always with me.' They looked at it. 'It is for everything,' Bernard went on, holding it up to the light. 'For the teeth, for the hair, for the body, for the clothes, for the insects and for the floor.'

'Fancy that,' said Keltie. Flo was on the point of asking if he often needed to clean floors on holiday but, still touched by the dignity of the desert, could find little to say about multi-purpose detergents.

'I think I'll go and see what Duncan's up to. Like as not glued to his lap-top.' Keltie gathered up her things.

'Monsieur Bernard.' Ahmed motioned Bernard to follow him to a room beside Reception used only by the family. Flo stood up. There was no point in hoping for a shower. She wandered back to the well. The carpet van had gone and the boys had put away all traces of the camping things.

'Laassell?' He was munching what looked like hay. 'Laassell?' He turned his big head towards her and before thinking she did her one, two, three, hop and was on his back.

'*Yalla*!' she said quietly. There was no response. '*Yalla seer*!' She kicked him. He rose to his feet and stood waiting for instructions. She leaned forward, grabbed the rope and to her astonishment he started off at a gentle pace in the direction of the nomads' tents. After a few minutes she gathered up enough courage to urge him into a reluctant trot, but the bumping nearly dislodged her. At her command he slowed down enough to grab at a prickly shrub with his yellow teeth. In a few minutes they were out of earshot of the Spanish revelry. A little black and white bird perched on a rock and stared at her, its head cocked as they headed slowly toward the foot of the mountain.

About fifty yards from the nomads' camp she pulled up. There were no men around, only a few children who ran part of the way towards her, then stopped dead and stared, as if she were spitting stones. One of them started to cry when Flo called out to it. Two women appeared in the doorway of the tent, dressed in dark garments with red-edged shawls around their heads. They folded their sinewy arms, encased from wrist to elbow in silver bangles and stared at her. There were no smiles, no *Bonjour, madame*, no requests for *un dirham, un stylo*, as they stared, their faces dark, leathery and lined, unmoving as the cliff of rock behind them. She lifted her hand in greeting again then let it drop. OK, ladies, two can play at that game. Without wanting to appear to be retreating, but stirred into confusion, she wheeled Laassell round. Eager to return to his hay, he picked up pace. Hanging on to the saddle bar, she allowed him (although she had little choice) to break into a gentle gallop. Flushed with pleasure, she arrived breathless at the well and dismounted. She had been out on a camel in the desert, on her own. True, it was only for about twenty minutes, but so what? Humming a little tune she passed through the gates and headed to her room, unaware of the figure in blue standing on one of the turret roofs. Jalil let fall the binoculars and hurried back to his duties for the evening. In her room, she lay on her bed listening to the strange noises coming from next door. At first she thought it could be Alex and

Omar snatching a quickie but no one, even in the throes of passion, could make noises like that. Grnt . . . whirr . . . whistle . . . grunt . . . clack . . . roar. It was someone snoring. She started to count the different noises of the symphony until Alex burst into the room.

'Good, you're still dressed. Come on.'

'Come on where?'

'Town. Omar's taking us to the *hammam*.'

'Have you done this before?' asked Keltie, clutching her sponge bag as they stood on the steps outside the *hammam*. From inside they could hear screeching, laughing and singing coming from a slit window high above.

'No.' They all looked at each other.

'In the guide book it says you have to keep your knickers on.' A woman with dark eyes and a big smile beckoned them inside.

'What about verrucas?' murmured Alex.

'Too late.' The woman all but gathered the three of them into her arms and ushered them into the dark interior of the first room, full of women in varying stages of dress or undress. The large woman kept her eye on them. Keltie was ready first, wrapped in a tartan towel, and was instructed to take a bucket from the stack and go into the next room. Alex followed cautiously, clutching shampoo and conditioner. Flo's zip got stuck.

'Your purse.' The large woman held out her hand for it.

'My what?' The woman nodded to a ramshackle desk by the entrance where it would be safe. Flo shrugged and gave it to her.

'And these?' She indicated her jumper and the baggy

pants she'd managed to drag off. A young girl standing near gazed curiously at her bra. 'Oh yes.' Flo took it off and as instructed kept her pants on. Wrapped in her towel, she went to get her bucket. A naked giantess loomed in front of her and grabbed it. Flo hung on. The giant woman braced her legs and pulled. Laughter echoed round the room and gusts of steam billowed out from the darkness into which Alex and Keltie had vanished. The woman pulled again. Flo stood firm as an undignified struggle started which she was bound to lose. Suddenly a tiny black woman, dressed in nothing but Y-fronts, darted from the steamy darkness and put a claw-like hand on Flo's arm.

'*Comme ça!*' It was then that she realised she'd taken three buckets jammed inside each other. There was more laughter. The tiny woman beckoned her to follow. Black, brown, deep aubergine, apricot, plump with mammoth buckets, thin with wizened, tear-shaped dangling breasts, about a hundred women scrubbed and scraped and lathered each other and their small children, who were eating tangerines and throwing the skins at anyone who passed. Flo joined Alex and Keltie and the three of them sat like plucked white chickens wondering what to do next until the little woman hustled them towards a tank of water overflowing from a running tap. She warned them it was very, very hot. Flo looked up at the ceiling wreathed in steam escaping from the one thin window high up on the wall. It was almost dark outside before the little woman deemed the water cool enough to use, produced an article much like a brillo pad and began to scour each one of them. Alex, her head buried in her arms, shuddered as she was sluiced down. Keltie, her skin pink, smiled at a young woman who, driven by curiosity about her hair, approached, putting out a tentative hand and touching the damp, white locks.

'It's real,' is what they thought she said to her equally curious friends. The children gathered round and stared with wide eyes. The noise rose, shrilling, squealing, shouting, singing as if they were in a giant aviary of shrieking birds, lost somewhere in the thirteenth century.

'Yes, yes, take it!' Alex thrust her shampoo into the eager outstretched hands of a woman who was nearly bald. The woman slopped off through the water and tangerine peel and displayed her treasure to a group of younger women who passed it round, sniffing and giggling.

'Oh God,' Alex turned to Flo. 'I think I've lost a contact lens.'

Jalil was waiting for them at the Café Timbuktu where Omar had promised to be.

'Where's Omar?'

'He had to see the mechanic. He said you were not to catch cold after the *hammam*. You would like to sit inside?' With every muscle free of tension, every pore scrubbed free of grime, hair soft and silky and their faces shining clean, they all agreed that they were ten years younger and possibly five pounds lighter.

'You would like to sit inside?' Jalil asked them again.

'No. Let's sit out here,' Flo said, watching the street alive with people and New Year's Eve in the air.

'As you wish.' He called the waiter and ordered their teas and coffees as they exchanged *hammam* stories,

Keltie winning with the glory of her white hair, Flo second with her battle of the buckets and Alex a poor third for thinking she'd lost a contact lens.

'It was', she pronounced with a shudder, 'the most awful experience of my life.'

'No,' Keltie and Flo disagreed, 'it was magnificent.'

Awful; magnificent; they were running out of words to describe the intensity of one happening after another.

Their chatter tailed off as a policeman approached the table, ignored the women and stood directly in front of Jalil.

'Your papers,' he demanded. Jalil produced a card from the sloping pocket of his robe. The policeman looked at it, then walked ten feet to another policeman. They stood together shooting surly glances at Jalil.

'What does he want?' asked Flo. The three women turned their heads and stared at the conferring police. Jalil shrugged.

'It's nothing,' he said, but his alertness indicated he was worried. The policeman came back holding the card.

'You know this man?' he asked them as a group.

'Of course,' they chorused.

'You are sure?'

'Of course we're sure.' Flo elected to speak for all of them. 'He works where we are staying. He is a friend.'

'Where are you staying?'

Alex told him, wishing Omar would come back.

'Come with me.'

Jalil rose and followed him to the second policeman. They stood talking out of earshot. There was much waving of hands, protest and explanation. After a few moments he returned and sat down, obviously shaken.

'What was all that about?' they wanted to know.

'He thinks I am a *faux guide*.'

'But that's ridiculous.' Flo remembered poor desperate Jacoub in Taroudant. 'You're not, so it's all right.' Jalil tried not to look at the policeman who still shot glances at him.

'He has kept my identity card.'

'Is that bad?'

'Very bad.'

'Don't worry. Omar will be back in a minute, I hope.'

'What can they do to you?' Flo noticed that his big hand was trembling.

'Put me in prison.' He made it sound matter-of-fact.

'Prison? How long for? What for?' exclaimed Alex.

'This is ridiculous.' Flo stood up and started towards the policeman, who at that moment approached the table. She sat down.

'What is this all about?' she started angrily. Keltie kicked her under the table.

'You know this man?'

'Of course we do. He is a friend. We already told you.'

'We do this for your own protection, madame,' the policeman replied.

'Protection.' She was about to get very angry and ask where they'd been when she was in the carpet shop.

'Keep out of it,' Keltie muttered, wishing she had her camera with her.

'Omar!' cried Alex, as he drew up with a screech of brakes outside the café.

'*Bonsoir! Bonne année!*' He was out of the car and had

an arm round each of the policemen and dealing with things in very fast Arabic. They thought they saw some crumpled money passing hands.

'One rule for some, another for others,' murmured Keltie.

Golden sparks flew up into the sky from a large, clay kiln by the tent where they had roasted a whole sheep. Six old musicians from the village, all dressed in white, filed past with drums, horns and tambourines, to play out the last moments of the year. To their bewilderment, they celebrated twice due to the time difference, as the Spanish insisted on singing it in an hour earlier. Then they danced on tables, popped balloons, threw streamers on to tables littered with remains of lamb, salad, couscous, nuts, dates, bottles and glasses.

'Great cheese, this,' remarked Duncan who was very stoned and pretty drunk as he unpeeled a triangle of Vache Qui Rit. 'I think,' he went on, stuffing it into his mouth and accepting another drag on a joint from Jalil who was passing by, 'I think that this is a school for spies. Spies in training to venture to far galaxies.'

'What?' shouted Flo above the din.

'This is the mayor of the village.' Omar presented a wizened little man to Keltie, gave Alex a shameless squeeze and hurried off.

'Aha!' Keltie shunted up to make room for the mayor with a gleam in her eye. Alex, serene and smart (in a little black dress), looked lovingly after Omar. Keltie poured a glass of wine for the little mayor, who held it but didn't drink.

'I said,' shouted Duncan across the table to Flo, 'I

said, this is a school for spies.' Omar reappeared with Bernard from Alsace.

'*Eh, mon ami.*' He pushed him down between Alex and Flo. 'These are our English friends. We have many English.' He embraced Alex again, took a swig of whisky someone had produced and went about being mine host to the Spanish who were clacking and stamping round the courtyard.

'What do you think?' Duncan was still on about his spy school.

'Could be,' Flo agreed, having drunk two whiskies herself and a lot of wine.

'And . . .' Duncan talked intimately to his tape recorder for a moment.

'Excuse me?' said the bewildered Bernard, trying to get into the swing of things.

'And these', continued Duncan, 'are the final exams.'

'Could be,' said Flo again wisely, and leaned over the table to Duncan. 'And he,' she hissed, nodding back at Bernard, 'he is the Examiner, the Grand Examiner.'

'What reason do you have to suspect that?' Duncan thrust the microphone at her.

'Because . . .' She paused for dramatic effect, somewhat lost in the din. 'Because he snores in code!'

Without thinking she accepted the joint from Jalil who had perched beside her on the banquette.

'I shouldn't if I were you,' advised Duncan.

'Why not?'

'You might get diarrhoea. Then again, you might get insights into the unknown.'

Flo drew deeply on the joint. She could do with a few insights into the unknown.'

'What is the password?' Duncan demanded of Jalil, pointing his mike. Jalil grinned from ear to ear.

'Pizza Hut!' declared Flo. 'The password is Pizza Hut, isn't it, Bernard?'

Although he didn't understand the joke, Jalil shook with laughter.

'Excuse me?' said Bernard.

'Pizza Hut,' Jalil informed him.

An insight into the unknown? Flo hadn't laughed so much since she was fifteen or maybe ten, or maybe never.

The Spanish had gone. The boys had gathered up the tatty carpets and were trying to sweep up little hills of confetti and streamers tangled round the table legs. Keltie and Flo sat together drinking the first coffee of the New Year.

'Would you mind changing places?' Keltie asked suddenly.

'OK.' Flo thought she might be hungover and the sun was in her eyes. She leaned forward.

'Look.' Flo turned. The little mayor was sitting cross-legged outside Keltie and Duncan's room.

'He's been there all night,' said Keltie.

'Why?'

'Beats me.'

'Perhaps he fancies you.'

'Don't be daft. I was only asking him if I could photograph the women in the village.'

'What did Duncan say?'

'Pizza Hut.' As she spoke Duncan opened their door and stared down at the little mayor, who made no attempt to move.

'*Bonjour*,' said Duncan pleasantly and stepped over him. 'What's he doing there?' he demanded when he reached the table.

'He's been there all night.'

'Why?'

'I don't know.'

'God knows what you said to him in your awful French.'

They started to squabble about each other's French.

'All I said was could I photograph the women of the village. *Femmes . . . photograpie!*'

'No wonder. They all know about European women on the loose.'

'What *do* you mean?' Keltie was pink with indignation.

'They're easy, only come here to get laid.' Duncan started trying to bribe Adi to bring him breakfast.

'What do you mean, easy?' Keltie insisted but couldn't prevent herself from an involuntary glance at the door of the Kitten room. Flo spotted the look. Keltie knew she had. There was nothing for it but to keep going.

'Yon Alex is pretty quick on the draw.' Keltie braved it out. Flo stiffened. It was all very well for her to have her own opinions about Alex on holiday but she wasn't having anyone else having any.

'Yes. Isn't she?' she returned with a touch of pride in her voice and went off to start her packing.

It was dawn with a long drive ahead, the bills paid, the tips distributed and addresses exchanged. Duncan and Keltie were taking a lift as far as Agadir.

'I wish one didn't have to book tickets, set dates. Why can't one take planes like buses?' Flo burst out as Jalil pushed the last of her silly parcels into the boot and closed it.

'Costs,' said Duncan in one of his rare moments of ordinary reality.

'How much this cost to hire?' Omar slapped his hand on the car and was shocked when Flo told him the rental price of the Peugeot.

'You should buy a car and leave it here. It will cost much less and I can meet you every time, no matter where. Even Tangier.'

'I'd rather buy a camel,' said Flo, taking a last look at Laassell.

'I am desolate that you leave,' said Omar and flung his arms round Alex, holding on tight.

'If we're going to catch this damn plane we'd better go.' Flo looked at her watch for the first time in two weeks. Reluctantly they started to get into the car, Flo and Keltie in the back, Duncan in the passenger seat because of his long legs, and Alex at the wheel.

'Wait!' Keltie leaped out again as two early rising women in black appeared against the skyline. She raised her camera but they were too quick for her and with a scuttling movement vanished into a dip at the side of the road.

'Of course you know why they wear those veils?' Alex murmured to Flo as she held the door for Keltie.

Flo raised her eyebrows. 'No. Why?'

'It's to hide the great smirks underneath. Moroccan men are something else!'

'You are impossible.' Flo hugged Alex who hugged her back. Things were back to normal.

'You're looking good,' Alex commented. By which she meant Flo's eyes were clear and she looked ten years younger. Flo took it to mean she'd lost weight. High praise. With relief they grinned at each other again.

'Oh, look.' Keltie pointed to the lonely little figure of the mayor making his way back to his village.

'Oh, *le pauvre*. He is in love.' Omar sighed.

'Goodbye, goodbye, *bonne continuation*,' said Jalil.

'Come back, come back,' shouted Omar.

'We will, we will.' Flo turned and took a look through the back window, trying to imprint the last golden moments and the lifting shadows of the dunes on her brain. The mountains looked close and it was going to be a beautiful day. Her eyes filled with tears of rage at the tyranny of a silly ticket. Tears of sadness because the magic stillness she had found would soon be torn from her. Tears which blurred the sight of Omar and Jalil leading a line of camels to be saddled for the day.

PART TWO

'**B**UT MUM, YOU'VE only just got back.'
'No I haven't . . . Christmas was ages ago.'
'But I thought you only went for Christmas.'
The New York daughter was put out by her mother's
change of routine. Christmas in Morocco was one thing,
established now, twice or was it three times, but here
she was, off again.

'I told you, darling, it's different this time. A long
trek into the desert . . . Fifteen days, I think.'

'Is Alex going too?'

'Yes, of course she is.'

'Well, I suppose it's all right then . . . What's the
weather like?'

'Here? Ghastly.' Over Christmas she'd been told
it was wonderful then as if to punish her for her
annual escape, January had been the most appalling in years. February was even worse, high gales
tearing down the trellis in the garden and a large
branch of the horse-chestnut tree from next door
crashing through the wall. Alex had fared no better in Spain where torrential rain had washed away
great stretches of the main road and the sewers had
overflowed.

'Well, have a good time, Mum, and take care.' Flo promised her daughter that she would.

'I will, oh yes, I will,' she murmured to herself and turned back to her packing.

With a million vivid memories stamped on their minds there was no need for sightseeing or meandering over any mountain ranges. The idea was to get to the hotel as fast as possible. After three Christmases and now a spring, they'd been upgraded from tourists, to visitors then 'family'. The fastest route Flo discovered, was flying via Paris to Ouarzazate, arriving in the Draa Valley before sunset then leaping into a taxi (without haggling, but this she kept to herself) and she could be at the hotel for dinner. A miracle. Alex made her own way from Tangier. 'Somehow . . .' she said bravely.

She had bumped into Sam, a neighbouring ex-pat, at the opening of an exhibition of an octagenarian artist she'd discovered in a shack near Ronda.

'The most enchanting primitives you've ever seen . . . masses of them. Sam bought two. Then we got talking about the desert. He said he'd always wanted to do the Lawrence of Arabia thing so I told him all about it. Well, not quite all. He gave me a lift all the way in a blacked-out Range Rover with air-conditioning. His name's Sam,' she said again.

'How is everyone?' Flo asked as she unpacked in the familiar little red-mud room. A small mountain of undies, T-shirts and lighters for the boys, reggae tapes for Jalil, Old Holborn for Muad, the night-watchman, hair stuff, face stuff and every medication she could think of.

'Much the same. Omar gets depressed and works too hard . . . They still haven't fixed the lav seats. Oh, really, Flo! What on earth is *that*?' It was a mosquito net, wrapped round a bottle of Glen Morangie for Omar. Flo looked up for a peg or nail to hang it on as Alex inspected the cotton dress with long sleeves that Flo had searched for for weeks. Flo sat on the bed and looked doubtfully at the Pentax she'd bought on impulse at the Duty Free. The assistant had told her it was so simple that a child of three could use it.

'Oh dear.' One look at the handbook told her there was more to it than met the eye.

'Do you know how to load this thing?' She looked at a roll of film in one hand to the camera in the other.

'Haven't a clue . . .' Alex inspected the pile of twelve books on the floor and picked out a Moroccan phrase book.

'You could stay here for years,' she commented looking at the cluttered room.

'I'm starving.' Flo, bored with unpacking swept up the bottle of Glen Morangie.

'What's that for?'

'It's for Omar.'

'Look,' said Alex, 'it's up to you, but I think it might be better if you didn't give it to him.'

'OK.' Flo rewrapped it and shoved it into the side pocket of her smallest bag. If Alex was uneasy about her giving whisky to Omar it was all right with her. It would always come in handy for someone else.

'Is everything all right with you and Omar?' she asked as they headed to the courtyard.

'Of course.' But it came out a bit too quick. 'Although I do sometimes ask myself, "What's a nice Jewish girl like you doing in a place like this?"' Flo cut short her giggles as two plump Dutch matrons made a sedate passage towards the showers in thick, candlewick dressing-gowns.

'Good Lord.' She looked after them.

'Wait till you see the others,' Alex warned her.

They sat at their usual table, the one Jalil had guided them to on that very first day. The cat-scratched legs and crooked plant pots were still reassuringly the same. But something was different. Something in the air. But not the unchanging menu which Joseph gave them with a welcoming smile. At the far end of the courtyard the tables had been pushed together to form one long one. There sat the party of their soon-to-be fellow adventurers, mostly largish middle-aged ladies and a few stolid couples. A man in a turquoise anorak and a black *shesh* sat at the head of the table which he banged with a spoon and waited for his group's full attention.

'My God, it's Bernard . . . Bernard from Alsace.' Flo recognised him from that first New Year's Eve.

'Yup, it's Bernard all right,' Alex said, then added, 'You know, you weren't so far off when you said he was a spy even if you were stoned. He's a tour operator. He was incognito and sizing up hotels for their trekking potential.'

'There you are!' Flo was triumphant. 'Insights into the unknown. What's he saying?' Bernard was addressing his group of Austrians, French, Belgians, Dutch and a few Swedish in his guttural French on how they should conduct themselves in a North African culture. They must always eat with their right hand. Should they be invited into a Moroccan home they must take off their shoes. It was very inadvisable for them to buy any souvenirs (carpets) at the end of the trip without being guided by him to a reputable shop. Tomorrow, at o-eight-hundred hours they were to be ready with all their needs for the desert neatly packed by the well. Any questions? Nobody seemed to have any. Bernard then issued them all with a bottle of his miracle detergent and sat down.

'Blimey.' said Flo.

At o-eight-hundred hours Flo and Alex stood with Omar who was a patting the magnificent black Range Rover. Bernard's group were packed, stacked and heaved on to their camels with squeals and nervous little shouts.

'How you got here from Ouarzazate?' Omar asked Flo.

'Taxi,' she admitted, watching Jalil tying her little cushion underneath the camel blanket.

'*Beinvenue*, Fatima!' Jalil called. Flo waved back.

'How much you pay for the taxi?' Omar insisted. Without thinking, Flo told him. Twenty pounds. Omar was horrified.

'You should get a car, Fatima, like my friend Sam. A Range Rover . . . *Magnifigue* . . .'

At this moment Sam approached through the archway with a neat rucksack on his back and wearing a black *shesh* at a rakish tilt. Alex introduced him to Flo. He was, she thought at once, a nice man, fair, slightly stocky with a firm handshake and twinkling blue eyes.

'Heard a lot about you,' he said.

'Oh dear . . .' Flo was as uncomfortable as anyone else whenever that was said.

'Good things, good things . . .' he assured her. 'Are that lot ours?' he asked Omar, excited as a schoolboy as he looked at the three unmounted camels Jalil was leading towards them.

'Yes, my friend, they are for you. Now you must mount.' Jalil helped Flo on to Laassell, Sam on to another large black camel while Omar heaved Alex on to the pretty one with long eyelashes. Flo settled herself comfortably. Omar spread out his arms.

'Twenty camels and all the boys . . . a real caravan,' said Flo.

'With that lot?' remarked Alex, snootily staring at Bernard's solid group who were either clutching their saddle bars or slathering their faces with sun-block.

'Alex, you must be nice,' Omar reproached her. 'It is very good, all nationalies . . . very good. Now we go! *Yalla*! *Yalla*!'

'*Yalla*! *Yalla*!' echoed Jalil and the boys as they moved off towards the south.

'Are you stiff?' asked Alex, as they pulled their boots off beneath a giant tamarisk, shady as a small church, its great roots pushing up in twisted shapes through the sand.

'No.' Flo hadn't had an ache or pain in several days. Her face was brown, she was eating like a horse and slept for eight hours a night on the hard ground.

'Look!' The camels were following Jalil in a docile line towards a well about a couple of hundred yards from the camp where the boys were pulling up buckets of clean, sweet water and pouring it into a stone trough. Without haste or gratitude, the camels drank their fill as the boys then filled half-steel drums left by other travellers, and set them to boil on fires already lit.

'Hot water tonight!' Omar told them and laughed as Alex, on her feet in a flash, was running towards the well, her shampoo in her hand.

'A bucket! I need a bucket!'

'Here!' Lahassan tipped a pile of potatoes out of a plastic bowl and held it out to Flo, who grabbed it and flew down the stony slope after her.

'This is the life!' Sam, stripped to the waist, was lathering soap all over his stocky body. 'You know something?' he confided to Flo, 'I've wanted to do this ever since I was a lad and it was now or never.'

'Why now or never?' she asked, sitting on the edge of the well, rivulets of water from her wet hair running down her clean T-shirt. Then wished she hadn't in case there was some awful reason why.

'Going back to England, packing it in in Spain,' he told her, scraping cautiously at his fair, new beard without a mirror. 'Drives you mad after a while. I made my pile; my wife wanted to lotus eat with the jet set. The marriage broke up and she went back to Deptford with the kids. I stayed on. Big mistake. Golf, drinking, sitting staring at your navel by a pool, more drinking, drives you potty in the end. I'm a working man,' he told her earnestly, as he wiped the soap off his face and screwed up his blue eyes. 'A working man and home's best.'

'But you're glad you came, aren't you?' Alex, her head wrapped in a towelling turban, gave him a smile Flo hadn't seen for a while.

'Glad? Look at it!' In a blaze of blood red and gold the sun was fighting for its life against oncoming night. A rogue cloud, caught in its light, a gleaming cycle shape that could have been a space ship.

'Look at the sky, Sam! Look at the sky!' Omar shouted from the camp. The three of them sat alone watching. No need to speak, no need to comment, until the cycle cloud dispersed and the sun was gone. They started to walk back to the camp. Alex linked her arm through Flo's.

'We do have some adventures, don't we?'

'Give us a listen,' said Sam as they settled themselves down. Flo handed over her Walkman. The cassette was Rachmaninov's 2nd.

'Bloody marvellous!' he said in surprise after the first opening bars.

'Keep it.' Alex was singing along to Bib Dylan on her Walkman with her eyes closed. Sam, giving little grunts of pleasure, conducted the concerto with his arms. Flo stared at the sky, content to let herself be overcome by the imponderability of space. After an hour's silence she remarked to no one in particular, 'Remember what Cecille said? Remember what she said about Venus not twinkling because it's a planet? It's not true. I thought so at the time. Look at it, it's twinkling away like mad.'

As the light grew stronger in the east, Flo was woken by a rustling sound. Propped on her elbow, she watched Laassell, who had hobbled and hopped into the middle of the camp and had his head stuck into a sack of vegetable peelings from the night before. Eventually he tossed it aside and headed for a new sack of tangerines.

'Hey!' She wriggled out from her warm blankets and in her pants and T-shirt walked slowly towards him.

'I don't think you're meant to be doing that,' she whispered, for fear of waking those still sleeping round the dead camp fire.

'Shoo! Shoo!' It didn't sound appropriate for one so large and noble. Laassell didn't think so either.

'*Agi, agi.*' It was one of the few Arabic words she knew and it meant 'here', not someone's name. Tempting him with a lump of stale bread, she grabbed his rope and led him from the storage piles towards a reasonably juicy-looking bush. Wide awake now, she slipped on her jeans, folded her bedding and looked round for her camera, then quietly started up a big dune for a dawn too good to miss. The sand was still cool beneath her feet as the colours changed from misty pinks and blues to gold and the shadows grew behind the tamarisks and rocks. No one else had stirred. Alex and Omar slept at a discreet distance in the brown sacking tent, now shaped into a tepee. Bernard, whose snores thundered through the silence of the night, had been banished several hundred yards away by his group, who were still dreaming on in their brightly coloured little dome-shaped tents. She looked at the instruction book to see what it had to say about wide-angle.

'Coffee, Fatima?' She started. Without a sound, Jalil had climbed the far side of the dune and was handing her a mug of milky, sugary liquid.

'How did you make coffee?' she asked, looking at the still dead fire.

'Magic.' He smiled and produced a little thermos from his pocket.

'Here.' She offered him a cigarette, which he took and lit as she trained her camera on the camp. Something white caught her attention. Omar's *shesh*. And he was wearing it, lying face down, spread-eagled with an empty bottle of wine beside him. Which meant he wasn't, as she had thought, tucked up with Alex. Which meant? Who could tell what it meant? Jalil smoke quietly beside her, looking thoughtfully at the clean, new day.

'Today, Fatima, you must wear a *shesh*. The weather will change and it will be hot.' He stood up and stared to where the camels were grazing in the distance. Then, without a word, he hurried down the dune and over to the sprawling Omar. He shook him gently, then more

110

firmly. Omar looked up at him with bleary eyes. They talked for a few seconds then Omar stood up and they both walked off into the desert. A little later they returned. Omar shook one of the boys, Zaide, awake. From where Flo sat, she heard the sound of an argument. Zaide lost. He filled a water bottle and trudged off towards the south.

'What was that about?' she asked Omar, who looked bleary and toxic.

'One of the camels went missing in the night. A new one. I bought it from the nomads near here and it must have gone to find them.'

He broke off to wave cheerfully at one of the group.

'*Guten morgen, schlafen sie wohl*? They could be any-where, the nomads . . .' He shook his head and told one of the boys to distribute the missing camel's load among the others.

Jalil was right. It was very, very hot. Hating anything on her head, but realising she'd be an idiot not to, she asked Omar if he had a spare *shesh*.

'Only forty dirham.' He pulled one from a pile of blankets on another camel. It was far from new. He showed her how to tie it.

'Very fetching.' Alex appeared from the tent. Flo put out her hand for a mirror.

'Oh God. I look like a nun.'

'*Yalla*, we go. But later we walk.' They rode for about half an hour and then dismounted at the start of a footpath zig-zagging up what looked like a sheer rock face.

'Now we walk. You must lead your camels, it is too steep to ride. Not difficult, not dangerous.' There

111

were a few protests from the group but Flo, Alex and Sam remained stoically British and started first, heads down, eyes fixed on the back feet of the camel in front. Sweat poured within minutes, throats became dry, some wheezed and puffed and Flo thought she heard someone swear. It took nearly an hour to reach the top where the boys waited with tea and water.

'We go.' Omar had them on their camels again, training Alex's binoculars for Zaide and the missing camel. In single file they plodded through a narrow gorge emerging into a wide, shallow, grit-black valley. Flo thought she saw a tree up ahead. Strange, one tree, stuck in such a wilderness. But heat haze and distance play tricks with vision. It was a woman, dressed in black, so still, so silent, she could have been Lot's wife. The caravan passed within ten yards of her but no one said a word. Not even Omar or the boys, as if the sternness of her stillness forbade greeting or comment.

'Did you see that woman?' she asked Alex later, when they stopped for lunch.

'Yes.' She sounded uncertain.

'D'you think anyone else saw her? No one said anything.'

'I know.' They both thought about it for a moment.

'Bit like that bus,' said Flo and lit a cigarette. A moment later she felt a hot stinging on her shoulder, like a vicious insect bite.

'Ouch!'

'Fatima!' Lahassan looked up from fanning the fire and let out a shout.

At the same moment Alex screamed, 'Flo, look out!' Then someone threw something over her head, smothering her. Something that stank of camel. She struggled, beating at it. Then her head was wrenched back as the cloth and *shesh* slid off.

'Oh, my God!' Ignited by a spark from her cigarette, the *shesh* had caught fire and burst into flame. Jalil had leaped and grabbed and now the length of blue cotton was burning from end to end. Within seconds it was no more than a strip of ash lying like a withered snake on the sand. She shuddered at what could have happened and turned to thank him, but he was back at some task involving ropes.

'Are you all right?' Alex hovered round her. With a shaking hand, Flo lit another cigarette.

'Are you all right?' Alex repeated and refrained from saying anything about smoking.

'I'm fine. Let's eat.'

Another ritual established by Bernard was the cause of much amusement, irritation or deep curiosity on the part of the boys. Every afternoon, after lunch, the group settled down in a stuffy, makeshift tent of blankets and listened as in guttural French then German he read aloud stories from *The Thousand and One Nights*. Those who could, sat cross-legged, and all of them took notes.

'What's he on about?' asked Sam, who spoke neither French or German.

'Is he reading the Koran?' Lahassan wanted to know.

'No,' Flo told him, 'he isn't.'

The voice droned on and on with heavy emphasis on words or phrases Bernard thought particularly significant and long pauses for dramatic effect.

'Give us a go with the Rachmaninov,' said Sam, who'd had enough and reached into her bag for the cassette. One of the camels, deep in a thorny thicket, raised its head then swung it violently from side to side. In an ungainly movement it backed, straining at its rope caught on a branch. Suddenly the rope broke free, tearing the ring from the animal's nostril. With blood spurting down its neck and making a high, screaming sound, it blundered past them heading out towards the desert.

'Jalil! Jalil!' But he was already there. After a lightning sprint, he flew eight feet through the air, landing four-square on the camel's flank. Together they crashed to the ground, Jalil's brown legs entwined with the camel's thrashing out in all directions and evil yellow teeth snapping inches from his face as he hooked his arm around its neck. The boys rushed towards them, dancing round, poking from a safe distance with sticks. Jalil hung on, his lips drawn back in a grimace as ferocious as the animal he struggled to subdue. Omar ran towards them with a leather bag.

'Oh no!' Alex and Flo looked away as he grabbed the uninjured nostril of the camel and produced a pair of pincers from the bag. With a deft movement he made a quick hole, inserted a ring in the nostril and looped a rope through it. Jalil slipped off the camel and looked ruefully at his torn, blue pants. The camel stood with its head down, blowing blood and froth from its nose and mouth.

'. . . and that night, so said Scheherezade to the Sultan . . .' Bernard droned on, he and his group unaware of the drama of desert life that had taken place less than twenty yards from where they sat.

The sun was at its highest. One of the Dutch ladies who was having trouble with her bodily functions, rode up alongside Bernard and made an urgent request. Bernard, who'd acquired a whip from somewhere and was living out some fantasy by insisting on leading the caravan, stopped, raised the whip and commanded everyone else to stop.

'You have a problem, my friend?' enquired Omar, still hungover and worried about the missing camel.

Bernard leaned down and muttered to him.

'No problem. Adi!'

Adi took the rope of the Dutch lady's camel and led it a short distance to a large rock. The camel knelt, the Dutch lady was helped off and hurried behind the rock clutching a lavatory roll.

'*Seer, seer.*' Omar told the rest of them to move on slowly. Moments later they heard a scream. The Dutch lady had remounted but the camel, seeing its companions disappearing over a ridge, jerked the rope from Adi's hand and was careering to catch up in a determined lolloping gallop.

'Greta! Greta!' her companions shrieked, then fell silent as the poor woman swayed from side to side like a large bolster. There was nothing anyone could do but wait for the inevitable. To make things worse, several of the boys ran towards them, arms outstretched but, too intelligent for such a ploy, the camel swerved sharply and, almost in slow motion, poor Greta fell into a large unhappy heap on the stony ground.

'Madame, madame!' Adi was beside her in tears, wringing his hands. Omar ran fast. Bernard followed at a more sedate pace on his camel. Her friends dismounted and stood around her as Omar and the boys tried to heave her to her feet. Greta made a valiant attempt to stand but fell back with a sharp cry. One of her friends gave her a swig of brandy. Omar relieved her of the flask as she set about making a splint.

'Jalil must take her back to the hotel,' he decided. Greta looked at her camel now standing meekly with the others.

'No!' she wailed.

'It is best if she continues with us,' Bernard said, overriding Omar. 'It is too far for her to go back.'

'No.' Omar was adamant. 'She must go back.'

'We are at the furthest point,' Bernard snapped, pulling out a map with a lot of swirling ridges, wells marked with little buckets and criss-crossed with goat tracks.

'There is a village not far. Jalil will take her. He will find a vehicle and then he will find a taxi and then he will take her back.'

'There is no village on this map.' Bernard pointed at it with his whip, obviously believing himself to be somewhere near the borders of Mauretania.

'Relax, my friend.' Omar, having finished the brandy, was feeling more relaxed and had no intention of telling him that they had traversed in a great circle and if he chose to look from the highest ridge, the water tower outside Mehemide would be clearly visible.

'I make the decisions for my group,' Bernard insisted.

'Oh, shut up!' snapped Alex. She'd had quite enough of Bernard, and quite enough of the desert for that matter. 'Do as Omar says. He is the *chef du caravan*. What he says goes.' One of the boys led the camel forward.

'No . . . no . . .' Greta's eyes rolled in horror at the thought of either remounting the mad beast or being abandoned in the middle of nowhere with a dark-skinned *homme du desert*.

'*Ja*, Greta. *Ja*.' Her friends encouraged her and looked as if the latter might be interesting.

'Have no fear, madame. Jalil is my best *chamellier*. He can track the flight of a bird by the scent of its path.'

'Please,' begged Greta, finally realising she had no choice, 'I must go to the toilet.'

Then the wind started,. preceded by a few miniature typhoons, spiralling cones of sand travelling fast and dispersing, and then tumbleweed whirled past in large, light balls. Soon, like a dragon from the south, the real wind came. Not the evil-tempered blast of the north-east at home. This wind was hot, callous and indifferent as it swirled in all directions, smothering everything from the largest camel to the desert beetles on the ground with a stinging rain of fine grit.

'Fatima!' Adi ran alongside, his thin djellaba flat against his skinny body, his hand shielding his eyes, the other holding out his own *shesh*. She grabbed it thankfully, and with no hope of winding or knotting, tied the flapping thing across her face, already masked with sand.

'How long does this go on?' she shouted across to Omar who was rocking side-saddle on one of the pack camels, brooding about the loss of a camel, one of his boys, Jalil, a damaged client and now this.

'Tonight, it is finished, inshallah.' There were three days to go. Flo let her head slump on to her chest. Some of the group shouted to Bernard and each other that they should stop, take cover. But where? Ahead was nothing but the emptiness of a wide plain. Beside her Alex, huddling into Omar's black burnoose, prayed for a miracle – like a taxi. Through the haze of cotton across her eyes, Flo saw Omar jump from the pack camel, kneel, pound the ground with his fists then raise them to the sky. At first she thought he was imploring Allah to make the wind stop. But she was wrong. Rage, not supplication had brought him to his knees as the last bottle of wine slipped from its sack and broke on the desert floor.

'Cheer up,' shouted Sam, then added, by way of a joke, 'Look at the sky, Omar, look at the sky . . .' and promptly got a mouthful of sand.

'Oh my God, a chair!' Sam staggered to one of the tile tables and crashed down on the first thing that hadn't shifted under him for days. Safe within the hotel walls the group began to acclimatise themselves to life without the wind which had hurled off somewhere else.

'Greta! Greta!' Her friends greeted her as she waited, serene and scrubbed, wearing a kaftan and sporting a plaster on her leg. She was the heroine of the holiday, but not to be outdone, the others related her tales of their perilous encounter with the elements.

'*Now* they laugh!' Omar flopped down beside Sam, took off his *shesh* and scratched his head.

'They loved, it, old man, the biggest thrill of their lives,' Sam told him but Omar didn't look too sure.

'Jalil!' he shouted. 'Jalil!' Joseph told him that after he brought the broken lady back he turned around and went off to find Zaide and the missing camel.

'They work hard, these lads.' Sam knew a worker when he saw one.

'Ah, Bernard!' Omar stood up, but Bernard strode past, tapping his thigh with his whip on his way to see Ahmed and to Register A Complaint. But his group, far from complaining, vitalised by their adventure, were popping in and out of each other's rooms like schoolgirls as they dodged round Joseph and the boys, who were beating blankets and sweeping six-inch piles of sand from under beds and windowsills.

'A big party tonight,' Omar promised everyone who passed. 'Couscous, music, wine.'

'I suppose it's too much to hope that there might be some hot water?' Still wrapped in Omar's burnoose, Alex was weary but immaculate as a movie star in a biblical epic. Flo, on the other hand, wondered how it was that she herself looked like a refugee from Greenham Common. Despite the *shesh*, her scalp was thick with sand, lodged in her hair, her eyebrows, the creases of her eyelids and ringed around her nose. It had infiltrated into every pocket of her quilted jacket, her navel and her lighter was jammed up.

'Omar,' Alex started, but he had gone to defend himself against Bernard's grumbles. She stared bleakly towards Reception and the sound of raised voices.

One by one, some carrying primitive-looking musical instruments, the boys slipped into the big tent to join the party. Jalil arrived last, astounding in scarlet jogging pants, a black T-shirt and his black *shesh*. He was carrying a tam-tam. A small cheer greeted him from the ladies of the group for having rescued Greta and found Zaide and the missing camel.

'How far?' Sam asked.

'Thirty, maybe thirty-five kilometres.' His answer was casual as he squatted down by the brazier to warm the skin of the tam-tam, smoothing it with his big hands. One of the boys plucked at a triangular mandolin, Lahassan began to scrape his fiddle and the others improvised with sticks, glasses, Coca-Cola tins on the tent-pole, tentatively at first, testing the mood of the group who were in high spirits. Greta hobbled round getting everyone to autograph her plaster. The boys, who couldn't write, drew a palm tree or a camel and signed with an x. Omar darted from person to person, desperate for allies to combat Bernard's threats never to come again. Alex gave up on him and decided to be polite to a Danish couple who'd expressed an interest in moving to Spain.

Jalil started up a steady slapping beat from one skin to another; the boys followed his rhythm with hard, sharp handclaps. The younger ones started to sing, their high shrilling voices taking on a mood as wild as the wasteland they had passed through. Two of the ladies attempted an enthusiastic but inept clap themselves and a couple rose and bumped around. Even Bernard stopped blaming Omar for the weather (for the moment) and reeled off the names of the instruments, *duff*, *guedra*, *oud*, *rebab*, then started telling a bemused and tired Zaide about the times of the Almohades who had ruled the south in the twelfth and thirteenth centuries. Jalil speeded up on his drums, looking out at the stars, and although it seemed the boys now played for themselves alone, the power of the music commanded the full attention of everybody in the tent. Sam begged a blank tape from Alex and recorded them on Flo's Walkman.

Joseph, urged by Jalil and blushing deeply, sang a local song in his harsh, young voice. Drawn deeper and deeper into the heart of the music, Flo felt a creeping languor, her limbs so loose she might be drowning in an unfamiliar sea. With difficulty she stood up when Joseph finished his song.

'I'm off,' she murmured to Alex, who was wondering where Omar had disappeared to this time.

Safe beyond the music still throbbing in the tent, too exhausted to remove her boots or jacket, she fell on to the newly shaken blankets. Later, two hours, three or maybe four, she woke to a scratching sound on her door. There was no electricity, no candle and her lighter was broken. The door opened quietly and backed by a faint light of stars she saw a figure in a black burnoose standing at the foot of the bed.

'Fatima.' The voice was rushed and nervous. 'Fatima, it is Jalil and I promise . . .'

But what it was he had to promise she didn't hear as without surprise or fear she heard her own sleepy voice replying, 'Jalil. Oh good, it's you.' She held out her hand. It was something she had never given a thought, something that had never crossed her mind but now that he was there beside her, it was as natural as the sun that rose and set each day.

He left her silently at dawn, murmuring, 'Rest, Fatima, rest.' Then was gone.

Immune, protected from the outside world by the wonder of his passion and her own fervent responses, she shied away from waking. Later the vibrancy of her body would be subdued by cowardice and caution. Even now, thought and feeling fused, something was whispering, 'Oh, Flo, things like this don't happen often, if at all.' The power of his innocence, when without silly comments he'd been puzzled by the complications of a bra. His tenderness and gratitude that she chose not to speak. No questions. No surprise. His silence when, exhausted by their beating hearts and gasps of pleasure, he wound his dark arms loosely round her. And later, his honesty as they smoked a cigarette and she asked, 'Are you married?'

'Divorced.'

'Me too.' No histories, no explanations.

'When you are not here, I am sad,' he told her. And with joy she forgave her years of loneliness. Oh, take care, Flo. Outside there are eyes and voices everywhere. She slept again, knowing that had she tried to rise, place her feet on the rough mat beside the bed, she might be blown away by the faintest breath of wind.

Outside her door the day went on. The spare camels had been ridden off. Bernard and the group had piled into their bus and were on their way to Marrakesh with promises they'd return. A young French couple were desperate to meet relatives in Zagora.

'I will drive you,' Omar promised rashly, since the battery of the Mercedes was flat and so were two of the tyres. Sam said he fancied a look around the town and that he'd take them. Omar, partly in order to avoid Ahmed, who was looking sour, said he'd come too, as he had things to attend to. Alex spent the morning re-washing her hair and giving away every garment that would never be the same again to the boys. There weren't many boys around and those she found were subdued and moody, which she put down to having walked so far and walked so hard.

'Flo . . . Flo . . . Are you awake?' She tapped on the door after midday.

'Just about,' Flo managed, the newness and the rightness of the night making her wish she could put 'Do not disturb, ever again' on her door, her forehead and all her clothes. But it was Alex whom she trusted more than anyone she knew.

Would he smile? Would he speak? Did it really happen? She looked in the mirror half expecting to see the face of an angel in its speckled surface. No angel, but a face she hardly remembered, with time smoothed out and eyes bright with expectancy, looked back at her. She opened the door and he was there, outside the gate, beside the car with a tyre in his hands. No waves, no familiarity but full acknowledgement flowed between the twenty yards that separated them.

'There you are.' Alex looked up from the guide book. Flo sat down and picked up a paperback someone had left. It was in German, something to do with the war and Rommel. 'You're very quiet,' Alex said, looking at her. Flo was different, with a strange almost translucent look. 'You'd better keep out of the sun for a bit,' she advised as Flo turned a page.

'Pity about Mussolini,' she remarked casually.

'Mussolini?'

'Yes.'

'What about Mussolini?'

Flo tossed the book aside. 'Mussolini, it's such a pretty word, like something wonderful to eat. Pity he was such a pig.'

Alex let it pass. Flo got a bit oblique sometimes and it was best to take no notice.

'What's the date?'

It was Flo's turn to look blank.

'Do you know what the date is?' Alex called out to Ahmed, who was walking past with a small tin cash box in his hands.

'The twenty-second, madame,' he told her, looking at a flashy watch that told him everything.

'Oh my God, it's Millie's birthday!' Alex jumped up. 'I promised to phone her. Where's Omar?' Ahmed waved his hand in the direction of Zagora and reminded her that he'd gone off with Sam.

'Damn!' She followed him to Reception. 'When will they be back?'

123

'Soon, soon, inshalla,' he replied, not having the slightest idea.

'But it's my daughter's birthday and I promised her I'd phone.'

'It is Sunday. The Post Office is shut. But tomorrow it is open.'

'Tomorrow is no good. I must phone today.' She was, he guessed, on the verge of a tantrum. At any moment she might start up about lavatory seats, inadequate water and the fact she'd waited over an hour for her breakfast and there'd been a fly in the butter.

'Jalil can drive you.' Ahmed came up with a solution. 'Jalil!'

His first reaction was one of delight but then he frowned.

'What's the problem?' asked Alex.

'The car, it will take more time.' Flo felt there was something else.

'Are you worried about the police and that *faux guide* stuff if you're with us?' He nodded, grateful she'd remembered.

'It's all right if Jalil drives us, isn't it?' Flo asked. It was important now that they should do something normal, very ordinary, like driving into town.

'No problem,' Ahmed assured her, having remembered quite a few errands Jalil could run for him.

'How long?' Alex, her hair combed, was ready to go.

'Ten minutes, maybe fifteen.' Jalil grinned at Flo and hurried back to the car. Ahmed shook his head and sighed.

'Cars, always problems with cars.'

'So I've noticed,' said Flo and before he suggested

she should buy a Range Rover asked Alex, 'Do you fancy a walk?' She was wondering whether or not to tell her about Jalil.

'Yes.' Alex, exploding with impatience, was ready to go anywhere. As they passed Jalil, she decided that it wouldn't be right. Not yet.

It took about ten minutes to stroll to the compound which Flo still referred to as 'that Foreign Legion place'. They'd meant to many times but whenever they or any of the other guests had asked what it was, Omar dismissed it – 'It is nothing' – followed by a quick change of subject.

From a sign planted in the stony ground, they realised it must be Cecille's four-star hotel, still far from presenting any competition to the Hôtel des Dunes. As they drew closer, a fair woman darted out of the main gateway, unlocked a car, got in, tried the engine, got out, and looked right and left as if expecting warriors with machetes to charge the place at any moment, slammed the door, locked it again and walked quickly back to where she'd come from.

'That was Cecille, wasn't it?' Alex was good at names and faces.

Her fine hair almost dragged from her scalp into an elastic band, Cecille was standing in a white tent in the middle of the compound having an angry confrontation with a plumber. There was one room built, nearly a kitchen which trailed off into what might, one day, be a dining room. At the other end of the plantless quadrangle was the scaffolded start of a two-storey building.

Alex and Flo approached her, walking carefully round piles of wooden planks and breeze-blocks.

'Have you got a needle?' Cecille was too distraught to bother with niceties of greeting.

'A needle?'

'Yes, a needle.' They looked at each other.

'No?' Cecille turned back to the plumber, whose nine-year-old mate was moodily kicking his tool bag.

'The spare part?' she demanded. 'The spare part? Will it arrive on the bus?'

'Inshallah,' said the plumber.

'Today's bus?'

'Inshallah.'

'And will you collect it? Will it fix the boiler?'

'Inshallah.'

'And will the boiler then work?' But the plumber had lost track and told the boy to put the tool bag in his car. Cecille was near to throttling him.

'Wait!' she screamed. 'Now, listen to me. Tomorrow, I will go into town, I will go to the bank . . .' At the word bank, the plumber stopped in his tracks. 'I will get the money for the spare part, I will get the money for this week, I will get the money for next week. Will you meet me outside the bank?'

'*Oui*,' said the plumber promptly and drove off.

'You see how it is?' Cecille led them into the partly finished kitchen and pulled three beers from a fridge which appeared to be working. 'It's always the same, always inshallah until it comes to money.' She tore the elastic band off and ran her hands through her hair. 'We've had every expert in Europe to de-salt the water, they all said they could, with every chemical known to mankind. Each one cost a fortune and none of them worked. And now that thing . . .' She glared at the boiler.

'Is your husband here?' Alex looked out at the empty compound.

'Moroccan men!' Cecille snorted and left them in no

126

doubt as to what she thought of them. 'Charming at first, then insistent, then jealous, then boring, then never there when you need them.' To Flo's surprise Alex agreed with a knowing nod.

'Not all, surely?' she was about to ask but had the sense to keep her mouth shut. Cecille buried her face in her hands.

'And now the damn car won't work.'

'Do you need a lift into town?' Flo offered. Cecille looked up.

'You got a car then? I heard you were going to.'

'Me? A car? Who on earth told you that?'

'Oh, gossip flies around here, the Arab telegraph they call it.'

'I might get a camel, but not a car.'

Cecille obviously thought buying a camel too frivolous to be worthy of comment.

'We're going into town with Jalil; he's driving us in Omar's car. When it's fixed.'

Cecille shot a black look towards the hotel. 'No point. It's Sunday,' she snapped. She busied herself shifting her handbag from the top of the fridge on to what was going to be a draining board. They thanked her for the beers and started back, leaving her to her four stars.

'Why do you think she wanted a needle?'

'It's unanswerable, like the vanishing bus.'

The police waved them down outside the town, then gestured them on without stopping. Jalil put a reggae tape on and brushed Flo's arm lightly with his fingers. Alex, absorbed in the guide book in the back, didn't notice. Jalil laughed and pointed out an old man on a donkey riding backwards.

'He is from my village,' he told them. 'The donkey

won't go if he sits the other way.' Further along the road, a thin man in a *djellaba* hopped up and down waving for a lift. Jalil drove on without stopping. As they passed him another car approached in the opposite direction. The thin man rushed across the road and hopped up and down again.

'What?' Flo looked back in amazement at this strange performance. 'What's he doing?'

'He just wants a lift. A ride in a car. It doesn't matter where.'

'Is he from your village too?'

'Yes,' Jalil admitted, and burst out laughing.

They found Omar and Sam at the bar of La Fibule with Ali Baba who had a few more gazelles in tow. By the look of things they had no intention of hurrying back to the hotel. Sam had three long rolls beside him, which could only mean he'd bought not one carpet, but three, possibly four. From the beam on Ali Baba's face, Flo was sure he'd made a handsome profit and Omar a tidy commission. She was learning fast.

'Fatima! Jalil!' Omar greeted them. Flo explained about Alex and her phone call. Omar, not interested, called for drinks all round. Jalil, completely unabashed by the elegant surroundings, struck up a conversation with the barman who also came from his village. Flo noticed several of the Fibule guests look him up and down and heard Ali Baba telling his gazelles that Jalil was a real Tuareg who had just arrived from Timbuktu.

'Eh, my friend.' Omar raised his glass in Jalil's direction, then turned to Flo. 'He is a very good boy, one of the family.' To her, that meant he *knew*. Not only knew, but was giving her assurance that everything was as it should be. He didn't press her or ask questions, as if the whole matter was perfectly natural and therefore there was no need for discussion. She wondered how long it would be before he told Alex. Alex, having got through to Millie after several false starts, and paid far too much for a three minute call, joined them.

'Quite a party,' she said, glancing up at the room she and Flo had shared so long ago.

'It would be nice to have a bath, a real bath.' Flo picked up on her thoughts.

'Wouldn't it,' Alex agreed fervently.

The days passed. Ahmed and the seldom-glimpsed members of the family kept themselves to themselves in the warren of rooms behind the courtyard at night. It seemed that with Omar there was a royal command and no one could retire until he had run out of wine, cigarettes and things to say as he and the boys talked on and on in one of the turret rooms. As she waited each night for Jalil, she read until the candle burned out, then alternatively slept, woke, smoked cigarettes in the dark, wondering if Alex had waited this way for Omar. A sort of Moroccan version of the men staying in the dining room for the port. But he always came.

'Fatima?' And it was always a question, as if she might not be there when he pushed open the door and then swept her into his arms. And it was always dark as he undressed, modestly turning his back towards her, and last of all, unwinding his *shesh* and letting a crop of dreadlocks spring up from his head. Tainted by European standards of what a desirable woman should be, she was grateful for the lack of light which hid the blemishes and flaws of time. Strange, though, he never gazed with merciless scrutiny, as other men had done, at her breasts, her bottom or her legs. He looked only at her face, his concentration aimed at something timeless. And for her part, she was thankful that the light did not reveal the beauty of his perfect, hard body, thinner and slighter naked, without robes or his eccentric baggy clothes. He touched her softly, as if she was a thing of such fragility she might shatter in his hands, then strong and hard, pressing her into his chest, stomach, groin and thighs to stop her ever leaving. Sometimes, after they'd made love, he talked to her in brief, enigmatic sentences.

'There are things here I can't explain, Fatima. You must watch, learn, listen.' Laughing she refused to believe there could be a serpent in this Eden.

'You will see,' he told her as he rolled a joint.

'I will be leaving soon,' she told him sadly. He turned his face away. 'Did you hear me?'

'Yes. I heard you.'

Alex turned down the corner of the page of her guide book at the Gazelle d'Or, one of the most expensive hotels in Morocco.

'Sam said he'd like to see a bit more of the country,' she announced, sipping lemon tea. 'I think we'll leave tomorrow.'

'Oh.' Flo stopped, her fork halfway to her mouth.

'But no, you cannot leave,' protested Omar. 'Fatima? You are leaving too?' Before she could reply, Jalil appeared in the far doorway of the courtyard, his blue robe washed, ironed and mended. In his hand he had a bunch of yellow wildflowers. Very slowly he approached the table. Joseph, Adi and Ali stood aside, like courtiers before a prince. He stopped at the table and, without a sign of a smile, he bowed to Flo and handed her the flowers. Blushing, she took them from him.

'*Les fleurs du desert*. So romantic.' Omar raised his glass to this very public statement but Jalil had vanished through the kitchen door. Alex, unable to believe her ears or eyes, looked first at Flo, clutching her flowers, and then at the kitchen door.

'And how long has this been going on?' she demanded in English, so low and rapid that Omar couldn't follow.

'About a week.'

'Why didn't you tell me?'

Flo was silent, searching for reasons and excuses, then told the truth. 'There just weren't any words. Well, not the right ones.'

Alex was laughing.

'What's so funny?'

'Oh, Flo. You certainly took your time.'

'What do you mean, took my time? I never thought . . . I never guessed . . .'

To Alex, such naiveté in a grown woman was almost past believing. 'Flo, he's been sleeping outside your door ever since we started coming here.'

'*What*?'

'Oh, come off it, Flo. You must have known.'

'I didn't, I promise. I . . .'

'Well, you must have been the only one who didn't. I thought you'd never get on with it.'

But now that it had happened, Alex was concerned. It was all right for her. She could love, laugh and leave. But Flo was different. She made up her mind to collar Omar as soon as she'd finished packing.

'What about Jalil?' she demanded, tracking him down in the turret room.

'Jalil is a good man,' Omar told her.

'Yes, yes. I know all about that *Homme du Desert* stuff, but what about women?'

'Women? He is always honest, even with women.' He was unaware of what he'd said that made her laugh. 'I tell you, he has never approached a client before. Although many have wished that he would. Some even approached him.'

'What about marriage?'

'Oh, that is finished, a long time. It was arranged by the family when he was very, very young. They do that here. But he is divorced now.'

'I'm deeply relieved to hear it – What on earth?' She dodged out of the way as a small football dropped through the high turret window, missed her by a few inches and landed on the pile of carpets. The boys were playing a sort of netball using the slit windows as a goal. Jalil, with the advantage of his height, had thrown and scored.

He looked round to see if Flo had noticed then said, 'Fatima. Would you like to promenade to the dunes?'

He led her, on Laassell, towards the dune, golden in the evening light.

'We climb?' He held out his hand as she dismounted. He pulled her after him, their feet sinking into the soft sand which fell away in little trickles. When they reached the top, he offered her a strong local cigarette. His hand in hers, they watched until the setting sun sharpened the shadows of the rumpled sand and then with a last blink it vanished and the passing clouds were tipped with gold. He withdrew his hand, searched in his pocket and casually produced a silver ring.

'It has a secret,' he told her and slid two sections apart to reveal a small, blue heart. 'You are pleased?'

'Oh yes.' She could hardly speak for the turmoil within her.

'Come.' They ran, slithering and laughing down the dune. Laassell knelt for her, but to her surprise, Jalil mounted first and held out his hand for her to ride behind him.

Etched against the deep red walls of the turret room, Alex was waiting for them. 'This,' she said, as Flo dismounted, 'is romance rampant.'

'I think I'm engaged,' Flo said weakly as Jalil led Laassell to join the other camels for the night.

'Take it easy,' Alex advised. 'When's your ticket home?'

'Soon. I might stay on for a bit.'

'If you think you can handle it. Just remember to take it easy.'

They sat down on the edge of the well. Flo lit a cigarette.

'You don't think . . .' she asked, feeling like Judas as she said it, 'you don't think it's, well, you know, sort of room service?'

'No,' said Alex firmly, 'I do not.' Then told her she'd checked out Jalil with Omar. 'Are you in love?' she asked curiously, as Joseph approached to ask them what they'd like for dinner.

'Love?' Flo repeated as if it was a strange foreign word that terrified her. Love . . . a dangerous word. A word she'd never bandied, never really understood. But if love was liking, liking on a scale as monstrous and all-embracing as the sky above them, she could only answer yes.

'Ring me.' Alex made her promise. 'If you run into

trouble, ring me.' She would fly, drive or even swim from Tangier, if ever, whenever she was needed. 'Have a good time. And don't get any thinner!'

Ahmed left for Fes, taking the spoils of Bernard's group. With his departure the hotel lapsed into an end-of-the-season lull. The few guests who came seldom lingered more than one night. Even 'les fourmis', the Japanese, Spanish, French and Germans arriving for a quick glimpse of the 'vrai desert', stayed only a few seconds at the dunes, taking snaps before scrambling back into their air-conditioned buses. Joseph, who wouldn't have known how to move fast even had there been a flood or fire, slowed his pace to that of an old man and spent his time trying to mend the cushions with a large needle and thick black cotton. Adi and Ali hadn't been seen for days, neither had the cook.

'Ça commence,' Jalil told her. It was starting.

'What is?'

'La grande chaleur.' The big heat of summer was on its way and with it the flies that buzzed around the cats and banged into the mesh-covered windows of Flo's room. The only thing cool enough to wear was the cotton dress, which she put on each morning, rinsed out at night and found it stiff and dry the following day. Fearing she might be lonely now that Sam and Alex had gone, Omar invited her into the salon de video, a large room, richly carpeted (for you, Fatima, a very good price), the domain of Ahmed and the family. Since the generator stopped at nine o'clock, the vast TV was then plugged into the battery of one of the old cars to flicker on to the end of whatever video Omar had brought back from Zagora. They were usually appalling, dubbed into French by the same group of actors, each plot almost identical to the last, making it difficult for Flo to know if she had seen it before or not. Far from being lonely, she felt herself to be in a lake of peace with no self-imposed demands, each little chore – washing her clothes, her hair, tidying the red, mud room and writing postcards – so absorbing there were no revisions of the past or questions of the present. Jalil appeared from time to time to look at her, hold her and whisper 'Fatima' before vanishing again.

Omar drove them into town to shop, like a benevolent chaperone, leaving them together to drink Coca-Cola, coffee or mint tea in the cafés, inside, away from the intrusive eyes of the police.

'I have bought new shoes.' Omar came to pick them up at the Café Saphire. He was limping. 'They hurt my feet. You wear them.' He took off a pair of thick leather thonged sandals with soles made of car tyres. 'Les Michelines,' he called them, 'tres chic!' He tossed them over to Jalil, who slid out of his worn plimsolls and squeezed his enormous feet into the sandals, a good three sizes to small. Flo winced.

'But what about Jalil? They'll hurt him even more!' They both looked at her as if this had nothing to do with anything. Master, slave, no problem for either of them.

'Now Fatima, what about this camel?' She shifted her attention from the sandals.

'Where does one buy a camel?'

'Goulamine, the camel market.' Jalil interrupted to suggest that they could buy one locally but Omar waved this away.

'Non. We must go to Goulamine before it gets too hot.'

*   *   *

Ahmed returned the following day, to everyone's surprise. Omar then announced that he was going off for a few days to Ouarzazate 'on business' and Joseph went on stitching cushions. Flo sat in the sun, drinking her third coffee and feeding bits of bread to the sparrows. Jalil arrived silently from behind the big tent with a camel saddle that needed mending in his arms. He stood by her chair and she smiled up at him, longing to run her finger down his big, work worn hands but it was daylight and forbidden.

'Would you like to have a meal with the family?' His sudden invitation was almost lost at the back of his throat and he looked away towards the camels. Her mind flooded with questions. He meant his family, not Ahmed, Omar or any of the other relatives that flitted in and out of the video room. It was a great compliment, but so soon? She was sharing her body and her bed with this beautiful quiet man, she had listened to his private murmurings as he slept and he perhaps to hers, but families were different. The boundaries of their precious secret world would be extended to scrutiny and speculation and with that, she knew, something treasured would be lost forever.

'Yes,' she replied, helpless and polite and nervous. 'Thank you.' He gave a great smile of joy.

'About midday?' Dear God, he meant today! In a few hours, not some vague, unspecified arrangement for the future. What on earth should one wear? A fatuous thought, but Alex would have understood. What on earth could possibly be right for a western woman, indeed a very much older western woman, to wear to meet her lover's mother? Because it would be his mother who counted: his mother, like all the others who ruled their vast families from the gloomy depths of a mud house in the village. She'd probably be wearing one of those black things, sprinkled with silver sequins, that she'd worn since she became an adult. Maybe her face would be veiled, leaving her open to the mercy of intent, enquiring brown eyes. The denim skirt and jacket. That was it. The skirt was calf length and she'd leave the jacket buttoned up all the time. Even if she died of heat.

She shifted her chair slightly, hoping Jalil would put down the saddle and join her for a moment, but Ahmed emerged from Reception looking sleepy and unwashed in the cheap slacks and green shirt he'd taken to wearing when there were no guests.

'*A bientôt*,' Jalil murmured and moved off to go about his day.

'Did you sleep well?' asked Ahmed in a sing-song voice which meant he was trying to be affable. Uninvited, he sat down opposite her.

'Very well, thank you.' She slept like an angel, waking to be loved and loved again and she was sure the smirk that Alex had talked of long ago was painted on her face. 'And you?'

He asked her for a cigarette. She shoved her packet over to him, watching Jalil, now without the saddle, walk towards the gates. There was the sound of a motor scooter, put-putting along the track. He raised his arm in greeting to a boy in a burnoose. The boy stopped the scooter and Jalil climbed on the back, having difficulty arranging his long legs. Ahmed, the cigarette in his mouth, was making a great to-do of searching for a lighter in the pockets of his trousers and the green shirt.

'Have you got a light?' She pushed her lighter across to him, knowing he was capable of expecting her to hold out the flame but damned if she was going to.

'Where's Jalil going?' She tried to keep it light and conversational.

'Probably to tell the family you are going to eat with them.' She was shocked, shocked that he could know. How could he know? Had he been listening under the desk in Reception? Lurking behind the big doors to the courtyard? What else did he know? It was true, Cecille was right. Every intention and desire was written on the air, available to all, and now she too was plugged into this awful Arab telegraph.

'Jalil! Jalil!' Ahmed shouted at him. Jalil got off the scooter and walked back, obedient, but without haste. Ahmed said something in Arabic. Jalil produced a pink card, covered in cracked plastic, from his big pocket. Ahmed took it, clicked his fingers at Joseph who was trudging sulkily towards the shower rooms with a mop and bucket. He pretended that he hadn't seen or heard.

'Joseph!' shouted Ahmed. '*Un café, vite!*' He stood up and beckoned Jalil to follow him into Reception where they both searched for a bit of paper but it was locked and Omar had the key. They came back to Flo's table where Ahmed tore off the outer cover of her cigarette pack and copied down what was on Jalil's identity card. Jalil looked at Flo as if she was the last thing he would see before he died. Ahmed gave him back the card and Jalil walked swiftly back to the boy on the scooter. Flo watched as they wobbled down the track. The wind filled out the sleeves of Jalil's robe like the wings of a great blue bird as they picked up speed and headed off along the road. Joseph dumped a coffee in front of Ahmed, who stirred in three lumps of sugar and took a long, slurping suck.

'We must go to Zagora today. You will need your passport.'

'Passport? Whatever for?' She was still watching the road.

'The documents for the police, for Jalil. He is a good boy, one of the family; with a document there will be no more problems. But we need a stamp and for that we must have your passport. There will be no problem.' He patted the cigarette pack, now in his top pocket.

'But I don't understand,' she started.

'No problem, no problem,' he assured her with the nearest thing to a smile, which he forced across his mean-spiritedness. Mystified, she gave up and went to her room to change into more modest clothing.

Their first stop in Zagora was at the Hôtel Palmerie, where they sat at an outside table and, with a worried frown, Ahmed ordered a mint tea for himself and a Coca-Cola for Flo.

'The documents must have a stamp,' he told her again then asked doubtfully, 'What should we say?'

Now that she understood, she replied calmly, 'It's quite simple. Just say that Jalil – ?' There was a question mark in the air as she waited for his surname.

'Jaliya.' Ahmed supplied it. She smiled and rolled the sound round in her head. Jalil Jaliya, so soft, like the wind in the reeds.

'African.' Ahmed jerked his head southwards. Flo pulled herself together. 'Jalil Jaliya is a trusted employee of the Hôtel des Dunes and has been so for many years. With our full permission and approval he is escorting Madame Lucas during her visit to Morocco.' He asked the waiter for some paper; the waiter then gave him the bill which he handed over to Flo. Ahmed was visibly relieved when not only did she pay it but started writing their statement on the back in French.

'How do you spell Jaliya?' Ahmed gave her the cigarette pack with the details. Jalil Jaliya . . . date of birth . . . Dear God! He was only twenty-six! The same age as her daughter, the California daughter who had already mentioned collagen implants. Born the year she wore white boots, which John had said were vulgar, and a twelve-inch mini-skirt until she got too pregnant. She was probably older than his mother! Maybe older than his grandmother, since they all got married at about fifteen. Crimson with shock, she fumbled for her own passport. Ahmed was scanning the street, his eyes darting from one car to another.

'We must hurry. It is Friday, everything shuts.' Flo's pen flew across the scrap of paper with her full name, passport number and then thrust the passport into the depths of her bag to hide those damning dates before they filtered through on to the Arab telegraph.

'What now?' she asked as Ahmed got to his feet.

'We must see the writer.'

The scribe's office was a small room behind one of the shops that sold buckets, nylon rope, Tide, plastic hair slides and dusty Johnson's Baby Lotion. The scribe was a tiny man in a grey burnoose who wore steel-rimmed glasses with one eye blacked out. For about five minutes he ignored them as he finished what he was typing on a vast old Olivetti. Then he unloaded the machine, read it through and asked Ahmed what he wanted. Ahmed explained in Arabic. The old man shook his head. Ahmed argued with him, but the old man kept on repeating one phrase.

'What's he saying?' asked Flo.

'He says he wants to see you write it for him, word for word.'

'But I've already written it.' She showed the old man the back of the bill.

'No. He must see you write it.' She grabbed a split biro from a pot on the scribe's desk and looked around for paper. With great reluctance he gave her a used air-mail envelope. Standing, she wrote at great speed then sat down on a stool with a bump and handed it over to him. She held out her hand to Ahmed for the cigarettes and offered one to the old man, who secreted it into a drawer. Very slowly he read what she had written. At last he and Ahmed reached some sort of agreement and Ahmed turned to leave.

'Where are we going now?'

'He says he will translate it into Arabic and that will take time.'

'How much time?' She looked at her watch. It was quarter to eleven. Jalil had said midday. Ahmed gave a 'who knows' shrug not bothering to disguise 'who cares'.

'I'll wait.' She sat down firmly on the stool again. The scribe gave her a sharp look with his good eye and started to load the ancient machine with three sheets of paper, each with carbons between them. Carbon paper! It must have been twenty years since she'd seen carbon paper. It took a long time with much readjustment and rewinding. When at last the machine was ready, the scribe looked doubtfully at the information on the back of the envelope, then with amazing speed, he began to poke at the yellow keys with two fingers. Flo got up and stood behind him, entranced by the delicacy of the Arabic lettering as it danced on to the paper.

141

They hurried along the main street, she side-stepping children playing football and men strolling two abreast, until they reached a large building which she took to be some sort of town hall. Ahmed led her down a long passage where an old man slept on a bench. There was no one else in sight.

'Wait,' he ordered.

'What?' She started.

'Photocopies, we need photocopies.' He vanished round a corner then reappeared.

'Have you got any dirham?' She gave him a hundred and he disappeared again. It seemed an hour before he returned with a sheaf of papers.

'This way.' He rushed her up the passage and peered into an office and was disconcerted to find it empty. The old man roused himself and pointed at the next door. Ahmed knocked and was told to enter.

The sun fell flatly on the pale wood of a cheap desk. Behind it sat a large man whom she took to be a policeman. He had a shock of grey hair and a thick black moustache. After he'd shaken hands with Ahmed, who apparently he knew, he was introduced to Flo.

'Madame.' He smiled at her to sit, his crooked teeth giving him an almost friendly air. She sat down and took in the stark room, a phone on the desk, a glass-fronted bookcase with four shelves, three books, what appeared to be a very thin telephone directory and a photograph of the king. As if by magic, the old man appeared with a tray of tea. Taking his time, the policeman poured it into the three glasses, handed them round then and settled back in his swivel chair. Nervously, Ahmed began to explain what they wanted. The policeman listened, then studied all the photocopies.

'Your passport, madame.' She handed it over. He

looked at her photograph for a long time, then at her, then gave it back. He opened a drawer and took out a tin with a rubber stamp. With great deliberation he pressed the stamp on to the near dry pad, then on to the top paper. He did this four times, then signed each paper slowly. It was very hot. Sweating from the seriousness of it all, she had to stop herself undoing the top button of the denim jacket and, to distract herself, looked out of the window. There was a rose bush, she noticed, just outside, with one red rose growing bravely and alone. Ahmed pulled her attention back from the rose as he expressed servile gratitude to the policeman. They all shook hands again and the policeman wished Flo a pleasant stay in Morocco. Outside the office, Ahmed told her to wait.

'Why? What now?'

'We must get a stamp.'

'But we've got a stamp.'

'No, another stamp, a green stamp from the office of the Procureur.'

She looked at her watch.

'A moment, just a moment.' Ahmed darted off again.

She sat down on the bench beside the old man who was fingering his prayer beads and realised with annoyance that Ahmed had gone off with the cigarettes. She closed her eyes, confident that Jalil would know where she was and that she was trying to reach him by midday. A few seconds later, a door opened and she heard a key turn. A shadow fell across her.

'Ah . . . madame . . .' She opened her eyes. The policeman with the crooked smile was holding out the red rose with a little bow.

'Thank you,' she said as the call to prayer started.

*   *   *

143

Ahmed opened the back door of the car for her. Surprised, but none too bothered, she slid in beside a large, brown paper carrier and heard the clank of illicit lager and caught a whiff of it on Ahmed's breath as he showed her the stamp. A real, green stamp on the top copy with another signature.

'From the Procureur himself!' he declared, sweating but pleased with himself. He started up at high speed towards the roundabout at the end of town. A column of blue emerged from behind some carpets hanging outside a shop. It was Jalil. The Arab telegraph, simple smooth and efficient. He greeted her as if they had been parted for ten years as he got into the front seat, his great hand reaching back and clasping her ankle.

'It is done . . . We got the permission,' Ahmed told him. Jalil looked at the precious paper without comment.

'You'd better look after it,' Ahmed told Flo and gave it to her. Permission! Like a licence for a dog. Unwillingly she put it in her bag.

Ahmed stopped at the beginning of Jalil's village, which sat either side of the main road. He leaned out of the car window as they started to move away and said something to Jalil that sounded very bossy in Arabic, then drove off at high speed, creating a cloud of dust.

'He drives very badly,' remarked Jalil, looking after the car. 'Now we will meet the family.' Flo smoothed her skirt and put on her dark glasses.

'*Yalla!*' she said, thinking had she been a Catholic, she would have crossed herself.

The family house was on a little slope falling away into a steep garden with sunflowers, sweet corn and carrots and then the desert plain stretching to the mountain ridge in its straight line north and south. Two little boys charged out to greet Jalil, followed by a young woman carrying a baby.

'The wife of my brother,' Flo was told, although not the girl's name. The children were suddenly still, shy and uncertain, their brown eyes wide with curiosity. Jalil told them to shake hands. Flo squatted down and held out her hand and was touched with the soft brush of their sticky fingers and bashful smiles. The baby hid his grumpy little face in his mother's shoulder. Jalil shooed them all into the house and beckoned her to follow. The entrance to the inner rooms was reached by a wide corridor with a broken bike, a scythe and piles of firewood. She paused at the threshold of the main room to take off her shoes as Jalil had done. The room was about fifteen foot square, with five doors leading off it, the only light coming from a slit in the ceiling. The floor was earthen, spread with plastic mats, and round the perimeter a wooden bench was stacked with brightly woven rugs. In pride of place stood a black and white television where, in a shower of white specks, the devout were at their Friday prayers. Above the television she noticed an electric clock with a painting of a man and a woman and a lot of roses backed by what looked like Naples.

'It is Friday,' Jalil told her; his mother was praying but she would return soon. He told her to sit and put a cushion behind her back. He sat himself, taking the smallest of the two little boys on to his lap, who looked at her hands, still clutching the rose the policeman had given her.

'Here!' She held it out to him. The child took it, his dark head bent in concentration, fingering each petal as if it were a thing of wonder.

145

'Smell it,' Jalil told him. The corners of the room receded into shadows, a sun shaft from the slit in the ceiling fell on the child's black hair, the red of the rose and the dusk brown of Jalil's hands, both caught in the blue haze of his robes. For a moment she thought her heart would stop. The young woman with the baby had disappeared through one of the five doors. Through another, the oldest boy arrived with a brass table which he set in front of Flo, and another young woman carried in a tray with glasses and a pot of mint tea. Jalil dumped the little boy beside Flo. Still fingering the rose, he smiled up at her as Jalil poured tea into the glasses, then back into the pot, repeating the process. Flo put her bag aside as he handed her the first glass, then gave one to each of the boys and the young women. The baby stared at her and started to cry. She took off her dark glasses, which did nothing to mollify him. His mother bumped him up and down and said something which either meant 'he's teething' or 'he's the difficult one'. Jalil laughed, wiped its runny nose with his *shesh* and asked the young women something to which they replied in soft Arabic.

'My mother will be here soon.' Conversation stopped. The children stared at her and then away. The young women drank their tea without needing to talk. Flo looked at her feet, stretched out in front of her, so white, almost dead-looking beside the calloused dusty feet of the young women and Jalil's violent tartan socks. There was a soft rustling sound, the slap of plastic shoes hitting the floor and Jalil's mother sailed into the room like a great actress making her first entrance. Jalil got to his feet and with a swift, continuous gesture of reverence, bent over her hand, almost touched it with his lips, touched his heart and then his brow and murmured in Arabic.

His mother, unveiled, received her due and pushed back the sleeves of her red blouse and approached Flo.

'*La bess*?' she enquired, her broad face breaking into a grin as wide as her son's. Her veil slipped off her head as she sat down beside Flo, revealing long gold earrings and a swathe of silver chains around her neck. Her voice was high, punctuating her laugh, as she plied Jalil with questions. They were talking about her. Where did she come from? How long was she staying? Did she find the weather hot? Why didn't she speak Arabic? She broke off to tell the youngest of the two girls something. The girl rose and vanished, returning with a pile of clean clothes which she placed carefully on a plastic bag beside Jalil's big shoes in the doorway. The mother turned to Flo and said something with a shrug.

'What did she say?'

'She said,' replied Jalil, trying to look dignified but failing, 'she said the only time she ever sees me is when I need my washing done.'

At this universal complaint, Flo laughed and so did his mother and the baby, instead of being frightened, rewarded her with a great, gummy grin.

'Here!' The young mother handed it over to Jalil, who dumped it in Flo's arms. It was a long time since she had held a baby. Terrified that it might howl again, she jogged it gently to the family's approval.

'No, here!' The mother pointed as the older of the two little boys arrived with a tiny packet of Tide, a bowl of water and a dish cloth over his arm. With relief, Flo handed the baby back to Jalil and washed her hands as the electric clock whirred for a moment, and the chimes of 'Come back to Sorrento' filled the earthen room. Startled, she stared at it then smiled.

'What is funny?' the mother wanted to know.

'It's . . . it's a wonderful clock,' was all that she could manage.

'*Couli, couli.*' They ate at two tables, Flo, Jalil and his mother at one, the young women and the children at another. The prayers on the television went on.

'*Couli, couli.*' She knew now this meant eat, eat, but she was stuffed with lamb and vegetables and could eat no more. Jalil told his mother to desist.

They washed their hands again and Jalil asked, guessing she must need a cigarette, 'Would you like to see the terrace?'

'Oh, yes please.'

From the rooftop they looked across the mountains. Jalil with his back to the view, leaned against the wall as he rolled a joint. He lit her cigarette, his face close to hers, shifted to light his own, moved away, decorous and disciplined, both aware of the relief of being alone for a few moments, both amused by the tensions this privacy brought with it – tensions of desire flaring up in both of them that must be quelled until darkness came and the power of this discipline so charged and so much stronger than public expressions of touching, kissing, fumbling. She stared out at the desert and then towards the outskirts of the village, where she could see the tops of the giant palms in the central square.

'Have you looked out at this every day of your life?'

'Except for the time I was in the deep desert.'

'You're not really like other Moroccans.'

Her remark pleased him. 'No. I am different.'

She wanted to say, 'Is that because you are black?' But didn't. There were a lot of dark-skinned people in the south and it was nothing to do with his colour. Instead she asked, 'Where do you come from, originally?'

'I don't know.' It didn't seem to interest him.

'But your grandparents? Did they live here?'

'I don't think so. No, they didn't. I never met them.' To her it was astonishing that anyone should know so little, claim no identity with the past.

'*Esclavage*.' He said it casually. Slavery, so shockingly recent.

'Maybe you came from Senegal? Maybe further . . .' she guessed.

'Maybe.' He turned towards the south. 'Maybe Timbuktu. I would like to go there one day, inshallah. One day,' he joked. 'One day, Fatima, we will go there, you and I.' It was the first time there had been any reference to a future.

The young women and the children stood in the doorway and waved. The mother embraced Flo in a tight grip, looked up at her son, her face alight with pride, then at Flo, humorous and shrewd. They exchanged a few untranslatable sounds, smiles and nods.

'What are you saying?' asked Jalil, curious at this unexpected line of female communication.

'We were saying how good, brave and wonderful you are,' Flo told him with a straight face, then giggled with his mother at his embarrassment.

'Come,' he said.

The village was very old and very special, he told her. There was no café, no pharmacy, not even a petrol pump. The only sign of its antiquity was a rampart on the far side of an open space with the slit windows of dark homes. The children darted forward: '*un dirham*,'

149

un stylo, un bon bon?' then retreated fast when they saw Jalil.

'That is the library,' he said as they passed it, but without showing any inclination to give her a guided tour. She already knew from the guide book that it was the oldest collection in the world of Koranic manuscripts, written in minute lettering on gazelle hyde, about Medicine, Astronomy, Astrology and the numerical system now used throughout the world. It was here that numbers started, here that all those awful numbers in her passport had been invented.

'And that is the sanctuary for the mad people.' He dropped a coin at the feet of an old man outside the entrance and walked on, leading her towards the palmerie, small, cultivated squares of brilliant green bordered by water flowing between low banks of red soil. They sat under a tall palm.

'Were you alone in the desert?'

'Almost. I had the animals. People sometimes passed, shared their food and for water there were always wells.'

'Weren't you lonely?'

'I learned to talk to the goats, the birds. Sometimes there were foxes and gazelles.' His face lit up with the memory.

'How old were you?' It was a struggle for him to remember.

'Thirteen, maybe fourteen. I was always in trouble before I went to the desert. I changed. I have always wanted to go back.' In a nonchalant way he told her that he'd found the nomads, that he'd lived with them and learned all he knew about camels.

'They were good people. But they moved on. My mother sent my father to bring me back. Since then,

I have worked for *them*.' He meant the hotel. His face turned expressionless again.

'I'm glad you were there for me.'

'I'm glad I was there for you, Fatima, and that you came for me. But . . .' He frowned. 'I have fear for you and me. I have another house—' He pointed to the ramparts.

'Why are you afraid?' she interrupted.

'Fatima, you must watch, you must listen. I cannot tell you, you must learn yourself. Things there are not good.' She protested that Omar was kindness itself.

'But he is part of the family. They all hide behind each other and there are many of them. They are people from Fes, not the desert. Only Omar was born here.' He changed the subject and told her that once, all Ahmed's hair fell out. 'He was shiny, like an egg. It was after an accident. He drives very badly, he has an accident nearly every month but this time the car overturned. He said it was shock, but I think it was magic.'

'Magic!' Flo was alerted. 'What magic?'

'They use it a lot here,' he told her in a matter-of-fact way.

'What for?'

'Everything. Mostly to make people fall in love. They give things to eat or drink. I don't believe in it, but a lot of people do. Mostly women. Ahmed drank some stuff to be strong and all his hair fell out.' He thought it very funny, then looked at Flo's watch.

'We must go back now. I have to work.' He put his fingers between his teeth and gave a shrill whistle at a taxi passing by.

Omar was back, they were told, but sleeping in one of the tower rooms.

'He has found you a very good car in Ouarzazate,' Ahmed, all smiles, told Flo.

'Car? But I'm not buying a car. I'm going to get a camel.' The smiles vanished.

'But, madame,' he said, coldly, 'I got the papers for Jalil.'

So it had been a deal. She had fallen into a trap. And she hadn't realised. Ahmed walked away from her. Jalil shrugged and squeezed her shoulders. And that night the door to the video room was firmly shut.

'Look, Omar . . .' she explained the next morning, when he appeared from the tower room looking more rested than he had for days. 'I never said I was going to buy a car, did I?' She glanced at Jalil who sat with them, ignoring Ahmed's black glances as he passed back and forth giving orders to Joseph and preparing to go, this time, to Marrakesh.

'I never said I was going to get a car. A camel, yes, but not a car. If I had said I'd get a car, I'd get one. An Englishman's word is his castle.' In French it came out very oddly. Omar and Jalil stared at her, then at each other. What Englishman? What castle?

'No problem, Fatima. No car, but we buy a camel.' Omar didn't seem the least put out. They discussed the practicalities. Omar didn't know how he and Jalil could leave the hotel at the same time now that Ahmed had decided to go to Marrakesh.

'Everybody comes and goes.' Although used to it by now, she said she found it odd they should go such long distances just for a day or two.

'He has business there. Maybe you and I could go?'

'No, Jalil must come too,' Flo insisted. 'We can all have a holiday.' She broke off as Zaide approached.

'*Bonjour*, Fatima. *Ça va bien*?'

'Where have you been?' Omar demanded, only just having realised he'd not been seen since Bernard left.

'Here and there.' Zaide didn't bother to explain.

'Maybe Zaide?' suggested Jalil.

'Zaide?' Like schoolboys planning to play truant, they discussed whether Zaide could be trusted for a few days while they went to buy a camel.

'I have never had a holiday,' Jalil told her. 'I must get more washing from my mother.'

In a back street in Zagora, Omar and the mechanic stared into the engine of the Mercedes. They unscrewed things, screwed them up again, got in, revved up, got out and shook their heads. Jalil filled four large plastic cans with water, stowed them in the boot then discreetly rolled a joint at the back of the mechanic's workshop. Finally the bonnet was closed on the mysteries of the engine.

'Right, we go!' As Jalil opened the car door for Flo they all remembered they needed cigarettes.

'Jalil!' He was already halfway down the narrow little street. From the other end a very new, very clean four-wheel drive approached. It stopped outside the mechanic's and a man got out. The woman passenger shifted over into the driver's seat; it was Cecille, who gave Flo the briefest of nods before driving off quickly. The man stood in the doorway of the mechanic's workshop, his cream linen slacks and silk shirt bright against the dark interior. The casualness with which he ignored the cans of oil, blackened chains and piles of greasy rags implied there were plenty more expensive clothes at hand. He lit a cigarette with a gold lighter and, as he moved to put it back in his pocket, Flo caught sight of a handsome Tuareg cross on a gold chain round his neck.

153

'Omar?' He had a slight drawl and an upward inflection, as if he wasn't sure. Omar shook hands but with no show of enthusiasm.

'Madame?' Omar introduced Flo briefly. His name was Bruno. Bruno glanced at the car.

'You are travelling?'

'Yes,' said Omar, offering no further comment.

'To Goulamine,' added Flo, not saying why.

'Goulamine?' Bruno's eyebrows shot up. 'But Goulamine is nothing. You must go to Sidi Ifni. Pure art deco . . . superb.' This was for her benefit, as if Omar could not understand such artistic significance. Bruno and she exchanged small talk, mostly centring on antiques. He told her that he visited London often and Leighton House in particular, which he found also to be superb.

'Would you care for a coffee, madame?'

'We are leaving. Now,' Omar said as Jalil appeared at the end of the street and Cecille started hooting from the other.

'What a shame,' murmured Bruno, eyeing Jalil. 'Perhaps another time. You must promise me not to fail to visit Sidi Ifni.' He told her the name of the best hotel and sauntered off towards the impatient Cecille.

'Who was that?' asked Flo, surprised by the coolness of the encounter between him and Omar.

'Oh, him. He is the *patron* for Cecille, for that *espèce d'hôtel*. He is her brother.'

'You mean he owns it?'

'Of course he owns it. He is millionaire, with hotels everywhere, a boat, an aeroplane . . . he has tea with the king.' Omar shrugged. 'Ah, Jalil, *mon ami*.' Jalil joined them with a big grin, four packets of Camels, six packets of the bitter-tasting Macquise, some pink yoghurt and a couple of Mars Bars.

'Mars Bars!' Flo pounced.

'*Yalla*! We take the piste, eh? It is quicker,' said Omar, backing out on to the main street.

The first police stop was only moments later, just outside the town and a few yards from the start of the piste track. They pulled over. Omar shuffled around for the car papers, got out and with much bonhomie engaged one of the policemen out of earshot. The second one strolled towards the car. He had mirrored glasses and kept his hand on the holster of his gun. It was obvious he'd seen too many bad videos. He leaned down and stared at Jalil through the front window.

'Salaam Maleikum,' Jalil greeted him.

'Your papers.' Jalil produced his crumpled identity card from somewhere beneath his blue robe. The policeman stared at it as if it were a dead rat.

'Profession?' he snapped.

'I am a *chamellier*.' The reply was polite and steady.

'It says here,' the policeman prodded the card with his white gloved hand, 'it says here that you are a painter.'

'That is what I was when I got the card.' It seemed a reasonable reply but the policeman wasn't finished.

'Where are you going?'

'To Goulamine.' The policeman looked as if going to Goulamine was a serious offence. Still unconvinced, he craned his neck and stared at Flo on the back seat.

'Your passport, madame.' She gave it to him and continued gazing down the dusty piste ahead. Omar hurried back to the car, keeping up a cheery flow in Arabic, the word tourist punctuating what he had to say. The policeman gave her back her passport. A ten-dirham note passed from Omar's hand into his pocket. The policeman gave Jalil back his identity card.

'Painter!' he sneered. 'Painter!' Jalil stared ahead, ignoring him as Omar revved the engine and jerked the car forwards, almost bumping into a signpost that said Tazenakht was sixty-four kilometres.

'What did he mean, painter?' he demanded. Jalil explained.

'Get a new card, man. No wonder they think you're a crook. Do up your seat belt.'

'Omar, Omar.' Flo tried to tell him she'd worked out it was only seventy or so kilometres by the main road, but he had already started a serious game of dodge the pot hole.

Except for a line of telegraph poles and an occasional heap of stones that could have been primitive dwellings, the shallow valley was devoid of all signs of life.

'Fun, eh?' shouted Omar after an hour or so as the car bumped up and down and a large rock hit the side.

'I suppose so.' Flo was unenthusiastic. Jalil held her ankle and Bob Marley sang on. Omar suddenly said he'd had enough of Bob Marley. Jalil put an end to 'So Much Things To Say' and changed to a Moroccan tape. A woman wailed, a passionate complaint, answered by a chorus of more women, even shriller, their apparent desolation tuning with the parched landscape.

'Which way?' They'd reached a distinct fork on the track but with no signpost. They got out and stretched. Omar offered Flo a beer but she said she'd rather have a yoghurt.

'You like the piste, then?' Beer in hand, he walked round the car kicking the tyres as Jalil topped up the thirsty engine.

'Which way to Tazenakht?' There was no one to ask. Jalil looked north, then south, then north again.

'Right?' suggested Flo, wiping yoghurt off her hands onto her jeans.

'Why right?' they wanted to know.

'It's the way the telegraph poles go.'

'Here,' Omar said, 'that means nothing.'

'Oh, come on. You're the desert men. You're supposed to know these things. Which way? Right or left?'

'It's all right or left around here.' Jalil took in the vastness with a sweep of his long arm.

'OK. We go right.'

'What's she singing about?' Flo asked as they got back into the car.

Jalil gave that a bit of thought then replied, 'The washing up. And a bit about Allah,' he added.

Flo was wrong. The telegraph poles led up an hour-long trail to a disused military bunker, then petered out. They turned round. To her relief, neither man blamed nor scolded the way John would have done. In silence they drove for what seemed hours. It was nearly half past ten. They'd passed Tazenakht without stopping and were approaching Taroudant, when Omar pulled up at a small hotel and restaurant at the side of the road. Flo woke from a half doze.

'Where are we?'

Omar said, 'I must eat. Now.'

The tired, grubby trio walked towards the hotel. The manager, a stick thin man with glittering eyes and wearing a Rastafarian cap, sized them up with a look of sheer hostility. Omar gave him one back. The light inside the restaurant was harsh and bright, casting ugly shadows on the faces of the diners.

'It must be the only bright light in Morocco,' said

Flo as they took in the minimalist decor of chalk white walls and a few big green plants.

'It's too clean.' Omar condemned it as they seated themselves at a table.

'The cook has gone home,' announced the Rastafarian with pleasure. Flo looked round at the French and Germans halfway through their meals and started to laugh. Omar announced, very loudly, that he was a Moroccan and as such expected Moroccan hospitality. The Rasta glanced at Flo and Jalil as though they were no more from Morocco than another planet. With vicious delight he said there was no more chicken, no couscous, no salad and no omelettes. Jalil, who had taken one panic-stricken glance at all the knives and forks set out for him, rose to bolt.

'Sit down, my friend. We will eat Moroccan style. Tagine. Even if I have to cook it myself!' He was shouting now. The French stared. The Germans went on eating.

'Tagine!' he yelled. The Rasta backed down, admitting that perhaps there was a little tagine left and dumped a basket of bread on the table. Omar tore at a piece, stuffed it in his mouth, tore off more and threw them at Flo and Jalil. The French went on staring. Omar stared back at them.

'*Bonsoir, mes amis!*' He saluted the starers and turned back to Flo and Jalil. 'We are bizarre,' he admitted, 'even for Morocco.' He asked Flo what the time was. It was very late. The Rasta tended to the other diners, then disappeared for twenty minutes, returning with the tagine. It was cold. And it was burned. Jalil, unconcerned now that he was free to use bread instead of cutlery, ate while Flo picked at a raw carrot and scraped the burnt bits off a potato. She longed for a cup of tea and a ginger biscuit. Omar took one mouthful, then another and announced that he had stomachache.

'We may be shabby at Les Dunes, but at least we don't poison people!'

He kept up his complaints as far as Taroudant, where Flo took a little pride in guiding him through the sleeping streets until they arrived outside the Hôtel Français.

'There it is!' The sleepers were in place on the pavement, but there was no sign of Jacoub and the boys. They knocked, they yelled, they knocked again, but the door stayed firmly bolted against the rheumy longings of the alcoholics and any possible late night clients. They parked in the middle of the square and looked around.

'Wait!' Omar strode off towards the only light, shining faintly in a doorway of one of the cafés. Jalil took Flo's hand as they waited by the car.

'Fatima?'

'Yes?'

'You are tired?'

'A bit.'

He kissed the top of her head and fatigue flew, weariness replaced by soft contentment.

'Come!' Omar beckoned to them from the dim doorway. 'Come, it's pretty awful, but clean. Well, almost. There's a tap in the passage,' he informed Flo over his shoulder as they followed him up a flight of stairs. Tactfully, he left it at that.

'This one is for you.' The door opened on to a small room with a double bed that took up most of it. 'And I am here.' He opened another door on to a second room with two beds and threw himself down on to the nearest, holding his stomach.

'Is he all right?' she asked Jalil, whose big, blue frame

almost blocked the door. Omar gave orders, for wine, bananas, cigarettes, another blanket, something to clean his teeth with.

'It's no problem,' Jalil told her. 'Get some rest.' He watched her as she went into her room and shut the door.

The ramparts were still, firm and sturdy against the haze of the moonlit sky. Down below the empty tables waited for the next day. She knelt on the bed, her arms resting on the windowsill, and realised it was the same café where Alex flirted with Jacoub and she had fussed about her silly skirt before buying all that junk. A beginner, two years ago, or was it three? She tried to work out how many visits now merged into a stream of bright, clear days and nights which had brought her here. On her way to buy a camel, which seemed startlingly normal. She would be the first to agree that she could sometimes be a reckless shopper, but had anyone ever told her that she would buy a camel (even one of her Tarot ladies) she would have protested long and loud for her sanity. But now she was about to do it.

'It's all right, really, it's all right.' She sent a silent message through the stars to the girls, so far away, so safe, so busy in America. 'You see,' she tried to explain, 'you see, sometimes maybe you have to be who you aren't for a long time before you find out who you are.' And she was Fatima on her way to buy a camel. She pulled the shawl around her shoulders and decided against relaying the bit about the camel across the Atlantic.

Later, as she knew he would, Jalil came quietly into the room. Omar was tucked up for the night.

'Is he all right?'

160

'Yes, he's all right. He is asleep now.'

'He gives you an awful lot of orders.'

'Well, he does, doesn't he?' she persisted. He stood in a square of moonlight and unwound his *shesh*.

'That's the way it is.'

'But it was meant to be a holiday for you too.'

'Have you ever been to Taroudant before?' He sat down on the bed beside her.

'Yes. Have you?'

'No.'

'It's pretty, isn't it? Peaceful.' They went up and looked out over the ramparts, the silence broken only by the crickets.

'I love you,' he said in English.

'So where is it? This Sidi Ifni?' They drove round the main square for the third time. The town was held in a vacuum, sea mist sneaking over the decaying architectural grandeur and through the elaborate grillework of dead windows. As Bruno said, it was very art deco, a strange style for a military enclave. They passed the Spanish Consulate again, which was closed, and a Moorish art deco church which indicated that it was now a court of law. This too was shut.

'Where is everybody?'

'Gone.' Jalil looked at the greyness of the sea and sky as Omar pulled up beside a long flight of crumbling stone steps that led on to an uninviting beach. He dragged a pink blanket from the back seat and wrapped it round himself.

'My glands,' he complained, fingering his throat. 'Go for a walk,' he ordered, pulling the blanket over his head and reaching under the seat for a bottle of wine. 'I'll be all right.'

161

Jalil and Flo got out of the car and walked slowly to the parapet, the wind blowing her hair back from her face. Jalil rewound his *shesh* tightly round his head as they walked down the steps and on to the rocky beach. A few children in thick sweaters played football round them as Jalil lifted his big feet in exaggerated steps over the little rivulets of water from the incoming tide. They reached the foot of the cliff and looked around for somewhere dry to sit. He sneezed and looked at her, astonished.

'That was the first time in my life.'

'The first time you've ever sneezed?' She was as astonished as he and used the English word.

'Sneeze?' He didn't believe her. 'Is that what you call it?'

'Yes, sneeze.'

'It's a very unusual word. Sneeze.' He looked out at the sea with a troubled face. 'Look at it!' The waves broke and pounded up towards them, then withdrew with a hiss. 'It keeps doing the same thing but you never know what it might do next.'

'Have you ever seen the sea before?' Obviously, for a desert man, the sea could be a strange and terrifying monster.

'Yes, in Casablanca, but not so close,' he replied, staring at the grey water, not taking his eyes off it for a moment. 'It's not good to get too close to the sea. My mother says that too.'

'Don't you like the beach?' Not that she could blame him if he said no to this particular stony stretch of shoreline.

'Too much sand.' He shook his robe to prove it.

'What do you mean, too much sand? You're a desert man. It's all sand there.'

162

'But it's not wet,' he pointed out as he pulled her to her feet.

'I could kill that Bruno,' Omar raged when they reached the car. 'We must leave this terrible Sidi Sniff Sniff at once. I must *enlever les glandes.*'

'*Enlever les glandes?*' Flo couldn't believe what she was hearing. *Enlever*, as far as she was concerned, meant to take out, remove.

'Take out your glands?' she repeated, horrified.

'Yes.' He demonstrated with his thumb thrust under his tongue and a circular movement of his wrist. '*Enlever les glandes*, clean them and put them back.' She shuddered at the barbarity of it.

'I don't believe you. Is it true?' she asked Jalil.

'Oh yes.' He nodded. 'There are doctors who do that. Old doctors.'

'You will find me an old doctor in Goulamine,' Omar ordered as he flipped through the *Rough Guide*, then tossed it over to Flo because it was in English.

'Well, what does it say, *ce Rough Guide*, what does it say about Goulamine?' A moment of triumph, one to report back to Alex, to be with two Moroccans in their own country, who finally had to resort to the *Rough Guide*.

The camel market was a walled-in space about five kilometres outside the town. Like any other market place, the vans and trucks collected outside the gates and the animals were herded into a stone-walled enclosure for the serious business. Goats, sheep, chickens, donkeys, but the main event was the camels.

'Have you got your camera?' Omar asked her.

'Yes.'

'Use it. Look like a tourist and don't come anywhere

near me. Jalil will look after you.' All morning he'd been insistent that if anyone caught even a whisper that it was she who was buying, they'd double, even treble the price. Casually she walked away, looking at groups of camels, pointing her camera from time to time and snapping at white ducks squeezed into crates. Not only was she the only European, she was the only woman, but unlike the starers in the cafés, these grizzled men were engrossed in their bargaining. To her relief, she might just as well have been invisible. As she sat down on a large stone alongside a row of elderly Hassani, who also apparently had nothing else to do but watch, Omar, his blue robes flapping and flowing strode around talking to those he knew and those he didn't. Jalil walked alone, looking carefully, running his hands down the necks of one or two camels, talking to them while searching for signs of age or decrepitude. For a long time he stood near a group of white camels, one much larger than the others. Omar, breaking his own rule, came up to Flo and asked her what she thought. It was, she thought, very fine, beautiful and disdainful.

'It's lovely, but . . .' she edged a bit closer and stared at him. Omar had a brief exchange with the owner who told him he'd have to buy the whole troupe, five females and one male. He turned away as another great beast, black this time, was led past.

'What about him?' asked Flo, staring at the sky. Omar dismissed him as ugly.

'*Un malign*,' he said as suddenly it plunged and rushed, scattering a small herd of black goats and creating chaos as it blundered towards the exit.

'You see!' He went off to see if there was anything lurking in the car park that he'd missed.

'There!' Jalil was standing behind her. She looked

towards another group of cream-coloured camels, thin and weary, taking little notice of their surroundings.

'They are tired,' he told her quietly. 'They have come a long way from Layoune, but look!' In the centre of the weary beasts there was one, his head up, turning this way and that, curious and almost amused by what he saw.

'Yes,' pronounced Flo as the camel stared directly at her. 'Yes, that's the one.' She went back to her rock and sat down demurely, keeping out of men's business and praying that he wouldn't be too expensive or come with a whole troupe. Jalil found Omar, who looked at the animal briefly, then, almost bored, asked if he could try it. The owner, a handsome old Hassani with bright eyes and wearing a soft leather coat, told it to kneel.

'Ouch, ouch.' Omar gave a great shout and with much flapping of his robes leaped astride, waving his arms above his head as the camel rose to its feet.

'Eeya!' he shouted as it sprang off into a loping canter. He rode it round the enclosure, making a lot of noise before returning it to Jalil and Flo and declaring, '*Pas mal.*'

He jerked his head at Jalil, who approached it, stroked its ears and nose before leaping lightly and quietly on to its back. He trotted him to the edge of the enclosure and allowed him to look at the view beyond. When he came back he was smiling.

'Go for a walk with Jalil,' instructed Omar and approached the old Hassani.

They sat in the back of the car as Flo counted out the torn dirty notes.

'I did well for you!' Omar crowed, taking a swig of wine from a new bottle.

'Three hundred, four hundred, five hundred . . .' It went on and on. In dirham it sounded appallingly expensive. In pounds, it came to seven hundred. But (she informed Alex, should she be tuning in) she had got a whole camel. At Aquascutum or Jaeger just a coat would be twice the price, if not more.

'And Jalil and I are rich. I got a very good price for you!'

'What?'

'I sold you,' Omar told her with wicked glee. Flo stopped counting for a moment.

'You *sold* me?'

'And got a very good price, eh, Jalil?' He said something in Arabic. Jalil looked blank then furious.

'I'd make a terrible slave,' she told him. 'Wouldn't I?' she asked Jalil, but his face was as expressionless as a block of wood.

'It is difficult for me to talk about selling Fatima,' he said stiffly and got out of the car.

'Oh, come on, man, it's a joke.'

Flo went on counting.

'The transport will be another hundred pounds, and food for the camel on the journey, another fifty.' Jalil leaned against the bonnet of the car, his arms crossed over his chest. Flo gave Omar the last of the grubby notes, which he thrust into a leather satchel round his neck.

'You drink?' Omar handed her the bottle and she took a small gulp.

'Cheers, boys!' He offered it to Jalil, who shook his head without turning round.

'Can we go over it just once more?' Flo asked. 'Seven hundred for the camel, one hundred for transport, fifty for food and the rest, expenses for the journey. One thousand pounds. Which is . . .' She punched the calculator Omar produced for her. 'Thirteen thousand, two hundred and fifty dirham at today's rate of exchange.'

'Exact.' Omar beamed and got out of the car and went to settle up with the Hassani. Jalil stayed leaning on the car looking angry. Flo got out and joined him.

'It was only a joke,' she said, nudging him. 'It didn't mean anything. That is what's bothering you, isn't it?'

'It is that, and other things,' he said, looking troubled.

The pick-up truck looked very small for such a large animal to travel so far. Omar, in high good spirits, stood back as they let down the ramp and the Hassani approached with the camel. Her camel. The old man handed him over to Omar.

'No.' Flo indicated that he should give it to Jalil. Jalil took the rope, let it drop, then ran up the ramp of the pick-up truck calling, '*Agi, agi, agi*.' They shoved, heaved, almost lifted it from the ground.

'Oh, do be careful.' Flo fussed as the animal's head tossed from side to side.

'One, two, three.' With a final push the camel was bundled into the cramped space. Jalil patted his neck and jumped down, smiling, as though he and the camel shared a secret joke. The camel looked round calmly, well satisfied with the commotion he had caused.

'That truck's a bit small, isn't it?'

'He will be OK. He is good,' Jalil assured her as they watched it jolting over the rough ground.

'So, what are you going to call your camel?' Omar asked Jalil as they headed back on to the road.

'Wahid,' he replied without hesitation.

'Wahid? You can't call a camel Wahid.'

'Why not?' Flo wondered if it had any religious significance. 'What does it mean?'

'It means unique.' Omar reached into the back of the car for another bottle of wine, then changed his mind as two policemen flagged them down.

'Don't worry.' He saw Flo's look of concern. 'It's only ten per cent proof.'

'Where are you going?' The policeman, who seemed quite satisfied with Omar and Jalil and the car papers, was curious about Flo. 'Are you alone, madame?' he asked.

'Well, no, not exactly.' She indicated Omar and Jalil in front.

'Madame has just bought a camel,' Omar informed them. The policeman was so astonished he did the only thing possible and asked for her passport.

'Housewife?' he said, querying her profession. It was difficult to explain such a meaningless entry even in English. When she'd filled it in there seemed little else to say.

'*Femme de chambre*,' she replied primly, then realised she should have said *femme de ménage*.

'*Femme de chambre*?' There was genuine puzzlement that an English chambermaid should be with two Moroccans and have bought a camel.

'Ah, *les Anglais*.' The policeman shook his head, accepted twenty dirham from Omar and waved them on.

'It is good to do business with the Hassani,' Omar announced after they had been driving for a couple of hours. 'No papers, no bills of sale, no receipts . . . none of that shit. Just a handshake. They are desert men.' This, she thought, was very commendable. She wondered why Omar had thought it necessary to mention this out of the blue. A handshake was all very well, but it wasn't *her* handshake and all she knew was that the camel's brand number on one flank was seventeen and eight on the shoulder on the other side. He was skinny, he was white, he was, Jalil had said, about seven years old and his name was Wahid. Breaking into Flo's thoughtful silence, Omar stopped the car. They were in a valley which rose above the road into high crags and down into green fertile depths where several goats grazed under the watch of two children leaning up against a well. Omar leaped out of the car, declaring that both he and it needed water. Tearing off his robe he charged off the side of the road, then dragged off his shirt and *shesh* and, hopping out of his baggy blue trousers, ran down the rest of the slope in his underpants shouting, 'We may be desert men but there is no need to stink!'

'The children backed away as he approached, then ran and scrambled up the far slope, screaming as if they had seen a demon. Omar waved and shouted, which terrified them even more. He reached the well, let down the bucket, pulled it up and began to splash icy water all over his body. Jalil laughed as he collected the plastic bottles from the boot.

'We have Wahid,' he said with the pride of man announcing the birth of a first son.

'We do indeed.'

He kissed her through the car window and at a gentle pace headed down to the well with the bottles.

They'd cut it too fine. Ahmed was already back from Marrakesh and very, very angry. Flo had been there long enough to tell the difference between a heated discussion and a real row. She sat in the courtyard with Jalil and Zaide, the pleasure of their days draining as the shouting and harsh sounds rose than the video room and it seemed only moments before Ahmed and Omar would start hitting each other.

'What's it all about?'

'It is because we left Zaide in charge.'

'But I did nothing wrong,' protested Zaide, tugging at his little beard. 'There were only two clients, Australians. They ate, they slept and when they left they gave me fifty dirham.' About three pounds fifty and to him a fortune.

'*He* wanted me to give it in to Reception,' Zaide went on as Ahmed's voice rose an octave, 'but it was for me, so I didn't.' Which, to Flo, seemed perfectly fair and she said so.

'It wasn't my fault – the turkey,' he added.

'What about the turkey?'

'Not my fault,' pleaded Zaide and told her he'd found it dead and all bloated up in the cistern. 'The stupid thing suicided itself. If it had told me it was sad I would have killed it and the Australians could have had a feast.' Suddenly the voices in the video room stopped. A moment later Omar marched out past them without looking right or left and slammed into the tower room.

'Big trouble,' said Jalil.

'You have bought a fine camel.' Ahmed sat beside Flo as she watched Jalil and Zaide run to greet the pick-up truck. They let down the ramp and Jalil started to unfold the cramped animal. Wahid looked round at his new home as Jalil massaged his thin legs. A few of the boys from the dunes sauntered past with murmurs of approval. Jalil gave Wahid a bucket of water and some dates. Wahid drank the water, investigated the dates then, ignoring them, gazed long and hard at Laassell and the other camels, who looked long and hard at him.

'He is amazing.' Flo still couldn't believe that this beautiful beast was hers. Since Wahid obviously didn't think much of dates, Jalil spread some hay on the ground and, still holding his rope, watched until he had finished it then led him a short distance from the other camels.

'He must stay apart for a few days in case there are any arguments.' He bent to hobble him and glanced round at Ahmed now sauntering back into the garden.

'There has been enough fighting.'

'A very fine camel, madame,' Ahmed assured her. 'Now we have seven camels.'

Seven camels? She was about to remind him that Wahid was hers and Jalil's but thought better of it and asked casually, 'I wonder if it would be possible to have a receipt?' It was taking a chance on offending him; maybe there would be more door-slamming, but it was a risk she knew she had to take.

'A receipt?'

'Yes. A receipt for the camel. And for the food and transport.' She went on quickly, 'You see, I need it for my accountant.' It was an idea out of the blue. She wasn't sure what accountant was in French and explained it was the man who helped her with her tax. 'Wahid might be tax deductible.' It was worth a shot.

'Ah yes, *l'impôt*.' Ahmed knew about that. He went into Reception and came back with a bit of the hotel's headed paper.

'It is best if you write it.'

She wrote: 'Received from Mrs Florence Lucas,' then her passport number, the date and the amount, 'in payment for one camel (white) bought on her behalf at Goulamine, brand mark 17/8 and paid in full. With thanks.'

'A stamp?' she asked.

'*Bien sûr.*' Ahmed produced the hotel stamp, pressed it on the paper and signed over it. She read it through carefully and then read it to him.

'Thank you,' she said and put it in her bag.

Jalil spent his time at the dunes, gently introducing Wahid to his working life. He was quick, obedient and very well trained. Omar stayed in the tower room for three days. Ahmed stayed in the video room. If they passed each other on the way to the shower room there was only the briefest of nods between them.

'What *is* going on?' Flo asked Zaide. She was puzzled by this drawn-out game of petulance and depressed by the malevolent atmosphere permeating every dark corner of the hotel.

'It is the drink,' Zaide told her. He made a tippling gesture.

'Ahmed? Drink?'

'*Bien sûr*, all the time. Omar, he drinks like a man. The Other One, he drinks in secret and pretends that he is good.' Zaide sighed and held out his hand.

'*Au revoir*, Fatima.'

'Are you leaving?'

He chose not to answer directly and told her he was going to his family for the festival, then broke off to admire her bracelets that she'd bought in Taroudant.

'How much you pay?' He was sure she'd paid too

172

much. So was she. He pulled a bangle from his pocket.

'I have better bracelet, very good, real silver. Tuareg,' he added for good measure.

'Oh, Zaide, not you too. Go home.' She laughed and gave him a hundred dirham. Zaide grinned, put it in his pocket and marched out of the front gate. No preparation, no packing, no bags or bundles, just stand up with a hundred dirham in your pocket and leave. She was amazed by the simplicity of it.

It was too hot now to sit in the sun. She settled into the big tent with Graham Greene. No sound, no movement, heat permeating every stick and stone, flies buzzing round her feet and pinpoints of light above her head where the tent was torn. She put her book aside and went to look for Joseph in the kitchen.

'Joseph? Joseph? *Un* Coca-Cola?' The kitchen was empty, the stone sink clean with a dirty dishcloth hanging over it and the large, old-fashioned fridge was chained and padlocked. Slowly she walked back to the tent, an idea forming in her mind.

'Fatima?' Omar emerged from the tower room, bleary and blinking in the bright light.

'Where is everyone?' she asked him.

'The festival.' He shrugged and flopped down beside her in the tent. 'My feet are hot,' he grumbled, then shouted for Jalil. She told him he was with Wahid at the dunes.

'He is OK, the camel?'

Flo assured him he was fine then went on.

'I've been thinking about Wahid,' she started slowly. 'I was thinking it would be better if I made him over to Jalil. After all, it's silly for him to wait until I'm dead.'

Instead of the *'bien sûr'* she expected, Omar leaped to his feet.

'What?' He was glaring down at her but with his back to the light, his face in shadow, she couldn't make out if he was pleased or angry.

'That way,' she went on, 'Jalil would have some sort of security for himself.'

'What!' shouted Omar again, leaving her in no doubt that he was furious. 'If you give that camel to Jalil, I will slit its throat!' What she proposed was treason. Gone was the big-hearted *homme du desert.* Shocked, sweat now pouring down her back, she stood her ground.

'But, Omar, it is what I want to do.' She thanked heaven for the receipt in her bag. Omar paced round, shouting at her.

'If you give that camel to Jalil, he will get a big head. That camel belongs to the hotel. I bought it!' The full significance of what he was saying began to dawn. It was all right for her to buy a camel, a silly tourist with a whim. It was all right for her to play games, calling it Jalil's camel. But anything real, such as Jalil being the legal owner, was unthinkable.

'If you give him that camel, he can never, and I promise you, never, work at the Dunes.'

'Omar, please.' He flung himself down again and groaned, then yelled for Joseph.

'He's not here,' she told him. He got to his feet and went off to the video room to have another row with Ahmed. A few moments later he stormed past the tent again, shouting as he headed towards the Mercedes. Ahmed ran after him, demanding the keys. They stood beside the car, yelling at each other.

'OK. OK. I take a taxi, I hitch a lift. I walk!' Omar pounded off towards the road.

'If you're going into town,' Ahmed shouted after him, 'we need more potatoes, Coca-Cola, jam.'

'Get 'em yourself!' Omar shouted back and whistled down a passing truck.

'It is the drink.' Jalil sat on the edge of her bed, confirming what Zaide had told her. 'It is always the same, always some blah, blah, blah.' He produced two strawberry yoghurts and a spoon for her. He drank his from the pot then started to unwind his *shesh*.

'*C'est la vie.*' He ran his hands through his springy dreadlocks.

'It got much worse', she told him, 'when I told Omar I was going to make the camel over to you.' His hands dropped on to his lap.

'You told him that?' She nodded. He gave her a great grin then looked serious.

'Big trouble.'

'Yes. He was furious.'

'That is natural.'

'But why?'

'It is always the same. Everything for themselves. I told you to watch, to listen and you are learning.'

'But Wahid is not for them. They knew that. He's for you. I can give him to you if I want. At home it's called a Deed of Gift.' She explained what that meant and asked if it was possible to do that here.

'Yes. But it must be done in my village. Not Zagora.'

'Why not Zagora?'

'In Zagora there are big mouths and backsheesh everywhere. In one hour they would know.'

'So what if they do?'

'Fatima.' He took her hands. 'Fatima, you don't understand. Everything is for themselves. Even the

175

tips for the boys. Why do you think Adi and Ali left? And now, even Joseph. There is not much work in the south. The boys are very young. Sometimes they get paid a little, but not often. They rely on tips, they rely on food left over from the clients, they rely on one blanket for the night.' Shocked, she listened to the hidden politics of the hotel as he explained without rancour, his face still, the face of one who had learned to live by his own perceptions of hard experience.

'Omar has no choice. He is not the real *patron*. He is a relative without resource. Ahmed owns the hotel and he is from the city, a city man greedy for whisky and money for the family. He comes, he goes, he takes every sou with him and puts nothing back. Omar is of the desert. He was born here but he can do nothing. He gets angry, but in the end he will always hide behind the family.' It was the most she'd ever heard him say, and now things began to fall into place. The discontent of the boys, after Bernard's trek. Omar's anxiety that it should be a success, the shabbiness of the disintegrating cushions and the lack of fundamental needs like lavatory paper.

'But you? What about you? You are still here. You could work anywhere.'

'I would have left a long time ago,' he told her, his voice deep in the dark, 'but I waited for you. I waited since the first day you came. I knew you would come again.' She asked him why. His hand moved to her breast. She clasped it between her own.

'I waited because you are like me. And because your eyes smile, but I have fear for you and me.'

'Why?' She told him she had more fear for Wahid. 'Let's go and see him.'

'Wahid? Now?'

'Yes, now.' She looked around for her clothes.

'No,' he said. 'Like that.'

In her white nightie and her slippers, Flo held his hand as they tiptoed past the silent tower room.

'*Une cigarette*?' A voice came from the shadows. It was Muad, the night-watchman. Jalil gave him one and they talked together for a moment in soft Arabic. Jalil patted him on the arm and laughed.

'What did he say?' she asked him as they walked towards the dunes.

'He said he was happy for me that I have found a very good lady.' Flo felt a rush of gratitude towards the toothless old man.

'Look. He is there!' Jalil spotted Wahid, ghostly white, staring thoughtfully at the stars.

'Wahid, Wahid.' He turned his head, for a moment then looked back at the sky.

'You see, he knows his name. Here.' He held out his hand as they started to climb the dune. When they reached the top, Jalil took off his robe and laid it on the soft sand.

'A shooting star!' he pointed and they watched it blink away. Then he reached for her and slid off her white nightie.

'You are beautiful,' he told her as she lay down on the blue robe. Above her, the dialogue of his eyes was aimed at her alone as his warm, smooth body closed in on her. The slight breeze stroked her skin, the soft sand shifted underneath them. A warrior? A prince? A Nubian king? The knowledge that they'd known each other since the start of time swept over her and she knew she would never be so cherished or so loved again.

*   *   *

The official in the village town hall, who Flo took to be some sort of mayor, was young, wore a neat, grey suit, had a close-shaven head and piercing black eyes.

'You understand what you are doing, madame?' he asked her for the third time. She assured him that since there wasn't much call for camels in Notting Hill Gate, this was the most practical solution. She didn't mention any opposition from Omar and Ahmed, but she had the feeling he suspected as much. The paperwork done, the photocopies of everything, passport numbers, identity cards, receipts all stamped and signed, he then gave her the paper. It was in Arabic and she didn't understand a word. He made Jalil read it through.

'Here.' He gave it to her when he'd finished reading.

'No. You keep it and, for goodness' sake, don't lose it.' With his hand on his heart, Jalil vowed he'd guard it with his life, which amused the mayor, who shook hands with both of them and wished them a happy festival.

'I will give it to my mother for safe keeping,' Jalil told her as they ran down the steps of the town hall, excited and defiant as a couple skipping off to Gretna Green. He started to cross the road. 'You come?'

Flo shook her head and sat down on the steps. A visit to the family would be a long affair, shoes off, hand washing, tea, maybe a meal. She felt tired, jubilant and restless, not sure what she wanted to do next. But if they went straight back to the hotel she'd have rebellion written on her face, and there'd be more rows.

'No, I'll wait for you here.' She watched him as he sprinted down the road and round a corner, wondering where, in that crowded house, his family hid their humble treasures. She lit a cigarette, then decided that what she needed was a very large drink.

*   *   *

'I would like to visit a friend,' Jalil told her when they arrived at La Fibule. She gave him the rolls of film from Goulamine and asked if he could get them processed. She said she wanted to write postcards. He promised he would not be long. La Fibule had turned into a deserted Arabian Nights Palace with not a sign of visitors or staff. There was no one at Reception, no Ali Baba, no gazelles. The bar was open but unattended. Flo helped herself to a few postcards from a rack and found a table by the pool. It was cool and clean and comfortable. To the girls she wrote:

'Having a wonderful time' which seemed a bit understand. To her parents she wrote: 'Morocco is a very interesting place. The more you get to know it, the odder it becomes.' To Keltie and Duncan she wrote, 'Everyone sends their love,' which she was sure they would if they remembered who they were. To friends, 'I'm sure you'd love it here.' She had to think about what to say to Alex: 'Spent last night naked at the dunes in the moonlight'? She decided to wait on that one and stared into the aquamarine water of the pool.

'Hullo,' said a voice. 'You still here?' It was Cecille, with Bruno, her hair shining, in a white linen dress, expensive sandals and bag. Bruno gleamed away in white as well.

'We meet again. May we join you?' They sat down at her table.

'What are you drinking?' asked Bruno, crossing one elegant leg over the other.

'There doesn't seem to be anyone around.'

'It's the Festival des Moutons. Totally barbaric and totally wonderful.' For Bruno, as if by a silent royal command, a waiter appeared. Flo ordered a vodka and tonic, Cecille the same.

'*Comme d'habitude pour Monsieur*?' enquired the waiter. Bruno gave an almost imperceptible nod.

'Wonderful?' Cecille shuddered, disagreeing with her brother. 'They kill a lamb, a sheep or goat or something that's been fattened up for weeks, treated like a saint with flowers in its hair, then they slaughter it and eat it. Raw!'

'Raw?' Flo couldn't believe it.

'My dear, that's not all—'

'But why?' Flo interrupted her.

'Something to do with Abraham.' Cecille was vague.

'But I thought Abraham was Jewish.'

'He is. Was. Don't even try to understand and try not to get invited to a Moroccan house. I warn you, if you do, you'll be the guest of honour, since you are a foreigner.' Flo was about to ask why again but Cecille went on.

'The guest of honour is given the great delicacy. And that, my dear, happens to be the genitalia.'

'And you eat it? Raw!'

'Or cause offence. My dear, I've done it, and it's torture trying to swallow without vomiting.' The waiter arrived with their vodkas tinkling in long thin glasses. Bruno's usual was a lightly chilled sherry.

'Is this ice made of mineral water or from the tap?' Cecille asked the waiter. Bruno started talking about Degas. When he'd finished with Degas, he changed subject seamlessly and told Flo she reminded him of Jeanne Moreau (in her younger days, of course). Taken off guard by such an outrageously inaccurate compliment and the unaccustomed hit of vodka, Flo laughed, realising she hadn't spoken English for some while. Bruno then tiptoed into the who are you game. Where did she live? Who had she been married to? Did

she know the Princess Irene Someone-or-other? He'd
heard of John (he said) but never met him, but he lit
up when she mentioned her father.

'Sir Andrew . . .'

'Do you know him?' she asked, thinking, 'If you do,
it's more than I do.'

'Not in person, alas, but I have read his books and for
many years have read of him. A great and very elegant
scholar.' Elegant. A curious word to describe her father,
of whom it was well known that he'd never been seen
in anything but the same torn shorts and straw hat for
over thirty years.

'I hear you bought a camel.' Cecille had finished with
the waiter and looked at Flo with wide blue eyes. 'Take
care,' she advised, then asked how long she was staying.
Flo's ticket was now ten days out of date.

'I'm not sure.'

'Bruno and I could give you a lift,' offered Cecille,
'in the plane.'

'You have a plane?' Flo was impressed.

'Only a small one.' He dismissed it modestly. 'But
you have a camel, how very romantic. But then,
there has always been an intrepid type of Englishwoman lured by the desert.' He was fishing and she
knew it.

'How is the hotel coming along?' she asked Cecille,
changing the subject.

'No, no, I don't want to think about it.' Cecille gave a
little scream and put her hands over her ears. 'Bruno is
rescuing me from hotels, plumbers and dead sheep for
a whole week.' It was then Flo realised her handsome
husband was neither there nor had been mentioned.
Cecille, reminded of the hotel, launched back into her
problems.

'Your friends at the Hôtel des Dunes aren't exactly helping matters,' she declared, finishing her drink, calling for another, and was off on a long story involving Ahmed, rights of way, feudal attitudes to territory and possible litigation. Flo was about to admit to the furore concerning Wahid but Bruno had had enough.

'My dear,' he begged Cecille, 'enough. It will be dealt with. Aaaahhh . . .' His brittle voice softened as Jalil appeared through an archway of bougainvillaea. Flo waved at him. Jalil looked at his watch.

'Superb.' Bruno raised his glass to Flo who didn't know whether to blush or say thank you. Cecille turned her head.

'Ah, Jalil of the desert.' Jalil bowed to her. 'The best *chamellier* in the south. A charming boy and the only Moroccan who has never tried to sell me anything.'

Bruno, still gazing at Jalil then back at Flo, murmured, 'Pure Othello.'

'I hope not.' Flo rose to pay for her postcards.

'Oh, surely, you are not going?' She apologised and said she had an appointment.

'An appointment, in Morocco? How original.' Too grand to have a card, Bruno gave her a fax number and told her one of his secretaries could find him at any time. He raised his glass again.

'*Bonne chance*, madame.'

There were two cars she hadn't seen before parked by the well, but no sign of anyone except Ahmed. He was dressed in white, his arms folded over his chest, waiting for them.

'Where have you been?' he demanded with a face as

sour as a lemon. No *Bonsoir, madame, ça va*? Not even a *Bonsoir*. She stopped dead. He remained seated at the tile table. She turned and went into her room, changed her mind and came out again to see Jalil following Ahmed towards the courtyard in a subservient shuffle instead of his usual sure-footed stride, which infuriated her. She stood still for a moment until Ahmed left the courtyard. Still angry and ruffled, she sat down. Jalil turned back and, looking troubled, told her he'd find some eggs and went off to the kitchen. The generator was suddenly switched off. She sat in the light of one candle stub. There was no Joseph, no cook and even old Muad, who usually shuffled from his shack behind the broken cars at sunset, was nowhere to be seen. Jalil then appeared with a plateful of eggs mixed up with fried onions. He said he wasn't hungry.

'What? No scrambled eggs?' He liked the word scrambled.

He waited until she'd finished eating then said, 'He knows about the camel. He knows about the papers.'

'How?' she asked, dabbing her mouth with a Kleenex. She lit a cigarette for herself and one for him.

'Maybe someone saw you on the steps of the town hall.'

'But I was only there five minutes. And even if they did, it doesn't mean that we were . . . oh, so what!' It was ridiculous that one camel should become such an issue. 'It is legal now and he can't do anything about it.'

'Yes, Fatima, there is. There is something else that I must tell you.' He sounded worried, his voice flat.

'What?'

'He said I am forbidden to come to your room.'

'He said *what*!' So it was open war. 'Where's Omar?'

she demanded. Omar would soon put a stop to all this schoolmasterish tyranny.

'He is in Casablanca.'

'Casablanca? Why?'

'He has gone to see his wife.'

'His *what*?' Her head was spinning, but he'd used the word *femme*, which in French could mean either wife or woman. Before she could ask which, Ahmed appeared in the doorway of the courtyard with the small boy she had seen on that first day. Jalil was summoned. As he rose, Flo caught hold of his robe.

'When's Omar coming back?' Jalil shrugged.

'Soon, maybe tonight. He is bringing more of the family for the festival. Some are now here.' She let go of his robe and he walked slowly towards Ahmed with his head up, as if he'd made a decision. They talked for a moment, Jalil nodding, then protesting. Ahmed turned away and Jalil came back and sat down.

'Now what?'

'He said I must go and sit in the big tent.' It sounded as if he was being sent to stand in the corner.

'Whatever for?'

'In case tourists come past. I must sit in the tent and look like a Tuareg.' It was nearly eleven o'clock. It was dark. There hadn't been a tourist near the place for days.

'The man is mad,' Flo decided. 'Barking mad!'

'Not mad. Jealous.' He stood up.

'Where are you going?'

'To the tent.' He gave a half laugh.

'If you are going to the tent, I am too.' She grabbed the remains of the candle, blew it out and tucked a bottle of water into her bag. Jalil cheered up as he guided her out of the dark courtyard.

'Tomorrow is the Fête des Moutons,' he remarked. 'The family would be happy if you came to share the feast.' Oh God, sheep's balls. She pretended he hadn't said it.

He piled the softest of the cushions, found a blanket and lay down beside her covering them both with the prickly wool. For a moment they lay quietly looking out through the tent flap into the silent, silver-lit garden. He slid his hand under her shirt then down, tugging at the zip of her jeans.

'I'll do it.' She sat up, aware of every sound, her bracelets, the slap of her sandals as she threw them over to her bag, the rasp of her jeans and the small ping of her bra. Jalil tore off his baggy pants underneath the blanket and drew her to him. He held her fast, loving her with urgency and haste, hard, as if he almost wanted her to cry out loud, then fell back, his head resting on her naked breast. The explosions in her body ebbed away but even in the comfort of his nearness, no sleep came.

The day ran through her head. 'You are sure you know what you are doing, madame?' Cecille and her pale eyes: 'Take care, my dear.' 'They eat it raw.' 'But there had always been an intrepid type of Englishwoman.'

But she wasn't intrepid. People like Kate Adie were intrepid. All she'd done was buy a camel and give it to her lover. A man known and trusted, 'one of the family', and then Ahmed's chillingly insulting 'madame'. She sat up to drink some water and caught a flicker of white whisk round a corner. She watched, her eyes straining to the furthest corners of the garden, as Jalil snored softly beside her. Then she saw it again, this time unmistakable, no ghost but Ahmed, looking like a mediaeval priest in his white robe standing ten feet from where they lay.

'Jalil.' She shook him. He opened his eyes.

'It's Ahmed,' she hissed, guilty as a schoolgirl caught behind the bike shed.

'*Tant pis pour lui*,' he muttered, which meant 'too bad'. Ahmed hovered for a moment as if uncertain, turned, walked a few paces, then turned again.

'Jalil!' His low tone was more chilling than a shout. Jalil rolled over and started to make a joint. Ahmed called again, something in Arabic. Jalil intent on finding his lighter didn't reply. Ahmed repeated what he'd said. Jalil made a brief reply, lit his joint and blew out smoke. Ahmed gave a short snarl of disgust and disapproval.

'What did he say?' Flo struggled into her T-shirt and searched under the blanket for her pants.

'He said, "Is the woman there?"' Oho! So it was 'the woman' now.

'What did you say?'

'I told him to go away because you were asleep.' He took a drag of the joint. 'Relax, Fatima, sleep.' He stubbed out the joint, lay back and within moments was asleep again. She reached out to her bag for a cigarette and froze again as the slight figure of the small boy flitted past the tent then back again.

'Jalil. He's sent the child to spy on us.' Jalil gave a slight grunt and patted her stomach. Still as a tree in a night of prying eyes, she smoked her cigarette. A wild dog howled somewhere in the desert. A cat leaped from the kitchen window and slunk across the garden. Then she heard a car, perhaps two cars, draw up at the far side of the hotel. Then silence. Then more murmuring as two figures, one Ahmed, one Omar, stood together by the tower room. Ahmed left. Omar went into the tower room, returning to the garden with a sheet and a white blanket. He spread the sheet on one of the tiled tables, climbed up and lay on it, pulling the blanket up over his head. She stared in horror at the corpse-like figure, keeping guard between her room and the tent. But she wasn't in her room. None of it made sense. The cat jumped back into the kitchen. Something clattered from the windowsill and she couldn't bear it any longer. Clamping her jangling bracelets to her wrist, she struggled into her jeans, then tiptoed past the figure on the table to her room where she lit all the candles she could find, dragged her bags from underneath the bed and packed, belongings layered in order of necessity for whatever might come next. La Fibule . . . another hotel . . . the desert? She didn't care. Fully dressed, she lay on the bed dozing in and out of sharp and frightening dreams.

'*Bonjour*, Fatima! Did you sleep well?' Omar greeted her cheerily as she opened the bedroom door. The nerve of the man!

'No, I did not,' she snapped and heaved her bags out of the room, which made him laugh until he realised what she was doing.

'But, Fatima . . . What is this?' He looked down in dismay at her luggage. 'What has happened?'

'Ask your Uncle Ahmed.'

'Is it about money?' was his first question.

'No, not yet. But it probably will be.' Quickly she told him that she'd made the camel over to Jalil which didn't seem to worry him any more. Then she told him that Jalil was not allowed into her room any more.

'Why now? It was all right before. Why is it suddenly not allowed?' She looked across to the tent, for the hump of Jalil still asleep underneath the blanket, but it was smooth and stacked beside the cushions.

187

'But it is no problem . . .' Omar insisted as she carried her bags towards the gate where Jalil was standing watching the road for any passing vehicle. Whether it was the Arab telegraph, telepathy or common sense, he too knew it was time to leave.

'But where will you go?' cried Omar.

'Anywhere. Another hotel? The desert for all I care.'

'But with Jalil, another hotel is not permitted.'

'OK then, the desert.' She was shouting now. 'At least we'll get some peace.' Jalil hailed an ancient taxi which bumped up the track to where they stood by the well.

'But in the desert you will need blankets, a tent,' cried Omar, opening the boot of the Mercedes and flinging cushions on the ground.

'Are you ready, Fatima?' The taxi stopped and seven impeccably dressed old men stared at her from under their *sheshes* through the window. Jalil picked up her bags and shoved them in the boot already stuffed with sacks and secured with a bit of string. He retied the string and held the door of the taxi open for her.

'Jalil, Fatima!' Jalil ignored Omar's pleas for them to stay.

'Where are we going?' she asked Jalil. Not that she cared.

'The family,' he told her. 'You will be safe. You will be free and today is the festival.' Oh Lord, raw balls. She'd forgotten that.

'Please, Jalil, not today. I don't want to be rude, but not today.'

'But you will be free,' he repeated.

'I'm free already,' she said and got into the cab, squeezing up beside an old man holding a bicycle wheel. Jalil got in the other side. The driver closed their doors with a spanner with a quick deft movement he'd done a million times before. Omar shook his head and walked slowly back into the garden.

There were nine of them in the taxi, the maximum allowed was five. The old men squashed in beside the driver, three men between them and another with yellow teeth and bad breath crouched behind the seats, hanging on to the rest of the bicycle. Flo stared out at the yellow plain.

The road was deserted as the landscape that they creaked through. No shepherd children by the road, no sheep, no goats, perhaps all hiding or mourning for the chosen now being sacrificed. The cab stopped and let out the old man with the bicycle wheel. The driver opened the door with the spanner and untied the string of the boot, releasing the man with bad breath and the rest of the bicycle. Together they set off across the stony ground with no sign of a destination. The cab jolted on again. Jalil looked at her worn face.

'*Ça va*, Fatima?'

'*Oui, ça va.*' A spiral of dust sprang up in front of the taxi as they passed through Amerzrou, followed by a fierce blast of wind, centring on the middle of the village. A flurry of young women appeared, dressed in black with pink shawls round their heads, then they scattered like a shoal of fish and vanished, giggling, up and alley.

'Where to?' the driver asked Jalil, who told him in Arabic.

The taxi creaked and wheezed along the road, jolting them until their heads bumped on the roof.

'Up there,' Jalil told her, hanging on and pointing in between the two mountains outside Zagora. 'Up there is a trap door in the rocks. They say, if you are a good man, on the last Friday of the year, if you open it, a river of gold pours out.'

Flo looked up between the mountains.

'It is true. I have seen the trap door.'

'Have you ever tried to open it?' He laughed and told her he'd never felt good enough to dare.

'Ah, *voilà*!' The taxi jerked to a halt outside a long wall and a notice that said Camping Scheherezade.

Jalil had to bend to pass through the wooden door in the wall. Behind its blank face lay a low building with a vine-covered terrace overlooking a small green park surrounded by a fifteen-foot wall. The park was reached from the terrace by a drive, guarded by two spiked gates, wide enough for caravans and trailers to wind around the dense green bushes and tall palms. Jalil walked ahead with Flo's bags. She noticed a small compound just behind the terrace and stood on a large stone to investigate. There were three camels, staring morosely at an empty trough. As camels went, she didn't think much of them.

'What are we going to do about Wahid?' she asked as she jumped down and followed Jalil.

'He will be all right,' he assured her, with total confidence in the Arab telegraph. 'If there is anything wrong, the boys will tell me. Hamide?' he called out as they entered the main building. At the far end of a long room overlooking the park, a slight young man was cutting up lengths of plastic with yellow flowers and fitting them on the half a dozen tables.

'Jalil!' He dropped his enormous scissors and ran towards them, shaking hands and exchanging the five kisses of good friends.

'Welcome,' he said to Flo in perfect English. Flo

sank on to the cushioned seat by the window and looked down on to a quick-flowing stream bordered with bamboo.

'Do you like it here?' Jalil sat beside her.

'Yes. It's safe.' From the nearness of the two mountains she knew the town was close, the garden was green and the high walls shielded her from the endless challenges of dry desert.

'Safe?' Hamide raised his eyebrows as Jalil told him what had happened. She picked up the words, Ahmed, Omar, camel and *stupide*. As Jalil talked, Hamide darted around the room. In white flip-flops, khaki trousers and a crisp blue shirt, everything about him was neat and fast as he plumped up cushions, tidied away the plastic and adjusted old New Year decorations from the ceiling lights. He listened, shaking his head, nodding but not particularly surprised.

'Here you will be very safe,' he told Flo and darted off.

'Was it Hamide you went to see yesterday?' she asked suddenly. Yesterday, only yesterday, when she'd been writing postcards at La Fibule and talking to Bruno about Degas and the romance of the desert.

'Was it?' she asked again. Jalil tried to look innocent and failed.

'You *knew* something was going to happen, didn't you?'

'Sooner or later, yes.'

'We have rooms, new rooms. One for Jalil, one for you. You are free and you are private.' Hamide returned with the keys. 'Later,' he turned to Flo, 'later we can watch cricket.'

'Cricket?'

'Yes, I like cricket. England versus Pakistan.' He

191

pointed to a large television in the corner of the room.

'Cricket? What is cricket?' Jalil wanted to know. Flo tried to explain, and that cricket was also those things that chirped all night in the trees. Jalil couldn't stop laughing.

'But we have no crickets on Moroccan television.'

'But now we have satellite.' Hamide rushed them outside to look at the large white dish on the roof.

'The water is cold, but now that it is hot by the sun, it is hot,' Hamide explained as he ran along the path ahead of them, bending to throw a cigarette carton into a large wicker basket, and pointing at two impeccable showers in the garden. He headed on to the far end, to a building hidden behind a mass of bougainvillaea and bordered with a flower bed.

'Hollyhocks!' Flo cried out in delight.

'Hollyhocks . . . crickets!' Jalil shook his head as Hamide opened the first door on to a room, a table beside it, a mirror and a row of wooden pegs. Beside the bed was a small bunch of roses in a glass.

'Almost as if we were expected,' Flo murmured innocently. Hamide gave Jalil another key and told him there was another room next door for him.

'Clients!' Like a bright-eyed robin, Hamide cocked his head at the sound of a vehicle on the pathway.

'Cricket later,' he promised and ran off. Flo sat down on the bed. It had clean sheets and was as hard as the desert floor.

A mosquito settled on her bare brown arm.

'Yes, mosquitoes,' Jalil explained as she swatted it. 'The river is close by.' Just beyond the wall, he said.

'No problem.' She unzipped one of the bags and from the bottom pulled out the mosquito net Alex had laughed at. Jalil examined it carefully, stood on the bed and fixed it to the ceiling with the suction pad provided.

'Very good,' he approved. Flo crawled on to the bed and sat in the white gauze tent.

'It is for a princess. All you need now is a *tapis volant*.'

'A *tapis volant*?' A flying carpet.

'May I come in?' He parted the white folds.

'Welcome,' she said and held out her arms.

The terrace at the Scheherezade was a meeting place for the young men of Zagora. Like out of work princes in their robes or jazzy T-shirts they passed their time lounging, gossiping and drinking tea under the green shade of the vines and waiting, waiting, waiting. Maybe a tourist would buy a bracelet, hawked and spurned before, maybe a carpet or a kaftan from a 'cousin's' shop rewarded by a tiny commission. Dodging the wary eyes of the police, always on the lookout for *faux guides*, they crowded round the CTM bus every morning when it arrived from Marrakesh.

'Very good hotel, very cheap, very tranquil.' They guided weary, bewildered tourists to whatever star-rated hotel they gauged they could afford. On a really good day they might fall upon a couple of 'gazelles', Spanish, French, Australian or English, travelling without a male escort to help them scratch a living for a few more days. But the big heat was rolling in and most of the tourists were heading back towards the north. There were only two trailers in the gardens of Scheherezade and a couple of bikers who would soon be putting on their leathers and their crash helmets and roaring off.

The claim of tranquillity was no exaggeration. For

Flo, Scheherezade was paradise. No one shouted. She fell asleep in Jalil's arms to the sound of crickets and the barking of the bullfrogs by the stream. The water in the showers was unsalty and warm and the food was good. Just the usual, tagine, couscous or brochettes cooked by Hamide. He rented them two bicycles and they pedalled into town. Flo bought a bedside lamp to read by and Jalil, revelling in his new freedom, made quick visits to his friends.

'Eh, Jalil! Salaam Malekeum.' They could walk no more than ten paces along the main street without a greeting. But friends he never claimed as family.

'You will excuse me, Fatima. I must see my father. I will not be long.' His father, he told her, was working with his brother as a mason not far off.

'Do you play Scrabble?' Hamide asked Flo. She said she did.

'We will play later. I like Scrabble. It is good for my English.' Hamide sat beside her. 'My fiancée bought the Scrabble for me.' He sighed. 'She is very beautiful. Her name is Maggie and she lives in Australia. And I wait and wait and wait.' He had met Maggie three years before. It was, he told her, love at first sight and they wanted to get married.

He was a real chef, he told her, trained in a big hotel in Casablanca and was just filling in time as manager of the Scheherezade until he could go to Australia. Maggie had found him a genuine job in a Moroccan restaurant in Sydney. Bit by bit he had gathered all the paperwork and proof needed for immigration requirements, but each time they wanted something else. Each time a blank refusal, followed by a cold suggestion that he try again in six months' time. 'Another problem,' he told Flo. 'Her father doesn't want her to marry some

194

fucking Moroccan. It is very hard.' But Maggie held firm, wrote to him once a week as they weighed the options of their future. 'Inshallah, it will happen,' he told her. As he related this sad story he kept jumping up and looking towards the big gates.

'You move more and faster than any Moroccan I've ever met,' Flo told him.

'I know. It is true. Maggie calls me Speedy.' He looked as his watch. One of the boys called out and he replied in Arabic. The only word she understood was telephone.

'Telephone?'

'Today, inshallah, we get a telephone. The *patron* asked for it three years ago.' Three years, it seemed, was the allotted time for anything to happen.

'I will save all my money and telephone Maggie on her birthday.' He broke off as an elderly man in a stained *djellaba* made his way to a corner table.

'Ah . . . le Philosophe.'

The Philosophe was a retired schoolteacher who had known all the young men since they were born. Every afternoon he arrived, sat at the same table, drinking tea and smoking whatever cigarettes he was offered or could cadge from the guests and from the boys, which he did with mysterious charm, half gratitude and half imperious. Before Flo was seated, he was already lighting up one of her Camels and offering to light hers with a flickering match trembling in his long fingers. He crossed one bony leg over the other, his skinny foot tapping on the table leg.

'*Un thé.*' He waved his gaunt hand at Hamide. 'Would you do me the honour of joining me, madame?' Flo said she would. Hamide managed to settle in a newly arrived biker, make tea for the Philosophe and keep an eye open for the arrival of the telephone all at the same time.

'Tell me something, madame.' The Philosophe looked at her earnestly. 'Have you read Charles Dickens?'

'Yes. But it was a long time ago.' A wide smile of triumph spread across his face, revealing dangerously loose teeth beneath his drooping moustache.

'Congratulations, madame.' To the Philosophe, Dickens was the greatest writer of all time. His only regret was that Dickens had never, to his knowledge, visited Morocco.

'It is a pity, because in his soul he was in truth Moroccan. Don't you agree?' It was a question she was hard put to answer. As she thought about it, Jalil spun down through the big gates on his bike, past a figure sitting on a box, shelling broad beans.

'*Voilà*, Joseph,' he told her. 'A very good job for him. Sit all day. Open the gates. Close the gates. A very good job. If he remembers to close the gates.'

'You mean Joseph? Joseph from the hotel?' Flo stood and waved. It was the same Joseph.

'The merry-go-round, madame. They come, they go, a job here, a job there, and then they start again. The young, always in a hurry,' the Philosophe told her as Hamide sped by and pointed towards the gates as Omar in the Mercedes swept past Joseph.

'Omar. He is here.'

'Here we go,' said Jalil, or the nearest equivalent in Arabic.

Omar strode up the steps to the terrace.

'Fatima! *Et toi, mon ami*! *Ça va*?' He was obviously going to pretend that nothing had happened. Flo excused herself from the Philosophe and shook hands with Omar, who sat himself down at a table and asked her to join him. Jalil followed slowly and stood behind the chair.

'*Ça va*? *Ça va*?' Omar rubbed his hands together and

shot a quick look at the bikers drinking beer at the next table. 'It is good here.' He looked round. Jalil, still standing, said nothing.

'What is the matter with you, my friend? Sit down, sit down.'

'Now what about Wahid?' said Flo, breaking all the rules and rushing into the topic on all their minds.

'Wahid? No problem. He is well. He eats.'

'Good.' Flo rose. 'If you will excuse me . . .'

'No, no, sit down,' begged Omar. 'And you, Jalil, we must talk.'

Jalil and Omar talked for half an hour, Flo not understanding anything, reading smiles and gestures, the Philosophe, behind his newspaper, listening to every word. Omar, now knowing Jalil owned the camel, had obviously decided to make the best of things. His proposition, that from whatever Wahid earned, the hotel took one third, his food another and the final third being for Jalil. Or Flo. To her it seemed a steep price, but obviously some arrangement would have to be made.

'You think that is agreeable, Fatima?' She looked at Jalil, who looked neither pleased or otherwise.

'I suppose so.' Suddenly there didn't seem very much more to say. Omar waved at a couple of boys in the far corner of the terrace and ordered a coffee. Hamide, who was leaning over the edge of the terrace, gave a shout.

'The telephone! It is arriving!' and ran down the steps towards a small van. The boys all stood up. The Philosophe put down his newspaper.

'A telephone?' said Omar, getting to his feet. 'Very modern.' They shook hands but there were no promises to come back soon to the hotel.

'*Au revoir*, Fatima. Soon I take the family back to Fes.'

Omar left, unnoticed in the excitement of the telephone.

'That seems OK, doesn't it?' Flo asked Jalil. 'About Wahid?'

'It means nothing, Fatima. One third, one third, one third. What does that mean? It is only words. You will see.'

'What does Monsieur le Philosophe think?' asked Flo since the old man had obviously heard every word. He shook his head and held out his skinny hand for a cigarette. All he had to offer was that this was the south, jealousy was rife and that it would be a long, long story.

The next chapter didn't take long to unfold. In the late afternoon, Jalil went to do another errand for his father.

'It's nothing. I will be back soon.' He leaped on to the bicycle to pedal into town. Flo walked slowly from the blue room to the terrace. As she started up the steps, Joseph whistled. She turned and saw Ahmed driving down the path. He came to a jerking stop at the foot of the steps. He had come with her bill.

'*Bonjour*, Ahmed,' she replied to his greeting with as much civility as she could. Why didn't he just go away? Send the wretched bill with someone else? What right had he to infiltrate this peaceful garden?

'I need a word with you, madame,' he said and, as expected, pulled the bill from his pocket.

'Certainly.' She continued up the steps. Ahmed hung back.

'Could we not talk here?' he asked, pointing to a patch of green grass by the car.

'I think not.' Ahmed, on alien ground, followed reluctantly, looking right and left. Flo chose a table as near to the Philosophe as possible, dropping two cigarettes for him as she passed.

'What can I do for you?' Ahmed gave her the bill, which she read through with care. As far as she could tell, everything was as it should be except for one item.

'I am not going to pay for the last night.' He looked puzzled.

'I slept, if you remember, in the tent, not in my room. What do you charge a client to sleep in the tent?' Ahmed managed, with extreme difficulty, to subdue his rage.

'Ah, madame, you are so *drôle*.' *Drôle* or not, she insisted she was not going to pay for that last, horrible night. He conceded the point. She opened her bag and counted out the money to the exact dirham, asked him for a receipt and made him sign it.

'There is one more thing. You have not charged for Wahid's food. How much does it cost per day to feed a camel?' Ahmed waved this away, distracted by the loud plop as the German bikers opened a bottle of wine. For her, the encounter was over and she longed for him to go. But he had something else on his mind.

'Is it your wish, madame,' he lowered his voice, 'that Jalil should leave the hotel?'

'My wish?' The Philosophe moved his chair a fraction closer.

'Yes. Is that your wish?'

'I would suggest that is a question for him, not me. He is a grown man and the matter is between you and him.'

'Madame,' he wheedled, 'Jalil has worked with us

for many years. He is like one of the family. He must advance his life.' The Philosophe's newspaper trembled.

'Then why,' asked Flo, 'why don't you let him have his camel?' Ahmed had no answer for this and repeated that as a young man, Jalil must advance his future.

'In my country,' she replied, 'in my country, if someone has worked well for many years, the boss helps them to advance their careers. They get promoted, they get paid more.' Ahmed looked at her as if what they did in her country was of no consequence.

'It is not wise for him to leave the hotel.' It could have been a statement of fact, it could have been a threat, but she was saved from commenting as the telephone rang loud and clear for the first time. Hamide skipped into the big room and the Philosophe put down his newspaper, but it was only the engineer testing the line. Ahmed, irritated to have lost her attention, went on.

'Is it your wish . . .' To her intense relief, Jalil appeared, carrying the bicycle up the steps.

'I think that is a question for him. Why not ask him?' she replied. Ahmed spun round and Flo went to sit with the Philosophe.

As with his conversation with Omar, Jalil talked very little and Ahmed a great deal and very fast. Flo flipped over the pages of her phrase book.

'Do not worry, madame,' said the Philosophe. 'They only know fifty words and they just go round and round.' Finally, Ahmed stood up, put his cigarettes in the top pocket of his shirt and started down the steps. He stopped, turned and looked at Flo.

'*Merci*, madame.' His sarcasm was aimed at maximum dramatic effect. '*Merci*. You have stolen our best *chamellier*, you have stolen our camel, you have made problems with me and my family . . .' He caught sight of the figure by the gate, still shelling broad beans. 'You have even stolen Joseph!' There was a soft ripple of laughter from the listening boys.

'Oh, go shit in your hat,' she muttered and turned to Jalil. 'What on earth did you say to him?' Jalil, unperturbed, watched as Ahmed crashed his gears into reverse, revved, bumped into a nearby caravan then with a screech of tyres drove up the path in a cloud of blue exhaust smoke, covering Joseph with dust.

'He asked me if I wanted to remain at the hotel.'

'What did you say?'

'I said yes.'

'You said *what*?'

'I said I would, but only if I was free.'

'What do you mean, free?' His ambiguity was beyond her. 'Why didn't you say if you got paid?'

'Madame, this is the south,' the Philosophe reminded her. The telephone rang again.

'It works, it works.' Hamide danced past Flo. 'And tonight it is Oprah on the telly.'

Then the wind came back and life moved from the terrace into the big room, where the ceiling fan pushed the warm air round and round. The temperature rose several degrees in twenty-four hours. Flo washed the cotton dress out every day, its blue pattern now faded into a grey swirl, and sticking to her within moments as she sat in the big room where only flies had the energy to move.

'Jalil, what are we going to do about Wahid?'

'If I move fast, I always fall in a hole,' he told her. One of the boys raised his head and said something to him.

201

'He says Wahid looks thin.' They sat thinking about it for a few minutes.

'Why don't we just go and get him?' Flo could bear it no longer. 'Just go and take him. I'll tell them I'm going for a ride and I won't bring him back. But then, where would we take him?'

'Here,' suggested Hamide, who was making up her bill.

'That is no problem. We can leave him in the garden with the family.' Jalil meant that little strip of vegetables and sunflowers behind the house in the village.

'I suppose so,' she said doubtfully and looked at her bill made out in Hamide's neat writing. Apart from Wahid, there was another problem pushing to the front of her mind. The bill wasn't very much but she was running out of money. Three weeks had stretched to seven and she had bought a camel. And there it was, the last traveller's cheque in her wallet.

'You are right, Fatima. We must take him. But there will be a big noise.' Jalil had made his decision.

'Not if madame goes with you,' suggested the Philosophe. Flo told him not to be too sure.

'We could do with a decent camel,' Hamide urged, looking towards the windswept compound.

'We will take him when the wind stops.' Jalil had the last word.

Three days later, the sun rose on a calm, innocent day and it was over ninety-five degrees by eight o'clock in the morning. Flo dressed carefully in jeans, a white T-shirt, her linen hat pushed down over her nose and sunglasses, and thought about Kate Adie. She loaded the camera with a new film and tucked Wahid's receipts into the pocket of the case. Jalil tried to look calm, but kept jumping up and down at breakfast for orange juice and more brown bread which he didn't touch. The Philosophe arrived early in the oldest car she'd ever seen. He said he'd drive them to the hotel.

'But I will not stay there,' he said.

At the hotel, two cars were being loaded up with bags and cases by Moroccans whom she'd not seen before.

'The family,' Jalil told her as the sound of high female voices screeched from the video room. The plump lady, still at her crochet, waddled past.

'*Bonjour*,' said Flo and was rewarded by the plump lady turning her face away.

'Ah, Fatima, *ça va*?' Omar pounded out of the court-yard with two bulging suitcases. He stopped, put them down and, to her astonishment, offered her a cigarette. She shook her head.

'What are you doing here?' he asked. She explained that she wanted to take Wahid for a ride. Just to the village to take photos of Jalil's family.

'But why today, Fatima? It is so hot.'

'It will be just as hot tomorrow,' she pointed out, 'if not hotter.'

'That is true.' The small boy in the front seat of the car pressed the hooter. One of the Moroccan women slapped him. He started to cry noisily. Omar shook his head.

'I have to take the family back to Fes, but I will be back in two days. Just two days.' He picked up the cases and with unwilling steps trudged to the cars. They watched him get in and drive off, followed by an uncle in another car.

'We go?' Jalil walked over to the well where Wahid was standing with the other camels. Flo thought he gave a flicker of recognition. The boy at Scheherezade was right. Wahid was thinner, his hindquarters soiled and flies crawling round little open sores around his eyes.

'What is that?' Flo reached up and touched a bleeding patch.

'He has been scratching himself on the bushes. He needs medication.' Jalil heaved one of the saddles on to his back.

'Down, down.' Wahid started to bend his legs.

'What do you think you are doing?' Suddenly Ahmed was there, standing between them and Wahid.

'I am taking the camel for a ride,' Flo told him.

'That camel belongs to the hotel and you are not taking him, madame.'

'That camel belongs to me and I am taking him to the village to photograph Jalil's family.' She patted the camera bag. Jalil continued to adjust the saddle. Little Lahassan appeared from the tower room and stood looking from Flo and Jalil, to the camel, then to Ahmed and back again.

'That camel belongs to the hotel,' Ahmed shouted and she caught the smell of whisky in the hot air.

'Why do you wait until Omar is gone before you take the camel?' Ahmed thought he had the trump card.

'Omar knows we are going. I told him less than five minutes ago.' In despair she looked at the empty road. 'It was quite OK with him, and even if it wasn't . . .' She held out her hand for Jalil to give her the rope.

'Oh no!' Ahmed leaped and grabbed it from her. 'You are going nowhere!' Spittle flew from his mouth and landed on her cheek.

Think of Kate Adie, think of Kate Adie . . . With as much calm as she could muster, and praying Wahid would bite him, Flo opened the camera bag.

'How many times?' She shoved the receipts under his nose. 'Be reasonable.' But it was a word he'd never heard of.

'That camel belongs to the hotel. He has eaten on my land and therefore he belongs to the hotel.'

'I have asked you more than once . . . how much does it cost to feed a camel for a week? For a day? I will pay you, right now.' She had no idea how she was going to, but Ahmed pushed her aside and she fell back against Wahid. Wahid stared from one angry face to the other, then at the mountains in the distance, having decided that it was nothing to do with him.

'If there is any more of this bullshit,' said Flo wearily, 'I shall have to call the British Consul in Casablanca.' It was a card she felt ashamed of playing but he had left her no other option. But the British Consul cut no ice. Ahmed, the rope in his hand, began to lead Wahid into the garden. Wahid looked with interest at the tiled tables and the shower room. Flo ran after them. This time, Ahmed pushed her quite roughly.

'Enough!' shouted Jalil, who until now had been silent. He grabbed the rope from Ahmed and tossed it to Little Lahassan.

'No!' screamed Flo, forgetting all about Kate Adie and rubbing her elbow. 'Get on him, get on him! Gallop off!' Ignoring her suggestion, Jalil clenched his hands into two enormous fists and advanced on Ahmed. His face scored with rage, his lips drawn back into the same snarl she had seen when he felled the wounded camel in the desert, he started to shout. Out came the words, the pent-up history of resentments, insults, exploitation and injustices. As he yelled, he lifted his fists above his head.

'Oh my God, he's going to kill him!' Flo ran towards

Jalil and the cowering Ahmed, but was pulled back by Lahassan.

'Don't touch him! Don't touch him!'

Jalil's hands fell to his sides and he unclenched his fists.

'Come,' she begged, sweat pouring down her face. 'Come, let's leave.' Boiling with humiliation, she started towards the road, stumbling over stones, heat rising in her to match the blazing sun and at any moment, she felt fire would blaze out from her nostrils.

'Wait, Fatima! You go too fast!' Jalil caught up with her and threw his arm around her soaking shoulder. 'Relax!'

'What do you mean, relax!' she shouted at him.

Hamide thought that they should go at once to see the Procureur. He was, apart from the Caid, the most important man in town for settling disputes. 'Other than the Tribunal.'

The Philosophe advised them to go straight to the top and see the Governor of the area in Ouarzazate. Jalil thought they should see both of them. All agreed that Flo's suggestion that they wait for Omar to return and sort things out was a waste of time.

'Come, I will go with you to the Procureur.' Hamide changed into a clean pink shirt.

'I will drive you,' said the Philosophe and within moments they were in a passage in the town hall.

'You speak in English and I will translate for you,' advised Hamide as they settled down for a long wait.

Flo said her piece, Hamide translated and she produced the receipts for the Procureur, a tiny man in black trousers, patent shoes and an open-necked white nylon shirt.

He listened without speaking, his fingertips together, as Hamide translated in a calm, serious voice.

'The other one,' he said at last, sending for Jalil, who had been told to wait outside. Jalil repeated the whole story. The Procureur leaned back in his swivel chair and thought about it, staring at his telephone. Eventually he opened a drawer, filled in a form and gave it to Jalil, telling him to get it stamped. He shook hands with all three of them and went back to staring at the telephone.

'What is it?' Hamide and Jalil were dancing in the passage.

'It is a convocation.' They looked with glee at the paper.

'What is a convocation?' She was so tired, she didn't know if she was speaking French or English. A convocation, they explained, was a summons. Ahmed was ordered to appear before the Procureur the following morning with Jalil.

'Wow!'

'Quick, Fatima! The bus!' Jalil and Hamide rushed her across the road to the bus stop, where the bus was just starting up. Jalil leaped in and had a word with the driver.

'He will stop at the hotel and give that malign the convocation within the hour.'

'*Une cigarette*, madame?' said the Philosophe apologetically as he got out of his car. '*Felicitations.*'

Flo's presence was not necessary for the meeting with the Procureur. Jalil and Hamide set off, leaving her in the care of the Philosophe who appeared earlier than usual again. For a while, they talked about *Great Expectations* and he told her how he'd wasted his time telling the story to the children at his school.

'Have you ever had a child you thought might go far, a really clever child?' she wanted to know. Sadly, he shook his head.

'They are not interested. Sometimes the boys, but the girls . . .' He shook his head again, 'The girls just laugh, laugh, laugh. They were very exhausting and sometimes I got very angry.'

'Did you beat them?' He looked too frail and gentle to have ever thought of such a thing.

'No, but I had my methods.' He gave a reminiscent smile.

'What did you do?'

'madame, I threw them out of the window!' He assured her the schoolroom was on the ground floor. By the time she stopped laughing, Jalil and Hamide were back, triumphant.

'What happened?' The lounging boys pricked up their ears.

'It is the Procureur's decision that Ahmed must hand over Wahid at once. Himself.'

'Thank heaven!' But they hadn't finished. In a mixture of French, Arabic and English, the story unfolded. Ahmed, furious at being summoned, had at first insisted that the camel was his, (a) because Omar had bought it from the Hassani and he had the papers to prove it.

'But I thought the Hassani never signed anything.'

'No, there is more.' Then he changed his story to (b) and said Flo had bought the camel for the hotel out of the goodness of her heart to replace one that had died. Then, they both went on to tell her, came story (c), he was keeping the camel because Flo hadn't paid her bill.

'But the Procureur didn't believe him and said he must give back the camel at once.'

Three days and three nights passed and there was no word or sign from Ahmed or Wahid.

'Are you supposed to go and get him?' she asked Jalil.

'No. He must bring it to me.'

'And while we wait, we will play Scrabble.' Hamide had telephoned his girlfriend, Maggie. She had rung back and they'd talked for nearly an hour. She had plans, he said, to go to England and work at Oddbins.

'What is Oddbins?' Flo explained as he handed her the bag of letters.

'Oddbins. A good word for Scrabble.'

'Not really, it's a name.' Jalil and the Philosophe sat over the table watching every move they made. Flo won the first round.

'It is good Scrabble. I will play,' Jalil announced, picking out the plastic squares from the bag with his big fingers.

'But in what language?' Jalil didn't seem to think that mattered much. The Philosophe suggested the game be multilingual and he would arbitrate. Strange words spread across the board as Jalil, deep in concentration, made most of them up winning with 'piu' which was 'well' and 'track'.

'The road to the well,' he declared, landing on a triple word score.

'And now, Oprah!' Hamide switched on the television.

'Do you think Omar will be back tomorrow?' Flo asked but Jalil was engrossed in a savage, tearful fight between three mothers and three daughters, urged into astounding revelations about having stolen each other's men. Jalil, his eyes wide open, stared at the screen as Hamide translated for him.

'But these things are so private!' He was very shocked but still kept watching. 'So private. But she is nice, Oprah. She is clear. I understand what she is saying.'

'Do you think Omar will be back tomorrow?' Flo asked again.

'I told you, he hides behind the family.' Then she remembered something.

Later, in the blue room, as she tugged at the tangles in her hair with a broken comb, she asked him, 'You know when you said Omar was going to see his wife? Did you mean wife, wife or woman?' He shrugged as if it didn't really matter much, one way or the other.

'He has women. One in Tafraoute, one in Ouarzazate and maybe one in Marrakesh.'

'And you?' She gave him a sideways look and raised her eyebrows. For the first time, he looked angry.

'I am not like that, Fatima,' he said stiffly but she went on.

'What happened to your marriage?'

'It was not correct.' He closed the subject down. Not correct. So accurate, so simple. A visit to the town hall. Divorce. And that was that. For him, there was only now. No disappointing past and no frightening or wonderful future around the corner.

'Will you write to me?' she asked.

'Write?' He looked surprised. 'Why write?'

'Jalil, I must go home soon.' It was something she had dreaded saying.

'You are leaving me, Fatima?' He sat on the bed and looked at his big feet.

'Jalil, I'm not leaving you, but I have hardly any money.' She showed him what was in her wallet.

'But you don't need money. You can live with me and the family. We will feed you.' To him it was as simple as that.

'Jalil, I must go home. You have Wahid. You will find another job and I will come back soon.'

'I will never work for someone else again,' he said. 'Never.'

The next day she bought some stamps and envelopes and addressed each one carefully to herself.

'There. Now you can write to me.' Still he looked worried.

'You can write, can't you?' He told her that he could. A bit. In Arabic.

'But what would I say?' This loomed like a mountain in his mind.

'I will ask him what he feels and write it for him,' volunteered the Philosophe through a haze of blue smoke.

'Fatima, there is something I want to show you.' Jalil stood up, tucking the envelopes carefully into his pocket.

'In a moment. I have to see about my ticket.' He sat down again, looking as if someone had struck him. She went into the big room to try the airline for the fifth time. The first time there had been no answer, the second two times it was engaged for hours and the fourth, an answerphone telling her to try again the following day. This time she got through. Yes, they said, they could reserve a ticket with her credit card. Her heart sank. She had to pick it up the day before the flight. The flight, the only one with a seat,

211

was for the day after tomorrow. The only flight with a place for two weeks. She said she'd take it and walked back to the terrace, feeling that she'd lost a limb.

'Ça va?'

'The day after tomorrow. From Ouarzazate.' Jalil looked away.

'I have relatives in Ouarzazate,' said the Philosophe, although he didn't look to enthusiastic about them. 'I will drive you. But, madame,' his long fingers plucked one of her cigarettes from the pack on the table, 'there is something I must urge you to do.'

'What?'

'Maybe the camel is in danger. There are acts of vengeance when the heart is black and pride is involved. I think it would be advisable for you to talk to the Governor before you leave or they will make life for this young man a hell.' To her surprise, Hamide nodded in agreement.

'What sort of vengeance?'

'Poison. That is usual.'

'Poison?' It sounded too far-fetched to believe but the three men were serious.

'How do we get to see the Governor?'

'You just go to the palace and ask to see him. We will go tomorrow.'

Jalil, holding his baby nephew, stood beside his mother on the roof of the house, looking out towards the desert. A group of black-robed women, inked in against the deep red of the distant building, sent up a wail to the sky. Jalil's mother crossed her arms over her breast and shook her head. The two little boys begged to be picked up so that they could see. His mother said something,

'There is a child missing in the desert. He has been gone for one day and one night. He is only seven.'

'How long can you last in the desert?'

'About forty-eight hours without water. That is all.' As the sound of the weeping women rose, Jalil's mother turned to the two boys and told them, in no uncertain terms, that they must never, ever go into the desert on their own until they were grown men. She spoke in Arabic, but to Flo the intention of what she had to say was perfectly clear. With serious brown eyes the two boys nodded. She turned to Flo and said something, looking at Jalil. This time Flo was lost.

'She says', he told her, 'that I was always disappearing when I was that age. Sometimes,' he remembered, 'she used to tie me to the kitchen table by my leg!' He laughed, handed the baby over to his mother and took a last look towards the horizon and a line of men, heads down, walking slowly, intent upon their search.

'Come. There is something I want to show you.'

His mother turned to Flo and embraced her in an iron hug, asking Jalil, 'Why is she going?' Jalil made some response which didn't impress her.

'She says, will you come again, inshallah, and will you stay next time with the family?' Flo, with a lump in her throat, bent to kiss the children.

They walked as far as the ramparts, where he asked her to wait for a moment. He walked over to a row of turbaned old men sitting in a silent row outside the mosque, bent to greet each one with deep respect, touching his heart and then a hand-shake. The last old man rose, looked for something in his pocket, handed it to Jalil who repeated the

213

handshakes along the row again then came back to where she stood.

'Come.' They walked up a small slope towards the entrance where a young woman sat, cradling a sleeping child. She stared at Flo with hostile eyes and made no sign of greeting to Jalil.

'Don't be afraid. Come,' he said again and led her through a wall of flies. The passage was dark, lit by wedges of light from the roof at twelve-foot intervals. She walked behind him until he stopped at the third door.

'A moment.' He tried three keys, turning and shaking until the door opened with a creak.

'Come,' he said as they walked into a dungeon.

The room was about eighteen feet high with beams filled in with straw. There was nothing there except some rusty farming equipment, sheaves of long dried bamboo and a pile of empty plastic water bottles.

'There is a bathroom,' he told her, pointing to a tap in a niche beside a staircase leading to the roof. From the terrace, they could see the minarets of several mosques across the wide space where the children played and, in the distance, the irrigated palmerie where they had sat and talked before. She looked down. The children were all quiet, no football games, no running after bicycles; they sat in hushed groups, watched from a distance by very old women, crouched by the abandoned washing of the young mothers. The whole little world waited for news of the missing child.

'The village shop is closed,' he told her. 'It is sad but they will find him. Inshallah.'

'Look.' He distracted her with a large, zinc bath. 'For

the washing.' He turned her round, put his hands on her shoulders and looked into her eyes.

'Does it please you here?' he asked, desperate that it should.

'Yes. It pleases me,' she said and suggested that perhaps he could make a tent on the roof.

'I was thinking the same thing,' he replied with joy. The sound of a van broke the silence. A little girl in a red sweater looked up and pointed, then started running. Several of the children followed and then more, running fast on their bare feet. They crowded round the van as two men got out with a small figure between them.

'It is the boy, he is found!' The cry went round the village. Doors opened and old men and women hurried to the van, sweeping up the child and vanishing into one of the narrow streets. Within moments the wailing stopped, and a rustle of relief spread like soft music from the palms. Jalil leaned over the edge of the roof and shouted to one of the children, who stopped and grinned up at him, laughing as he told the story.

'He went to see a friend in another village. Allah *est grand*. They found him. But he will probably get a big beating from his father. I used to be like that,' he told her.

The hours wound on without mercy. Jalil sat on the edge of the bed, watching her pack. At first he made a childish face, his lower lip pulled down and then real tears filled his eyes.

'Oh, don't cry,' she begged, trying not to herself. 'I will come back, I promise.' Unable to speak, he shook his head.

'I will, I will. Look.' She rolled up the sleeping mat and unzipped one of her bags.

'Look.' She pushed the small pillow, her boots and quilted jacket into it. There was something hard at the bottom. The bottle of whisky that she'd never given to Omar.

'And this . . . and this . . . and this . . .' She threw in the last of her shampoo and some of her T-shirts. 'I will come back, I promise. You can keep these things for me.' She zipped up the bag and put it in the corner of the room.

The Philosophe suggested that since his car was almost as old as him they'd better get an early start. They left before dawn and drove past Jebel Kissane just as the sun touched the tip of its most tilted peak. No one spoke until they got to Ouarzazate, where the Philosophe had to ask directions to the Governor's residence. It was just behind the town, not far from the airport. As they got out of the car, a large plane took off, roaring over them.

'Your flying carpet,' said Jalil, watching as it banked and turned towards the north.

Once they were through the many waiting rooms and had answered endless questions asked by secretaries and had been scrutinised by armed guards and police, Flo alone was admitted into the Governor's room.

'This way, madame. No, just madame.' The Governor's secretary held up his hand to stop Jalil. With a sigh of relief, he sat down on a chair outside the office and stopped trembling.

She approached the Governor across a large stretch of thick carpet. A vast, crystal chandelier hung above her head and on the wall was a life-sized photograph of the king at worship. The Governor, a handsome man, impeccable in robes as white as his thatch of hair, waited until she was seated in a soft leather chair in front of the biggest ormolu desk she'd ever seen outside a James Bond movie.

'What can I do for you, madame?' he asked, although she was sure one of his many secretaries must have told him.

'It's about a camel,' she started, longing for a cigarette. The Governor listened gravely to the whole story, from the day Wahid had been shoved into the pick-up truck, to the row by the well and the flies around his eyes.

'Look.' Flo produced a photo taken of Wahid at Goulamine.

'A very fine camel,' the Governor agreed and sank into a reverie. After a moment's silence he asked, 'And you, madame? What is it that you want?'

'Me?' She was startled. 'Me? I don't want anything. I just want Jalil to have his camel and to go in peace.' But the Governor appeared to want more.

'You see,' she explained, 'in my country, when you give a gift, it is unconditional.' She stopped, feeling quite pleased that although her dress was washed out and shabby, the varnish on her toenails peeling, at least her French hadn't let her down. The Governor digested this, then told her it was possible for Jalil to go to the Tribunal.

'But that', she replied, 'costs money. It takes time and Jalil is not in as privileged a social position as those that are against him.' The Governor got her drift.

'Madame,' he said, having come to a decision. 'Rest assured this matter will be dealt with immediately. I will be in touch with Zagora as soon as possible.' He smiled at her and added, 'But, madame, this is a Moroccan affair. It is best if you now withdraw. Please have no anxiety and please don't hesitate to get in touch with me, should you have need.' The interview was over.

He stood up and they shook hands across the big desk and she left, wondering if she should be backing from the room.

Jalil and the Philosophe waited in the car while she picked up her ticket from the airline office. The elation of their victory with the Governor drained from her as she looked through the window and saw Jalil's set face staring straight ahead through the windscreen.

'Seven o'clock at the airport, madame,' the girl told her.

'Seven o'clock.' Flo put the ticket in her bag. There were only fifteen hours left.

'Where now?' asked the Philosophe, his thin foot pumping on the gas with very little response as they jerked up the main street of Ouarzazate. With only twenty pounds left in her purse, Flo took the false economy option of credit card travel.

'Somewhere where they take a card.' The Philosophe stopped outside the first of Ouarzazate's many five-star palaces.

'Eh, madame.' She kissed him on his skinny cheek and thanked him from the bottom of her heart for all his kindness. He wiped away a tear and asked if he could have the rest of her pack of Camels. Jalil gave a small sob. They got out and stood beside a stone-faced doorman on the steps of the hotel.

'Goodbye, goodbye. *A bientôt!*'

'You are married to Monsieur?' asked the clerk in the cool marbled hall where fountains played and Muzak mingled with the sound of splashing water.

'No,' replied Flo, prepared to get as Mehim Sahib as her mother, should it be necessary. The clerk gazed thoughtfully at Jalil's Bob Marley T-shirt, baggy blue pants and black *shesh*, as if he, too, thought they were, if not bizarre, certainly spectacular. He sighed and told her with regret that it was against regulations for them to have a double room.

'But,' he said, as Flo opened her bag and withdrew her wallet, 'we do have a small suite.'

'Done,' said Flo.

The hall smelled of polish. The cleaning lady she sometimes shared with her upstairs neighbour had obviously done her stuff but put the ashtrays and the cushions back in the wrong places. The red light of the answerphone was winking on her desk beside a stack of letters. The tulips chosen with such care had been and gone and the vine was romping round the garden, strangling everything in its path. The horse-chestnut trees on either side had shed their flowers into two pink semicircles on her side of the wall. Flo shivered, pulled the grey shawl around her shoulders and shut the French windows. They'd be back in Zagora by now, Jalil and the Philosophe, in the big room watching television. She went into the kitchen, switched on the kettle and dropped a tea bag into a mug. The fridge was spotless but there wasn't any milk. Or maybe they'd decided to spend the night in Ouarzazate with the Philosophe's sisters. Or maybe Jalil had gone back on the bus alone. There was some dried stuff, she remembered, at the back of one of the cupboards. She stirred it into the tea, watching the granules that never melted swirl and settle round the edge of the mug. In the bedroom, her reproachful clothes tumbled out of her bags. The bed was smooth with cool sheets, uncrumpled pillow cases. The lights would all be out in the trailers at Scheherezade. Jalil would have given up his blue room. Maybe he was sleeping on the roof under a meadow of stars. He'd told her he always slept on the roof when the weather got really hot. She went into the bathroom and twisted the sand-gritted cap of her toothpaste, looking in the mirror at the straw-haired stranger who had come home to pay a few bills and tidy up the garden.

The room was dark and soft and smelled of tuber-ose. The bedclothes were hardly rumpled. She was alone and LA was on the line. 'Hi, Mum! You're back . . .'

'Yes, I'm back.'

'Did I wake you?'

'Not really, darling.'

'I left hundreds of messages . . .'

'How are you?'

'Great. I got a rise. They're sending me to Seattle for two months and I get to choose my own car.'

'Wonderful.' Flo was none too sure exactly where Seattle was.

'Did you have a good time?'

'Amazing.' Amazing. How cowardly. Why couldn't she say, I fell in love, bought a camel and got involved in a feudal dispute. Instead, she asked, 'Where is Seattle?'

'Oh, Mum, really.' The LA daughter told her exactly where Seattle was and that she might also be going to Denver.

'Colorado?'

'Yeah, Colorado.'

She tried to think of something to say about Colorado.

'Listen, Mum, gotta go. It's a madhouse here. Glad you're back. You can get me any time on my mobile.'

'OK, darling, glad you're well.' Flo rang off, wondering if her daughter had as many codes as she. Amazing. How pathetic.

'Hi, Mum, did you have a good time?' This time, New York. She made an effort to be honest.

'It was very interesting.'

'What was the weather like?'

'Hot and getting hotter.'

'Are you brown?'

'It's not that sort of a place.' It's a place where you cower from the sun and thank God for cool, green shade.

'Mum? Do you remember Tim?'

'Tim?' She didn't.

'Oh, Mum, of course you do. He lived in Parsons Green and rode a bike.'

'Oh yes, I remember.' Tim was a young man with fair hair, blue eyes, nice manners and always washed up his own coffee cup.

'Guess what? He's in New York. We've been out a couple of times. Oh, Mum, it's so great to talk to someone English.'

'Yes, I know.' Even to talk English, Flo thought, was like falling back on some long forgotten skill.

'Gotta fly, Mum. My hair's a mess. Talk to you at the weekend.'

Flo hung up. The spell was broken.

PART THREE

THE REAL WORLD, or what was supposed to be the real world, she did her best to keep at bay, apart from ringing Alex and getting no reply. The winking answerphone and the letters on the desk could wait. But not the garden. The vine had to be cut back, the new weeds pulled, the dead tulips replaced with white geraniums. To Flo's delight, she found the hollyhocks had seeded by themselves. Like those other hollyhocks outside the blue room far away. There was a whole film left in the camera, the film she'd meant to use for the dark-skinned family in the village. She started with the hollyhocks, focused on a fat pink rose and, kneeling in between the milk white mounds of alyssum, zoomed close into the heart of a crimson peony. Then she tried a bit of arty stuff, a trowel in a flowerpot and the water leaking from the lichen-crusted water butt. She tried Alex again. She sent Jalil a postcard of a London bus.

Unwillingly she sidled back with tiny steps into the almost forgotten routine. The laundry man delivered. Her upstairs neighbour asked if she would take in a parcel he was expecting. They came to read the gas meter. Reluctantly she ran the tape back of the answerphone. Someone said, quite crossly, that they would 'deeply appreciate it' if she would collect a skirt she'd taken to be altered. She'd missed a few invitations to dinner, dated at intervals between the girls' increasingly aggrieved messages telling her she wasn't back yet. Her dentist's secretary reminded her she'd missed an appointment and there was a surprise message from young Damian of Halliday and Ross. He thanked her for her card, said that they must get together soon and left his mobile number. She tried Alex again but instead of endless ringing she got the unobtainable sound. After a week she tried the television but snapped it off in horror, sickened by the sight and sound of men in suits telling their placatory lies to cover up the latest governmental blunder. She dialled Alex's mother in Maida Vale.

'She's very well, dear. Very well. She's sold the house and she'll be over soon.'

'You look wonderful!' Alex looked wonderful too, prettier than ever as she kicked off her new Manolo Blahnik shoes. Her hair was shorter and Flo could swear she'd put on a couple of ounces.

'Spaghetti's fine,' Alex said. Flo could hardly believe that she had heard right as she slipped a lazy pre-cooked meal into the oven.

'Did you get a good price?' she asked as she opened the last bottle of John's wine.

'I could have got more if I'd waited.' Alex waved away the sale of her house as yesterday's news. 'But you can't wait for ever and they bought the car as well.'

'The car?' Even in the darkest days, Alex had never been without a car. 'Don't you need it?'

'It's left-hand drive and I'm thinking of coming back to London.' London? Alex, who loved light clothes and sunshine and cafés that stayed open all night.

'I've been seeing a bit of Sam,' she mentioned casually, so casually that Flo looked up from making the salad. 'So tell me about this camel. What's his name again?'

'Wahid,' Flo told her. 'It means unique.'

Both claimed they were exhausted but talked until long after two. Alex said she'd stay the night in the spare room and they talked on, giggling and interrupting each other as Alex monitored Flo's wardrobe and borrowed stuff to do her nails, listening in horror as Flo told her in the greatest detail everything from the day she'd left with Sam, to the sad moment when she'd left a desolate Jalil in Ouarzazate. But never once did Alex mention Omar, even to ask how he was. Omar, for Alex, was now an experience to be happily recalled sometimes and that was it. Even so, Flo decided to keep quiet about the 'wives' in Tafraoute, Marrakesh and elsewhere. There was no point in re-creating something that might not even be true.

'Ahmed was such a shit.'

'Are you going back?' Alex asked her. You, not we.

'Of course. But not to the hotel.' That was out of bounds for ever. 'It's such a shame it all went wrong. I don't really understand. Just because of a camel.' Flo sighed and slipped into her dressing-gown.

'You upset the pecking order,' Alex said wisely. 'You're a foreigner. You are a woman. You fought back.' Flo tried to change the subject but Alex hadn't finished with her.

'Just remember, a ratio of one to ten. If you're still having fun, go for it, but for goodness' sake, get an open-dated ticket next time. Choice alters things. It shouldn't, but it does. Sam says . . .'

'How serious is Sam?' Flo asked.

'Very. Well, let's put it this way,' she replied, looking almost as surprised as Flo. 'I'm going to marry him.'

And she did. Three weeks later at the Marylebone Register Office at nine thirty in the morning. The only place to go at that hour was to the Ritz for breakfast. It was an intimate affair, with fewer than a dozen people. Alex, in a pretty Jasper Conran suit, promised, 'We'll have an enormous party later . . .' Sam, beaming, kissed her and confirmed this. He took Flo aside to tell her that Rachmaninov chap had written lots of other stuff. Alex had given him a Bang & Olufsen stereo and he was really getting into it. Alex blushed when she and he cut a three-tiered cake beneath the cherubs frolicking on the ceiling. Alex's mother, in a rakish red hat with a veil, sat next to Flo and sobbed for joy. Millie, in the shortest mini-skirt in London, read the telegrams. Sam made a speech telling everyone how he'd found his bride 'beneath the desert skies'. Clutching her bouquet of pink rosebuds, Alex sashayed down the soft-lit corridor, clutching her bouquet and Sam to where a white Rolls Royce was waiting to whisk them off to Paris. She turned, straightened up her mother's hat, told her not to cry and tossed the bouquet to Millie, who caught it with a languid arm and winked at Flo.

'Goodbye, goodbye.' Then she was gone.

Flo made her way back to the dining room to find her lighter with tears of thankfulness for Alex, who would never have to shop at Boots again and deserved a medal for the giggles with which she'd warded off the dark days that would have brought most women to their knees. The table had already been cleared and the waiter was setting out the lunch places.

'Can I help you, madam?' he asked.

'No, it's all right.' Flo spotted her lighter under her chair.

'Is everything all right?' he asked.

'Yes, everything's fine,' she assured him as she groped for the lighter on her hands and knees, wondering why it was the Ritz made her so emotional.

'Fine.' She retrieved the lighter. 'Very fine.' But the waiter didn't look as if he believed her.

To shake away the feeling of anti-climax there always is for those who stay behind when the bride and groom have flown away, Flo decided to risk sore feet in high heels and walk home. The Hyde Park trees were heavy with dust-darkened leaves and the flowerbeds blazed with regimented swathes of red and blue. Still the nannies pushed their boat-like prams with royal rights between the humbler au pair girls with plastic covered pushchairs. A group of Japanese tourists took pictures of the soldiers from the barracks riding past with chinking bridles, the horses polished as their boots. She wondered if they were the same tourists who'd taken pictures of each other at the dunes. She reached the Round Pond where boats responded to orders from remote controls. At Notting Hill she stood by a zebra crossing; wondering what Jalil would make of squat, black taxis and if he'd got his postcard yet. There was, she decided, a very easy way to find out and wondered why she hadn't thought of it before. Despite what she knew must be a blister rising on her left foot, she walked faster.

'What do you mean, they won't give Wahid back?' Jalil wasn't there, Hamide told her, when they'd got through his overjoyed exclamations. 'Ça va? Ça va? Is it hot? Is it cold? Hamdullah.' He was talking as quickly as he moved and she could guess that he was shifting from foot to foot, dusting everything within reach of the phone flex.

'Like I said, Fatima, they won't give him back.'

'But the Governor said he'd tell them to.'

'Maybe he forgot.'

'When will Jalil be there?'

'In one hour, inshallah, maybe tomorrow. He is very busy.'

'Busy? What's he doing?'

'He is thinking.'

With his brow creased beneath his *shesh*, and looking to the distance for an answer. 'If I do things too fast, Fatima, I fall in a hole.' Flo looked at her watch.

'Tell him I'll call again tomorrow, or maybe later on tonight.'

Dragging off her dress, her bra, her pants and stay-up stockings she flew around her room, muttering, demanding of the four walls in a rage, Why wouldn't they give Wahid back? How dare they keep him? How could they be so brazenly dishonest? How come they could get away with it? She stormed into the bathroom and set the shower at full. With shampoo streaming down her face, her eyes tight shut, she could see Ahmed, sneering at her. Through the hiss of water from the showerhead, she thought she heard the phone. Dripping water all over her scattered clothes, she picked up the receiver.

'Hullo,' she snapped.

'Flo?' It was young Damian, asking her if she would have lunch with him.

'Yes,' she said, her mind still boiling with unanswered questions. He told her crisply where and when. Still dripping water, she wrote it down before she forgot, put on her bathrobe and dialled Scheherezade again. Then again later. Jalil was not back. Then the following morning. The Philosophe sent his best wishes but didn't know where Jalil was. Time after time Hamide told her not to worry.

'Fatima?' Three days later and Jalil was on a line so clear she could hear the bullfrogs in the background.

'Fatima!' he was shouting, as if she was in some far-off Atlantis. 'Fatima! I have kidnapped him!' She could hear Hamide telling him how to say kidnapped.

'Kidnapped!'

'Yes.' He was laughing.

'Who? Ahmed?'

'No, Wahid.' They were all laughing now. Jalil, Hamide, the Philosophe and any of the boys listening and lounging in the big room. There was no other way, he told her. He had waited for them to be honourable but they didn't know how. They had ignored the Governor's message, so he decided to deal with matters himself. When the time was right. Which probably meant at the full moon.

'But how?'

'I went at night . . . Through the desert. I walked on the back route.'

'What back route?' He was going too fast for her to take it in.

'I left a message for them so they would know it was me.'

'What message?' What ancient desert lore was there to cover kidnapping your own camel? Flo lit a cigarette to steady herself. She could hear the click of

Jalil's lighter as he lit one too. Then Hamide was on the line.

'They cheered, Fatima, the people in the village cheered and the people in the town. And now Wahid is safe. He is here. He is in the garden.' For a moment, she thought Hamide was going to bring Wahid to the phone.

'Fatima?' Jalil was on the line again saying, 'You are coming back to me?'

'Oh yes, yes, very soon.' He told her that no matter where she was, he was beside her and would be until they both went to live with Allah.

'And even then.'

Hamide rang three days later to tell her that Jalil had been arrested.

'Arrested? But what for?' she yelled.

'This is Morocco,' was the only thing he could come up with before launching into a jumbled story, when she demanded to know what the hell was going on.

'They sent a man with a big stick to the family house,' he told her, then that it was all right because he wasn't there. But his mother was.

'She told that shitty gangster to piss off!' Appalled that they could sink so low, Flo had to smile. His mother, with her bangled arms across her scarlet blouse, her proud head thrown back and dark eyes pitching fire. It would have to be quite a gangster to deal with her.

'Then they sent the child here.'

'What child?'

'The young son, Ahmed's son, to weep crocodile tears and say he was lonely without his camel. Jalil refused to speak to him. Then Ahmed went away and a policeman came and arrested Jalil. He said he would rather go to prison than give up Wahid.'

'Where is Wahid?'

Hamide lowered his voice to a whisper. 'He is hiding by the river. I sent Joseph to keep guard.' This, she found not too reassuring.

'But why—' Her next question remained unanswered as the line cut out.

'But Damian, why me?' Flo almost had to shout above the din of media voices, would-be media voices and the voices of those who'd come to watch the media lunching at Kensington Place.

'Ah!' said Damian, who was wearing Calvin Klein jeans and Patrick Cox loafers. 'There is a reason.' He looked about eighteen but she guessed he must be about the same age as Jalil.

'Surely you must need someone younger?'

'That's just the point,' he said. 'I don't. The whole world,' he assured her, looking at her with his baby blue eyes, 'the whole world is getting older.'

'True,' she had to agree. And then he explained.

Halliday and Ross, as she probably knew, had gone to the wall. Tough times sort the men from the boys. The youth culture was all very well but overcatered for. The greater part of the population was over fifty. She told him she didn't know that. Looking around the restaurant, everyone looked under thirty. She put her knife and fork together, her meal almost untouched. As Damian put his proposition to her and the others shrieked and gossiped around them, Jalil was sitting in a prison which was probably swarming with flies, fighting for his camel against the ever-changing accusations. Damian was still explaining. He'd started a video production company. She forced her attention back to him.

'What?'

'I want to make programmes for the over-fifties. You know, like *The Oldie*. You know *The Oldie*?' Flo said she did and had found its tone a bit grumpy.

'Exactly. Now, what I'm looking for is someone like yourself, who understands the needs, the pleasures and the pains of the older generation.'

'Very much the same as the needs, pleasures and pains of the younger generation,' she replied.

'Good girl!' declared Damian. 'I knew you'd get it.' He asked her if she wanted a pudding. Flo shook her head. 'Channel Four are already interested. Now, the way I see it . . .'

But what could they do to him? Jalil had only to ring the Governor's office to confirm the camel was his. But would they let him? She prayed that he would think of it. Demand that they would let him.

'Of course, it won't be full time, but I think it's something you'd enjoy. And we've worked well together in the past.' She pulled her attention into the here and now. She was sitting in a trendy restaurant, she was fifty and this boy was offering her a job. It was something that most of her friends would kill for and this earnest young man opposite her obviously believed she was playing hard to get.

'So, what do you think?'

'Well . . .' She sipped her cappuccino. 'I travel a bit. I go to Morocco. It's a kind of home from home.' Her mind slipped again. And the sun comes up each morning on a new day, you never know what's going to happen next, there's a camel hiding by a river and a good man who's never heard of Channel Four is sitting in prison.

'That's exactly what I mean. Retirement and the freedom to do as you please doesn't necessarily mean bingo. Think it over, Flo, think it over and call me.' Damian waved for the bill.

There was a letter waiting in the hall. It was addressed to herself in her own handwriting.

> '*Sur le dos de mon dromadaire je vive dans le sable et je chante pour toi. Toute va bien? Moi, avec rien, je vois le soleil qui se leve, chaque jour, et se couche le soir et je vois les étoiles et la lune et je chante pour toi.*'

She told herself it made economic sense: it was no more expensive to live here than there. If anything it was much cheaper.

Flo picked up the phone. She made an appointment with her dentist for the following day and booked an open-dated ticket for the following week.

The police had run out of interest and Ahmed out of protests. Jalil was realeased with no apologies or comment.

The little stream ran slow and there were bare patches around the trailers. The worst of *la grande chaleur* was over, Hamide told her, but for Flo, the middle hours of the day were still hot enough for every movement to be calculated against the energy it took to lift a cup of coffee or turn the pages of a book. Jalil thought it was now safe for Wahid to leave his hiding place among the rushes by the river and he was tethered near the blue room, his rope tied round a stone to save him from the temptation of the great bundles of gold and amber dates ripening on the palms. Jalil joked about tying the

232

rope round his own foot at night. Hamide told Flo that when she was away Jalil had never slept less than five metres from his precious camel.

'Why not bring him in?' Flo suggested as he peered from the little window at the shadowy white form in the moonlight. 'I'm sure he'd like the mosquito net.' Jalil said he thought he'd probably eat it.

'You never told me what the message was,' she said as they sat, naked and shining with a film of sweat on the hard bed.

'What message?' He had forgotten.

'The message you left in the sand when you kidnapped Wahid.'

'Oh, that.' It was folklore now, in the village and at Scheherezade. 'I walked through the desert to the place where Little Lahassan leaves the camels for the night. He was late so I went to sleep until he came.'

'You went to sleep?'

'Beneath the big palm. Yes, I went to sleep. At last he came. When he had gone I walked three times round the tree. I wore my boots and I have very big feet,' he told her, raising one for her to see. 'I have the biggest feet in my region.' He brought his strong leg down across her body. 'They knew they were my footprints and so there would be no trouble for Little Lahassan.' He leaned back, stretched his arms above his head and blew a smoke ring. 'Allah *est Grand*.'

'Jalil was desolate when you were not here.' The Philosophe reached apologetically for her cigarettes, having already finished the carton she had brought him. 'He is not like the others. He has a big heart.' A small shriek of laughter reached them from the far side of the terrace. One of the boys had triumphed. He had captured not one, but two gazelles who had

233

unwittingly arrived on the CTM at the wrong time of the year. They wore skinny T-shirts, shorts and little boots and their captor guarded them with the ferocity of a leopard with its kill.

'*Le shopping*?' they heard him say. The girls conferred. Flo thought she heard the word carpet. The boy gathered them together before they could change their minds and strutted off, the girls prancing either side, towards the big gates and the minefield of boutiques that lay beyond.

'Ah, the young. Here today, gone tomorrow. But you, madame, you are not like them.'

'No,' Flo agreed, 'I'm very much older.'

'And thus, you too have heart.' The other boys had relaxed back into their torpor once the gazelles had gone. Waiting. There would be more, tomorrow, next week, the week after, inshallah.

'You see how they wait, how they hope. They hope that some day someone will take them off to Europe and they all become millionaires. It seldom happens.'

'It seldom happens in Europe.' Flo started to explain as she had done so often that it was not a Shangri La in the cold north and just because one had a credit card, it didn't mean a row of beans unless there was something in the bank.

'And then,' the Philosophe went on, 'hope dwindles and they think it is enough to be remembered, with a card, a letter or a pair of jeans but when the holiday is over, they are forgotten.' The Philosophe sighed.

'Maggie will come back.' Hamide started clearing away Flo's breakfast. 'You will see, she will come back.' His visa application had been rejected again and he had nothing left but hope for another six months. 'Maggie will find a way.' Flo prayed for him that Maggie would.

'You should take Jalil back with you to England,' Hamide remarked.

Jalil shook his head, as if he had suggested that he caught a plane to Hell. 'No! No! No!'

'Why not?' Hamide was at a loss.

'London is very big, bigger than Casablanca,' he told them. 'England has sea all round it. I have seen it on the telly.' He shuddered at the thought of that unfathomable grey water. 'I am a desert man. I belong here.' And that was that. A man who understood the folly of false dreams and greed, who knew that far away he would be trapped in a flat, in a house, in a street, in a big grey city where he could never see a star or a sunset. He reached for Flo's hand.

'One day, I will go south. You will come with me, inshallah.' He broke off and looked down into the garden where Wahid was munching his way through a pile of vegetable peelings from the night before.

'Watch! Watch!' Wahid had caught sight of a cabbage leaf just beyond his reach. He began to toss his head from side to side until he had manoeuvred the rope attached to the stone across his head. With a deft movement he nipped it between his big yellow teeth and raised the stone from the ground. With the stone dangling, he walked elegantly towards the cabbage leaf, allowed the stone to drop and claimed his prize.

'*Dhaki, dhaki*, I have never seen a camel do that before,' declared the Philosophe, who seldom took any interest in camels. Jalil beamed at him and then at Flo.

'*Dhaki*?' she asked.

'It means clever, intelligent, crafty,' Hamide explained.

'You must learn Arabic,' Jalil told her. 'The Philosophe

will teach you.' The Philosophe said that he would be
delighted. He shifted round his chair to face her, lit
another cigarette from the stub of the last one and
looked at her seriously.

'Madame,' he began, 'I have a proposition for you.'

'Yes?' She hoped it didn't have anything to do with
carpets.

'I am getting old,' he announced, and help up his
hand as she started to assure him that he wasn't. 'Yes,
madame, I am getting old. I am older than my car but
the human spirit is more enduring than a machine,
correct?'

'Correct.'

'But,' he admitted with a sigh, 'I have lost the battles
with the gears. Not all of them. Only the reverse.'

'There is nothing wrong with the car,' Jalil told him
as he had done many times before.

'That is as maybe,' the Philosophe agreed, 'but reverse
eludes me, I can no longer go backwards. This presents
difficulties.' He went on to suggest that Flo (for a very
few dirham) should rent the car from him during the
day. In the evening, Jalil would accompany him to his
house and turn the car around.

'That way I am in the right direction to return to
Scheherezade in the morning. What do you think,
madame?'

'What do you think?' she asked Jalil, punctilious as
any Moroccan wife. He said if it was all right with her,
it was all right with him.

'*Hna jit bezzef lmarrat.*'

'I have been there several times.' Flo started her
morning lessons on the terrace with the Philosophe.
The dates were ripe. With a rope around his waist,
Jalil frog-leaped to the topmost branches of the palms

untouched by the perilous, spiky trunk. When he reached the top, he struck the thick date stalks with a machete. Joseph, below, caught the bundles as they fell through the branches and laid them out on sheets of plastic to be graded.

'*Kayma chems.*'

'It is sunny.'

'*Bayne gli ghadie teh chta layoum.*'

'It looks like rain today.'

'No rain yet,' said the Philosophe. 'Maybe in the New Year.' Jalil waved at her from fifty feet above the garden.

'*Yllah nchoufour!*' he shouted.

'What does that mean?'

'It means he wants to take you for a drive.' Flo closed her books and ran down the steps and then towards the car. Jalil, his bare feet scarcely touching the palm, descended at high speed.

'*Yallah nchoufour?*' he asked, putting on his boots. He opened the door of the old car for her. Up on the terrace, the Philosophe closed his eyes and nodded off.

Every day they bumped around the palmeries to hidden villages to see his friends, who offered tea and sometimes sticky cakes. Flo answered questions from the women, Jalil condensing what she said in very brief translations. How many children did she have? Had she any medications? Did it always rain in England?

'This is a very special village,' he told her when they stopped. It was a kasbah, not more than four walls around a muddy square with a leafless tree in the middle. It seemed deserted and could have been for centuries.

'A *maribout* lives here. He is very famous.'

'What is a *maribout*?' From what he told her she

learned a *maribout* was a cross between a doctor and a priest.

'He makes mad people well again.'

'How?'

'He ties them to that tree.' He saw her horrified face and assured her that they were always given food and water.

'They always get well.'

'How long does it take?'

'A week, maybe two.' She looked at the bare tree and wondered what those soft-spoken therapists in Primrose Hill would make of it.

'But how does that make them better?'

'He shouts at them.'

'*Shouts* at them? What does he shout?' He told her that no one knew. It was a secret.

'And when they are better, they give him a chicken, some eggs or a goat if the family is rich.' So much for sixty pounds an hour.

'Is he here?' If Keltie had been with them, she'd be snapping away and demanding to meet this magic man himself. He told her that he thought the Maribout was away on holiday. 'In Casablanca.' She was thankful that he was.

'*Hde lwaggt nrajour lddar*,' he said but it was beyond her and she laughed.

'It means, it is time to go home.'

He sat behind the steering wheel, lit a cigarette but made no move to turn on the ignition.

'Shall we visit the family?' Before she could reply he went on. 'It would be good if you lived with the family, not in Scheherezade. My mother said she would like that.' Careful, Flo, careful. She could almost feel Alex by her side, but Alex's doubts about double glazing were not the problem. She sat still for a moment, considering. This would take all the tact that she could muster. She was content the way things were, safe behind the big walls at Scheherezade, her lessons with the Philosophe by day, evenings playing Scrabble with Hamide and sunsets by the river when she rode on Wahid with Jalil gently leading her. He was staring straight ahead through the windscreen. She took his big hand.

'But what would I do all day long if I stayed with the family?' And what thousands of tiny mistakes would she make? She'd got used to the little things, taking off her shoes, wearing clothes with sleeves, scooping up tagine with a bit of bread, but she knew there must be so many other hidden pitfalls. But the fears were not for cultural blunders, they were for Jalil and herself. Two people met, hurled together by some fate to complete each other's universe. It happened every day. Then their private world was invaded by a tribe of strangers, mothers, fathers, uncles, aunts, all with something to say, all with claims of history on their side. Those claims which could do nothing but diminish the power of the threads that held them together. She was already breaking all the rules and knew it. She was from a cloudy island in the north with cool English blood and he from hot, dark Africa. He was black and she was white. He was tall and she was small. His family were devoted Muslims and she was not. She was a stranger, a woman so much older who would be sleeping with their son in a room up on the terrace. She wasn't brave enough to face it.

'And,' she went on gently, 'suppose the family did something that was difficult for me and I had to leave?' Pack her bags and run, leaving him to face the rows and accusations. 'What would you do? It would be very difficult. We're OK as we are.' He listened to what she had to say. If he was disappointed, he didn't show it. Eventually he nodded and said that perhaps she was right.

'We'll talk no more of it.'

The days grew cooler and the nights grew longer. Hamide provided them with two thick brown blankets. The mosquito net was no longer needed but Jalil liked it and wanted her to leave it where it was. Evening life moved from the terrace to the big room, where Hamide lit four big gas heaters and the Philosophe settled into his winter corner and wore thick grey socks with his sandals. The garden was filling up with trailers, cars and caravans, the rooms all taken, and Hamide ran from first light until the small hours. When Jalil wasn't helping his father or his brother in the village or the town, he fell with natural ease into clearing tables and charming guests. Flo found herself becoming an unofficial information service for the visitors. What time did the bus leave for Marrakesh? Was it possible to get tickets in advance? How far was it to El Rachidia, and where was it possible to buy shoe laces or a chicken? Some of the them came and went within a couple of days, some stayed longer. A Dutch divorcée confided in her deep and intimate secrets and despairs but cheered up when one of the boys turned his gleaming smile on her, and she whisked him off to Essourira.

'He's scored!' declared his friends or the equivalent of it. A tiresome American woman who wore Moroccan clothes and was taking a PhD in Islamic Thought at Berkeley, California, dumbfounded everyone by scolding them for not going to the mosque more often. She informed them that the Arabic they spoke was wrong and corrected their pronunciation. She went too far when she accused Hamide of putting too much cummin in the tagine and Miss PhD was promptly moved from her room to the only one where the shower didn't work, to make room for two young Frenchmen. Hamide made a vague excuse that they had booked it long ago.

The two Frenchmen were very quiet and sat alone, studying maps of Africa. The only person they were inclined to talk to was Jalil, questioning him about the different musics from further south. They were going round the world later on the next year, they said, sponsored by a cigarette company. Africa, South Africa, China, Russia, then back to Paris. They were an advance party, waiting for their fellow travellers to complete the paperwork for such a massive trip and join them with three sturdy Land Rovers full of tyres, spare parts, spare passports, video and recording equipment. The trip was going to take two years, they said.

'Timbuktu?' Jalil's face lit up with longing.

Flo's birthday came and went but she said nothing, horrified at the thought of Hamide making her a cake. Instead, she wrote postcards to the girls and Alex. 'Guess what? And don't laugh. I'm making New Year decorations!' When Jalil was working she now ventured out to do some gentle shopping on her own in the town. She found some coloured paper, glue, sellotape, tinsel and silver foil. Joseph helped her cut up cardboard cartons, which she sprayed with gold paint she'd discovered in a garage. Happy New Year, in English, French, Spanish and Italian. She needed help with Arabic and Japanese.

'*C'est magnifique*!' The boys blew in wrapped in their

burnooses, slamming the door on the cold night outside and admiring her handiwork before settling down to watch the Marrakesh Song Contests, or at least that's what she took it to be. A series of Brylcreamed singers, sprung from somewhere in the thirties, poured out their souls to an ecstatic audience, followed by large, gold-laden women who sang longer and even louder. The Frenchmen made notes as they waited patiently for it to end and then politely asked if they could watch the news on Sky.

One of them turned to Jalil and said, 'Would it be possible to go into the desert for a day or two on the white camel?' Jalil hesitated. He'd been reluctant to allow Wahid to be demeaned by what he called 'tourist donkey rides'.

'Yes, it is quite possible,' Hamide interrupted firmly. He took Jalil aside and in very fast Arabic reminded him that he was a *chamellier* and here was a chance to earn a few dirham. The season wouldn't last for ever and soon the visitors would go. Jalil looked at Flo with a worried frown.

'Of course I'll be all right,' she said, intercepting his unspoken thoughts. 'You must go. It's your job. And if you don't, Wahid will forget how to work.'

They went into the desert for two nights and three days. The weather was clear, the stars were bright and it was about the time of the full moon. When they returned, Jalil was calm and happy and the two Frenchmen glowed with an almost mystical tranquillity.

'*Superbe! Superbe!*' A few days later they asked Jalil if he had a passport. He shook his head.

'It is easy to get a passport,' Hamide prompted him, 'but not so easy to go anywhere with it.' He produced his own, which he carried with him day and night beside his heart. Joseph, who was peeling potatoes by the gas fire, put out his hand. Hamide watched him like a hawk as the boy turned it over in his grubby hands.

'What is this?' Joseph looked at the words inside. Hamide explained how he'd filled it in. His name, his age and his profession.

'What does it say for profession?'

'Chef. I am a chef,' he said with pride.

Joseph shook his head and asked what he should put down by way of occupation. 'If, one day, I ever have a passport.'

'You?' said Hamide. 'You would put down *fellahine*.' There was a ripple of laughter.

'What is *fellahine*?' Flo wanted to know. The Philosophe told her it meant peasant. Flo was very shocked.

'Don't you have *fellahine* in England?' asked one of the boys.

'Not exactly.' But it was difficult to explain.

It looked as if it was going to be a very late night. The Frenchmen persuaded Jalil to play his tam-tam and Joseph began to sing. The other boys found instruments from nowhere, and forks scraped along a metal wastepaper basket. At three, Flo went to bed. Nearly asleep, she turned as Jalil opened the door of the blue room and stood for a moment looking down at her. She closed her eyes and listened, as she always did, to the rustle of his clothes and, as he undressed, the clunk of his big boots on the stone floor and the faint squeak of the bed when he ducked under the net and joined her.

'Be careful,' she murmured as he reached for his cigarettes on the floor and lit his lighter, which almost brushed against the white gauze. He reached for her hand and lay beside her, looking up and smoking.

'Fatima?' he said after a long silence. 'There is something I want to ask you.'

'Yes?' It was difficult for him to say the words he'd gathered up but then they rushed, the same way as long ago. 'Fatima, it is me, and I promise . . .' The promise that she'd never heard.

'Fatima? Would you be prepared to take out marriage papers?' It was a proposal. Very startled, very wide awake, she sat up.

'I have talked with the family and they agree.' Now that he'd said it, she realised that she'd always known one day he would. The only reply she had was a cruel truth.

'No, Jalil. I am too old.'

'It doesn't matter.'

'But it does. You are a young man. One day you will want children.'

'There are enough children in my family. Already the wife of my brother is fabricating another.' He sounded as if this was a catastrophe that he could do without.

'Jalil, I am old enough to be your mother.'

'I love my mother,' he said simply. She thanked heaven that he'd never heard of Jung or Freud or any of them. She had, but that was her problem.

'Fatima?' She clung to his arm, her face pressed against his shoulder and silently she cursed time.

'Jalil, I will stay with you. I will live with you. If I go home I will always come back.' And she meant it from the bottom of her heart.

Again she followed him down the dark corridor of the kasbah. This time, there were hardly any flies. A group of women, all in black, stood beneath the single light bulb outside the third door. They stopped their chattering and stared. Jalil ignored them as he took the keys out of his pocket.

'Oh! I forgot.' He laughed. There was something different about the door. It had no keyhole. 'Come.' He beckoned her to follow him back out into the sunlight, along a narrow path, then into the main square where they mounted a slope towards the outer wall of the kasbah. He had made a new door that opened out directly on to the square and he had painted it blue.

'*Voilà*. We will live here.' She looked round the dungeon. The only light came from a small window set in the three-foot-thick walls and just below the wooden rafters. It was blocked with a carton against sand and flies and dust. The clutter of farming implements and dead palm were gone and the door leading to the inner kasbah passage was now blocked up, with three-inch gaps on either side.

'There is a toilet.' He showed her where he'd made a walled-off space with a hole-in-the-floor lavatory, a tap and bucket. 'And a kitchen.' There was another space, no larger than a cupboard, with a two-ring cooker, a tagine pot and several empty Nescafé jars. He'd draped Christmas lights around the main room and made a niche with a small lamp that he'd painted with a camel. There was bright green plastic matting on the floor, a worn rug, a large mattress with thick blankets and two pillows. He turned to look at her.

'We will live here, Fatima. I am not a *faux guide*,' he told her seriously. 'It is not right for me to live with you in a hotel.'

'Yes,' said Flo. He had made a home for her, created it with his big hands and loving heart and there was nothing else that she could say.

PART FOUR

S OMEONE ONCE SAID, and Flo guessed he must have been Chinese, that it was cowardice to know what was the right thing to do and not to do it. She had done the right thing. But she never dreamed the price would be so high. Her desert boots and little things she'd collected had been dumped on War on Want, her bracelets given to anyone who wanted them and the snapshots of Jalil and Wahid hidden at the back of a deep cupboard in the spare room. It was several months now. Sometimes the days were almost unbearable.

'Put it out of your mind, Flo, let it go. You did the right thing.' Alex begged, wheedled and bullied her into at least doing something about her hair. She gave in but it was one of the bad days. She picked up a magazine and she saw the sickening photograph. Grannies on the Go! Go! Gambia!, women in their sixties, even seventies, on a package trip which all but guaranteed sex on the side, bulging from ugly bathing suits on a beach, lascivious smirks for the camera as they groped near naked black boys. It was supposed to be amusing. In tears, she fled from the hairdresser into the street, her wet hair dripping down her body. She poured a drink when she got home and turned on the television. Anything to blank away the memories pounding after her. It was *Coronation Street*, a programme she'd never watched before and, by some cruel synchronistic joke, somebody called Deirdre was anguishing about marrying a Moroccan.

'I know it hurts like hell.' Alex dragged her to galleries, auctions and Harrods, trying to distract her as she chose things (no expense spared) for her pretty house in St John's Wood that Sam had bought. 'But you've got to look after yourself.' Look after yourself. Love yourself. The commandment of the nineties, preached since the time of Jesus and now mantra preached by *Vogue*. Massage, exercise, aromatherapy. Love yourself. She did. But she loved Jalil more.

'I will be beside you all the time, until we go to live with Allah.'

His voice came back to her at night and she woke in tears and terror from dreams beyond her control. She searched for pills to find the strength to go into the kitchen and stood barefoot on the cold tiles as she made cups of tea she seldom drank. She never told Alex about the nights in case she suggested that 'she got some help'. Hardly fair, as Alex never would. Her job was to listen, which she did, poor woman, for hours, days and weeks.

'His mother came every day,' Flo told her, not remembering if she had told her that before. 'She used to blow in and stand facing the wall and pray. I always wondered what on earth she was praying for. It was a bit unnerving at first.' Then she suspected the daily visits from that queenly woman with such joyous eyes were perhaps for her protection. She was a foreigner, living openly and without shame with a young man of the village to whom she was not married. A target for hostile, sidelong

247

glances, half hidden by black veils and perhaps at risk from the odd pebble being thrown. Jalil removed the light bulb in the passage and blocked up the cracks beside the inner door and the women stopped looking and listening. Eventually some of the younger ones began to smile and say good morning. Jalil's men friends dropped in, one after another, throughout the days and evenings with gestures of respect and friendship and endless unconnected questions as they drank tea and shared their joints. Did she like Morocco? Did she live in London? Did she believe in God?

'His mother wanted to do my washing for me,' she told Alex as they wandered around Fortnum and Mason. 'But I wouldn't let her.' Unseen by the women, squatting outside their door with buckets, washboards and big bars of yellow soap, Flo ran the tap, soaked, swilled, rinsed and rinsed again, shook her clothes, and shook again, and hung them on the line Jalil had slung across the roof terrace.

'On high days and holidays we used to have pink yoghurt.'

Alex picked up a jar of marmalade with brandy which Sam particularly liked.

'Jalil used to do the shopping, he didn't trust me to get it right. He said I'd spend too much.' He bought two sachets of Nescafé at a time, a small tin of condensed milk, two tomatoes, a couple of onions and a few morsels of meat for the tagine. Mint was plentiful, big, fresh-smelling bundles, but jam and bananas a luxury.

'They used to keep the stale bread and take it to a sort of tip at the far end of the village for anyone to give their animals and chickens. In the evenings, we used to sit on the roof.'

They watched the children in bright clothes bowling tyres with bits of stick, kicking half-deflated footballs, running, laughing, squealing, humping the smaller ones from place to place, dumping them beneath a palm to play with the little stones. The sun began to vanish, and one by one the children drifted or were dragged to their homes as the muezzin called from the mosque. She sat with Jalil, smoking, drinking coffee, her grey shawl tucked around her and Jalil's arm resting on her shoulder as they tried to guess the names of the stars. Later on the music started, melodies escaping from the radios in kasbah homes, soft lit with oil lamps, and later the young men played their tam-tams and their lutes and sang songs of hope and melancholy.

'We saw Omar only once, after the row, but not to talk to,' Flo told poor, patient Alex, as they walked around a gallery in Bruton Street. 'He was passing in the car but he was with Ahmed and he turned his head away. He looked pretty glum.'

'I wonder if Omar—' she had started, but Jalil had cut her short.

'No, Fatima, it is over. We will speak no more of it.' Alex said she didn't blame him.

'Too feudal for words. You'd think it was still the thirteenth century.' And by all accounts, it was now worse. Little Lahassan was waiting for them outside the kasbah door.

'Ah, Fatima!' He'd greeted her with a great smile and hopped inside to have some tea. He was full of gossip. Jalil cracked big lumps of sugar and shoved them in the teapot as he told them things were not good at the hotel. Bernard's group no longer came. Cecille's four-star enterprise had been suspended. There was much boozing and many rows. Omar was depressed because Laassell was getting too old to work and had gone off to try and sell back some of the camels to the nomads. Jalil and Little Lahassan thought this was a big joke.

'But,' Little Lahassan shook his head, 'no work is no work.' Jalil had no work either but was too proud to speak about it.

'Oh, I forgot.' Little Lahassan stopped at the door as he was leaving. 'Hamide says there is a letter for you at Scheherezade.'

Jalil was in no hurry to pick up his letter. The wind was starting and he wanted to do something to the guttering on the roof. Out of sight, his mother blew in through the door, bunching up her skirts and settling down by the mattress. Flo was rinsing out the teapot. His mother asked her something but she didn't understand. She looked at the mattress, patted it then looked back at her, but she still didn't know what she was getting at. She stood up and walked towards her and, with a merry question in her eyes, patted Flo's stomach. Flo froze and backed away. His mother laughed again and mimed a rocking movement with her arms for a baby that would never be.

'It was after that,' Flo told Alex, 'that things started to change.'

The wind was brutal, callous and unending, stinging grit filtering through every crack and crevice of the kasbah and pushing drifts of sand beneath the doors.

'We went to Sindibad by bus. There weren't any taxis. I don't know how the driver made it. We walked from the bus stop. The dust was so thick, it was almost dark in the middle of the day.'

Alex had settled for Claridges for a shopping pit stop. She called the waiter and ordered lemon tea, still listening.

'When we got to Scherehezade, Hamide gave Jalil his letter. He played it very cool and pretended he wasn't really interested.' He'd taken his time to open it, then gave it to her to read for him. The Philosophe, a scarf across his mouth to keep out the wind, reminded him he was perfectly capable of reading French himself. Everyone knew the letter was from Paris. It was from one of the young Frenchmen who wrote that they were nearly ready to start their trip. They would be passing by Zagora en route for the rest of Africa. They had discussed the matter fully with their colleagues and wondered if Jalil would like to come with them as far as Mali. Timbuktu. They'd like him to advise them on the music that they found along the way. If he was interested, would he please get a passport immediately and fax them the details. They would arrange the paperwork needed but it took time. Speed was of the essence. They very much hoped that he would come. She finished the letter and handed it to Jalil, who put it in his pocket and turned to watch a Brazilian soap, dubbed into Arabic on the telly.

'Jalil, you must go!' She shook his arm.

'An opportunity from heaven,' insisted the Philosophe, but Jalil had sunk beneath his own horizon and was now glued to an advertisement for nappies.

'You must get your passport. Get your passport!' Eventually he told them all that he didn't want to go.

'Do you think he was afraid?' asked Alex, pouring out another cup of lemon tea.

'No. He wasn't afraid. He told me he didn't want to go because he didn't want to leave me. I told him it would be only for a while but he clammed up and wouldn't listen. It was only half an hour later that I got the call.'

'What call?'

'New York. One hour after Jalil got the letter, it was New York on the phone.'

'Hi, Mum.' New York loud and clear.

'Hi, darling. How did you get my number?'

'I rang Alex.'

'Is everything all right?'

'Fine. Fine. Listen, Mum, do they have chairs there? Are you sitting down?' New York was laughing.

'What's the matter? Darling, are you all right?'

'I'm fine, Mum, guess what? You're going to be a granny!' Flo sank on to the nearest cushion.

'Mum? Mum? Are you still there?'

'I think so.' Her voice was weak.

'Listen, Tim and I are coming back to London. Yes, you remember Tim. We'll probably get married or something. Mum?'

'Yes, I can hear you, just.' The line had gone static.

'I don't have any medical insurance. So I'll be having it in London.'

'When?'

'There's no rush. There are a few problems but nothing serious.'

'What problems?' She could hardly hear now.

'Don't worry, Mum. Everything's OK. Love you.' And then the phone went dead.

'*Ça va*, Fatima?' asked Hamide as, white as a sheet, she got up from the cushion and then sat down again.

*   *   *

'*Non! Non! Non!*' The electricity was off because of the storm and his shadow in the candlelight was enormous on the wall.

'Jalil, I must go home, and you must go with the Frenchmen. It is a wonderful opportunity.' She went slowly up the steps with a torch to find her clothes, dried and stiff and thick with sand on the line. When she came down he was sitting on the mattress, his head between his hands.

'*Non!*' he shouted as she dragged her bags out from underneath the stairs.

'My daughter is having a baby, she needs me. And you, you have your flying carpet.' He watched her as she searched behind the cushions for her slippers, his face suddenly much thinner.

'Why?' he asked again. 'Why?' He turned his head away to hide the tears as she rummaged through the plastic carriers in her bag and found something hard. The whisky that she'd never given to Omar. Perhaps a drink would make things easier.

'Have we any glasses?' She went into the kitchen to look. There were two, with tea and mint still in them. She washed and rinsed them and shook away the drops of water.

'Jalil! What are you doing?' He had the bottle to his lips and was drinking like a frenzied calf. The bottle was a third empty. She reached for it but he was too tall and held it high above her.

'Jalil, for God's sake!' He didn't drink. She had never seen him drink a thing except maybe beer.

'No . . . you will not go!' he shouted. She jumped again for the bottle as a dog jumps for a biscuit. It was her turn to scream and shout. But screams in kasbahs are ignored. It is the business between a husband and a wife.

'Please stop, please!' She jumped for the bottle again but it was empty and he flung it on the floor. His body smelled of desperation as he ripped off his T-shirt, tearing it to pieces, screaming back at her. He would die if she left him. He grabbed her arm and flung her on the mattress and kept on screaming, jumbled words, not French or Arabic but a sing-song rhythm of despair. He stopped suddenly, stared down at her then moved away. She prayed he'd gone to vomit. But he came back and knelt beside the mattress with a knife in his hand. A knife, small and sharp and shining. She shrank back in shock and fear. Think of Kate Adie, Flo, think of Kate Adie. But Kate Adie couldn't help with this. For an hour, he ranted, the knife held lightly in his hand. She thought of reaching for it, grabbing it, throwing it into a dark corner, but she knew she must sit very still. But even with that shining blade, six inches from her arm, he'd never hurt her. Not if she sat very still. The alcohol would wear off in time but how much time? An hour? Two hours? The village lay in darkness; the wind buffeted the carton wedged into the window above their heads as he ranted on, gasping for breath, as he wept and cried out to her, the words becoming thick and gushing until he fell into a silence of deep pain. He tried to stand, swayed and stumbled towards the lavatory as she sat like stone, listening to his sobs and retching. His face and body streaked with vile slime, he came back and fell on to the mattress, still holding the knife in his hand.

'Jalil,' she said the words as softly as she dared. 'Jalil, I'm very thirsty. Would you make me some tea?' She held out her hand for the knife. Like a bewildered child he gave it to her, rose uncertainly to his feet, went into the kitchen and was sick again. Stiff as an old woman she rose and led him back to the mattress. He slumped back with his eyes shut as she damped a towel, wiped his face and stroked his dreadlocks. He tried to circle her ankle with his big thumb and finger but his hand fell away and he slept. He didn't hear the muezzin at dawn. He didn't hear the klaxon of the CTM. He heard nothing until he woke after the next day and it was getting dark again. And Flo, her head full of common sense and her heart full of tears, was gone.

Exhausted by her story, she stood in the bay window of Alex's partly furnished sitting room and watched the snowflakes whirling round the garden in St John's Wood. Alex sat by the fire, sending shadows flickering up her newly painted walls.

'You did the right thing,' she told her for the millionth time.

'Did I?' Flo's voice echoed back. 'We thought we were invincible, you know.' She pitched her cigarette into the fire and watched it smouldering to nothing. 'But we'll talk of it no more.'

'Do you want to stay the night?' Alex asked her. 'I can easily make up the spare bed.'

'No, it's all right. I'll get a cab,' said Flo and walked towards the phone.

The baby was born on midsummer's eve. They called her Polly. There had been an awful moment when Flo thought they really were going to call her Titania, but from the second she was born, delivered with a golden skin, no scaly coverings or wrinkles and weighing over eight pounds, she was Polly.

'Isn't she the most wonderful thing you ever saw, Mum?' Her daughter laughed back, dark eyes and beautiful, banked with flowers and not a mobile phone in sight. Flo nodded. She'd already checked for the requisite number of toes and fingers, marvelled at the miracle of her round and undistorted little head with a satisfactory amount of damp, black hair.

'She looks a bit like you,' remarked her son-in-law, flushed with triumph and champagne. The baby yawned. Actually yawned and then raised a faintly marked eyebrow. What other baby could raise an eyebrow at only three hours old? Flo had quite a few friends who had recently become grandmothers who boasted and bored each other silly with endless anecdotes about these small new people. Flo felt sorry for them, absolutely sure that no other child could be as exceptional as Polly. As she stared into the crib she marvelled at the generosity of nature, another miracle, that had banished in a second all the vain ambivalence she'd ever felt about becoming a grandmother, over-whelmed by the unexpected certainty that this child was part of her.

'She's extraordinary,' Flo told the taxi driver who picked her up outside Queen Charlotte's and sped her home along the Goldhawk Road.

'Mother doing all right?' he asked and told her he was a grandfather four times over. He started off into a vivid account of his daughter's Caesarian. She listened intently to every gynaecological detail, while giving thanks for her daughter's indecently quick labour.

'Eight and a half pounds,' she exaggerated.

'A whopper,' the cabbie agreed, drawing up outside the house. She gave him twenty pounds and told him to keep the change. After all, he was a grandfather. He said he'd wet the baby's head when he got home, with his old lady. 'What's her name?'

'Polly!' cried Flo and all but danced towards her front door.

Laid out on the floor, a neat gallery of women stared up at her with roguish smiles, seductive smirks and distant languor. Nell Gwyn to Marilyn Munroe. Damian, true to his word, was keeping her busy and paying her quite well. This time he wanted mistresses, mistresses of history. He'd added Camilla Parker Bowles but Flo said she didn't count.

'I'm a grandmother!' she told those women, all with lonely faces, tongues of velvet and wills of steel. She flung open the French windows on to the still, hot garden. Next door were having a boisterous barbecue, the smell of charred meat drifting up through the horse-chestnut tree, then into the orange-tinted London sky. She fixed herself a drink with lots of ice and sat down on a creaking garden chair, listening to the middle classes barking through their party.

'Cheers, Flo!' Toasting her new status, she tipped her glass, the ice slipping into her mouth as she searched the sky for a star. There must be a star somewhere tonight. Polly's star. One of those stars she and Jalil had gazed at from the roof. How he would have laughed when Polly yawned. He must be, she thought, somewhere near Timbuktu by now. Enough. She pushed away the longing that was surging up, permitted only in the darkness of the night. She must ring Los Angeles, who was standing by to be an Aunt. And all the others she'd promised to let know at once.

It was only right and proper to ring John first.

'Jolly good! Splendid!' He was surprisingly benevolent considering, as she guessed correctly, that he'd left the table of a dinner party. 'I'll send a crate of something special,' he promised.

Then she rang her parents. Her father's voice answered, far off in New Zealand, whatever time it was over there. As she'd expected, he sounded preoccupied.

'It's me, Dad!' she insisted, since he didn't seem to know who she was. He promised he'd tell her mother, who he said would be delighted. Los Angeles wanted to know every detail, then said wistfully that she'd given up her personal trainer and was sick of California shit and sunshine.

'I'm thinking of coming home myself, Mum.' Flo felt a shock of pleasure.

'Oh do, darling, do come home. We all miss you.' She hung up and thought about it for a minute before ringing Alex, expected back by now from a picture buying trip in St Petersburg. She took an even bet with herself that she'd have brought back one of those Russian dolls entombed inside each other for the baby. She dialled and got the answerphone.

'It's a girl.' She laughed the rest of the way through her excited message. 'She's called Polly. Ring me, no matter what time you get in.'

With her head full of tomorrow and too wired to sleep, she went back into the garden. The party next door was winding down, people saying loud goodbyes and car doors slamming. A police siren wailed in the distance and someone was playing Grover Washington from an open upstairs window. What about Camilla Parker Bowles? She'd tackle that with Damian tomorrow. After she'd written little résumés for all the mistresses for his secretary to make neat on her word processor. And what else? She'd promised to chase up the carpenter, to put finishing touches to the nursery. The phone rang as she was pouring another drink. She went towards it with a smile.

'It's a girl!' The words were ready on her lips for Alex.

'One moment,' said an operator. Then the line went dead. She hung up. It rang again.

'Hullo . . . hullo.' The overseas distortions made her guess it must be Alex in some antiquated Russian hotel. Or maybe New Zealand ringing back. Her father was quite capable of forgetting if it was a boy or a girl. 'Hullo.'

'Fatima?' It was Hamide.

He said he hadn't had her number or her address, and to excuse him but he'd forgotten what her real name was. He'd been desperate to get in touch. And then, *grâce à* Allah, Jalil's mother arrived at Sindibad that day.

'She is here, beside me now,' he shouted above what she thought was someone weeping.

'She found an envelope in Jalil's pocket. It said London, someone told her it said London. I found your number with the lady at directory. It took a long time.'

'What has happened?' She knew that something had. Hamide was faint again, his voice echoing through the static.

'Wahid is dead.' His reply was stark, no sugar coating and she felt as if someone had thrown a brick in her face.

'What do you mean, dead? How? Why?'

'He was poisoned.' The line was clear as Hamide rushed on. They'd found him by the river one morning. The day before he was fine. And then he was dead.

'Does Jalil know? Where is he? Why didn't he tell me?' But Hamide was still telling her the story, of how they'd tried to move him with a donkey but he was so heavy the traces broke. Someone came by with a Land Rover; *grâce à* Allah and they towed him to the desert.

'Why didn't Jalil tell me? Does he know?' she shouted. Her sweaty hand slid down the telephone and she clutched it, pressing it to her ear.

'He thought that you would cry.' Cry for poor Wahid, as he had. For that great body, torn clean by vultures, somewhere behind the two mountains and, by now, his bones innocent, white and shining on the grey grit.

'When did this happen?'

'Three weeks, maybe four.' Yes, Wahid would be clean and gleaming now.

'Where is Jalil? Is he with the Frenchmen?'

'No, Fatima. He is gone.'

She heard a woman's voice crying out, 'Fatima! Fatima! Fatima!' It was his mother. She heard Hamide try to calm her.

'Where has he gone? Where has he gone?' The line was even worse.

'I'll call you back,' she shouted. Her hands shook as she looked for the number of Scheherezade, dialled again and waited. Next door the stragglers at the party were chatting quietly and the sound of the saxophone still moaned across the sweet-smelling summer garden. She dialled again, waited. Nothing. In a mad dream, she dialled once more. It rang. Hamide picked it up at once.

'Where has he gone?'

'The desert. He is running from the police.'

'Why? Why? Why?' Now what little air there was was sucked from her body and the room, as Hamide told her what he knew. Jalil thought that Ahmed had poisoned Wahid. They tried to persuade him that no one could be sure but he wouldn't listen. Jalil went and found Ahmed.

'And he damaged him.'

'Damaged? How?'

'He broke his jaw and knocked out all his teeth. Then he wanted to kill him. It took eight men to hold him. Ahmed ran away and got the police. But Jalil had gone, escaped.'

'But where is he now?' No one knew. Some said he was dealing drugs in Tangier; other people said he was working in a marble quarry near Casablanca. The phone was grabbed from him and a torrent of impassioned Arabic poured into the quiet sitting room. Hamide got the phone back from Jalil's mother and explained.

'She has never spoken on a telephone before.'

'What does she say?'

'She says that Jalil has gone south. That he chose his own punishment.'

'Where south? Where in the desert?'

'Fatima, the desert is very big, but today Zaide came here. He has seen the nomads. The nomads had seen Jalil. They were with him but the aeroplanes came over. They were frightened and thought it was the police. Or the army . . .' Zaide had met one of them, who told him that they'd crept off in the night, but that they left Jalil with food and water.

'But when?' she screamed. 'How long ago?' She dared the phone to let her down.

'A week, maybe?'

'Give the facts. Exact facts.' She was icy calm now and had a pencil in her hand.

'His mother says . . .' The phone went dead.

*　　*　　*

'You are not, and I repeat, *not* rushing off to Morocco!'
Alex leaned against the draining board in Flo's kitchen,
her hands on her hips and angrier than she had felt for
a long time. She'd had a dreadful flight on Aeroflot,
delayed by six hours, got home anticipating good news
of the baby and now this.

'But . . .'

'No buts, it's final. There's nothing you can do. If
Jalil chooses to piss off into the desert, that's his affair.'
Numb and distant in her dressing-gown, Flo stared at
the untouched coffee in front of her.

'There must be something.' But Alex wasn't having any.

'Yes, there is something. It's called life, your life.' With
an enormous effort Flo got up and switched the kettle
on again. Alex watched her, wishing with all her heart
that Jalil's wretched mother hadn't found the address,
that Hamide hadn't rung and smashed to fragments
the strength she'd watched Flo build with pain and
perseverance over the past months.

'What were you going to do today?' she demanded.
'And tomorrow?'

'What?' Flo stared, as if eating, sleeping, living out
the little things that kept a person sane were far
beyond her.

'What? Look in your book if you can't remember.'

'I was going to see the baby, finish off those mistress
notes for Damian's secretary and have lunch with Robert
tomorrow.' Absurd things.

'Robert!' Alex gave a cry of surprise. 'When did he
pop up? You never told me.'

'You weren't here.'

'Well?'

Flo searched her memory to remember what he'd
said. 'Canada. Yes, he came back from Canada.'

'Why?'

'He said they wouldn't take him in the Mounties.' Despite herself she gave a weak smile.

'Is he back again for good? What about his wife?' Although Alex never had much time for Robert, time had passed; anything could have happened by now and anything was better than all this anguish. 'What about his wife?'

'I didn't ask.' Out of the blue he'd rung, asked her out to lunch and she'd said yes. But she must cancel. She got up and went into the sitting room.

'What else were you supposed to do this week?' Alex challenged as Flo listened to Robert's answerphone and left a brief and unapologetic message as he had used to do. Before Alex could object she rang Queen Charlotte's to tell her daughter she'd got a bit of a cold and didn't want to pass it on to Polly and then made an excuse to Damian's secretary about the notes on mistresses.

'Right, now you've cancelled everything. Does it help?'

Her face buried in her hands, Flo had no answer. Alex would never understand. Jalil, a young king from another life, was calling out to her in this one.

'Didn't you care about Omar?' Flo asked suddenly.

'That was different. He was part of our trip, all those mountains, palm trees, stars and stuff.' Move on, move on, Omar discarded now like an empty bottle of suntan lotion. In a way, what she said was true. He was part of that yellow earth, wide valleys and purple shadowed canyons. But those canyons were still there, the tamarisk trees and desert beetles didn't cease just because a holiday was over and a suntan long faded. And Jalil was out there now, alone in the desert of sand, white relentless glass stretching to an undefined horizon.

'I must think.' Jalil himself had told her that forty-eight hours was the maximum that anyone could last in the desert. And how long had he been gone?

'No, you must not think.' Alex cut across her nightmare visions, 'There is nothing you can do, so leave it be. I'm not having you jumping on to planes and rushing off into that God-awful heat and hiring helicopters.' The moment that she said it, she could have bitten off her tongue. Flo got up, rushed to one end of the room and back again in a mindless frenzy.

'A helicopter, that's it!' She turned her haggard face to Alex, begging her to understand. 'We must find a helicopter!'

'How? How can you just find a helicopter? Remember what it's like down there to catch a bus. Remember that time in Tangier . . .'

'A plane! What was the name of that guy at La Fibule?' Alex looked blank. 'The one who had a plane and sprayed the locusts?'

'Claude?'

'Yes, Claude.' Memory was now razor-fine and she remembered. 'He gave you his number.' In those innocent days when it was raining and they watched the Sheltering Sky and Alex had been mortified that he'd been called away.

'That was years ago.'

'It doesn't matter. Ring him.' Flo grabbed her arm. 'Ring him!'

They argued for an hour. Alex told her she was mad and that this panic would make her and everybody else ill. She had a good job now, a family to think of, Robert was back and there was Polly.

'You're a grandmother, for God's sake!' It was below

the belt and she knew it and expected Flo to counter that feeling was not a function governed by age, but she just stared with hollow, anxious eyes.

'Please,' was the only word she had to fight with.

'Oh, all right.' Exasperated, she fished in her bag for her tiny address book, with a lifetime's numbers written minutely on the thin, blue pages. She turned her back on Flo as she pressed the numbers for somewhere in France.

'Hullo.' Her voice changed, charged with charm as a woman answered. She sounded very young. Alex asked if she could speak to Claude. The woman asked her who she was and she explained she was an old friend calling from London. The young woman replied that she was Claude's wife, he wasn't there and she had no idea when he'd be back. She sounded very French and hung up.

Of the random choices open to them, Alex decided on the view at Christies and bullied, wheedled and coaxed Flo into getting dressed, combing her hair and putting on some lipstick. She was after some Whistler sketches. With her attention on her catalogue, she walked ahead up the wide staircase, Flo following, her hand on the mahogany banister, her limbs held lightly together by willpower.

'I suppose it's a shame for all these things to be broken up.' The sale was for death duties. Treasures of centuries, collected on Grand Tours, ambassadorial postings, eccentric spendthrifts and keen-eyed agents were about to vanish into the homes and the collections of the wealthy. Alex didn't agree; most of the stuff, she said, had been lurking in dark attics and damp corridors for years. It was time they saw the light of day. She went off to find her Whistlers. Flo, without a catalogue, trailed past cabinets of eighteenth-century miniatures, plump women with pursed lips and men in ruffles and quiffed hair. She tried to concentrate, if only for a second, on paintings of long-necked racehorses, Georgian silver, Sèvres porcelain and ancient Chinese statues. She wished there was somewhere to sit down as she forced herself to stare at a dark icon, into the elongated eyes of a stern mystic, his golden halo all but worn away. The eyes looked back at her, eyes to be reckoned with, but she didn't have the strength.

'It is charming, is it not?' A man beside her spoke. It was Bruno, impeccable as ever. If he'd had a hat, he would have raised it.

'Ah, it is Florence, I wasn't sure.'

How could he be sure that this fragile woman was the one who'd laughed and sat with him in the dappled shade beside a sparkling swimming pool. She felt as if she were staring at an apparition. Bruno had an aeroplane. Bruno knew Jalil. With the smile of a lifetime, she turned to him and from a great distance heard him saying something about not having seen her in Zagora recently, something about *la grande chaleur*, how was her father and had she been to the antiques fair at Grosvenor House? Alex joined them and Flo heard her light laugh as she tried to introduce them, then her own voice rasping out the word 'plane'. Her hands reached out to Bruno then there was a rustling sound and a soft thump as she fainted.

She came to on a sofa, covered by a pink satin quilt, with half a memory of being partly carried into a car then into a lift.

'Where is this?' Within a second, her terror for Jalil was clutching at her throat again.

'Shhh.' Alex was at her side, looking worried as she told her she was at the Ritz in Bruno's suite. He said that English hospitals were barbaric and insisted that they should come with him. Bruno, looking in a gilded mirror, reflecting the tops of the trees in Green Park, was trying swathes of silk Sulka ties against himself.

'Florence, you are better now?' There was another man beside her in a dark suit, who took her blood pressure and her pulse. Alex told her he was a doctor.

'Just drink this.' She tried a weak apology. Bruno waved it away.

'Not at all, my dear. So charmingly eighteenth century to faint. And you did it beautifully.' Flo pushed aside the quilt and tried to stand. Alex and the doctor advised her to stay put.

'Would you care for a little lunch?' Before anyone could answer, Bruno talked to room service, ordering lobster thermidor for himself and Alex and a little bouillon for Madame. The doctor made out a prescription which he gave to Alex and told her he was available should he be needed. All that was required was rest and quiet, and the door closed behind him with a fat click.

'Bruno, you've got a plane.' There was no time for niceties and polite requests. 'You must find Jalil.' Straight as an arrow, Flo's demand flew from where she lay and to Alex's astonishment, instead of patting her hand and telling her not to worry, Bruno said very firmly to her and to his own reflection in the mirror, 'I will.'

Flo started to explain what had happened. Alex told her to relax because she already had.

'I was going south tomorrow, anyway.' Bruno said it as if he was passing somewhere and was casually compliant about running a small errand. 'But,' he added thoughtfully, 'I shall need a pilot's cap and a white scarf.' He rang a bell. A door which led on to a second sitting room opened and a secretary appeared.

'Yes, sir?'

'I need a leather flying cap, circa 1938, and a white scarf. Silk. Lockes,' he suggested. Without a change in his expression the secretary made a note.

'It gets very boring sometimes, being rich,' Bruno explained almost apologetically as the secretary left. 'And I've always wanted to be Biggles.' Alex was deeply impressed.

'Bruno is going to find Jalil,' she told Flo as if she were a child.

'Are you? Are you?' She struggled to sit up again.

'Of course. He is too beautiful to lose.'

'But the desert? Where in the desert?'

'Quite honestly, I don't know.' But Bruno didn't seem too worried.

'Maybe he's safe and sound in prison,' Alex ventured. Bruno looked at Flo just for a second and she looked back. He was deadly serious. They both knew, without a doubt, Jalil was not in prison.

'Of course, if anyone could find him, Omar could.' Alex wasn't thinking when she said it.

'Omar? That rogue? I've had a lot of trouble with that family. In the end I had to buy them out.' Again he said it casually, as if he'd bought a pair of shoes. Two waiters encroached upon his bombshell with a loaded trolley.

'You bought them out?' Alex wanted to hear more.

'Eventually. It was the only thing to do.' But it had taken time, even with his money and his influence, until Ahmed had seized on the offer beyond his greatest greed from an anonymous bidder, taken the money and fled back with it to Fes.

'Are you going to rebuild it?'

'No, no, no. Why should I?'

The waiters laid a table in the window and brought a tray with bouillon and warm, white rolls and set it tenderly on the coffee table next to the sofa.

'The moment it was mine, I razed it to the ground.' So the Hôtel des Dunes was gone and he'd no idea where Omar was.

'Hamide could find him.' Flo lit a cigarette and reached for a white phone on the coffee table. Alex snatched the cigarette away and stubbed it out.

'For heaven's sake, you just fainted.'

'Allow me.' Bruno took the phone from her and Flo was telling him the number at Scheherezade, each digit, fast and concise as if they were her own. The phone connected and rang on and on. Alex sipped champagne, and Bruno picked at his lobster thermidor with one hand. The door to the bedroom was open and two maids were packing two-foot piles of shirts into expensive luggage. The secretary came back with a pilot's cap, a silk scarf and some goggles. Bruno tried them on, declaring them to be superb, as he hung on. At last, someone answered.

'Ahh!' Bruno sounded surprised, as if he seldom used a phone. Alex looked up from her lunch and Flo lit another cigarette. Alex pretended she hadn't noticed. Bruno quickly switched from French to perfect Arabic and then slowed down.

'Is it Hamide?' Flo asked. Bruno was now making unconnected sounds, one after another as the voice at the other end kept repeating, '*Bonjour*.' Flo leaned towards the phone.

'Oh God, it's Joseph!' It might just as well have been answered by the bullfrogs. She willed the stupid boy to understand.

'The boy says, Hamide is in Casablanca,' translated Bruno.

'Ask him if the Philosophe is there.'

'The Philosophe is none too well and with his sister in Ouarzazate.'

'He smokes too much,' Flo muttered in despair as Bruno gave up. They both looked at the ormulu clock on the mantelpiece.

'I will be there tomorrow evening.' Bruno, in his flying cap, was unconquerable and made the statement like a holy vow.

'Let me try something.' She picked up the phone and asked for telegrams which they told her were now called telemessages, and said they'd put her through. Two packages arrived from Spinks as she, listened to 'Tales of the Vienna Woods' on the phone. An architect arrived. Bruno led him to another table, gave him champagne and became involved in a roll of blue-prints. Flo got through to the telemessages and spelled out Omar's name and the address of the Post Office in the village. With an English operator it took a long time. Another secretary arrived and Bruno, turning from the architect, told him quietly that he wanted a doctor with a glucose and saline drip standing by at Marrakesh. Alex heard him but Flo didn't, intent on spelling out her message, 'For the love of God and your old friend, find Jalil. Fatima.' She lay back on the sofa before anyone could again tell her to relax and, in spite of the warmth of the summer day, pulled the satin quilt around her shoulders. One of the maids asked Bruno if he needed all his dinner jackets and he said he did. A hamper arrived from Fortnum & Mason. Unable to move or think, she listened to the distant voices of the secretaries giving instructions rather than requests about aviation clearance. In the second sitting room the fax machine was going mad. Alex and Bruno were discussing tracker dogs. Alex speculated as to whether Zaide's information via the nomad was true, if indeed there had ever been a nomad. Was it even true that Jalil had punched Ahmed, or was it an endless circling of make-believe and sand-swept myths? Flo knew that Bruno didn't think so. The secretary told him he was wanted on the other phone by the President of France. Bruno flipped his scarf over his shoulder and went to talk to him.

'Do you ever feel as if you're living in a mad dream?' Alex asked Flo.

'Often,' she replied.

The cordless phone was never more than inches from her hand by day and night. Callers got short shrift, only her daughter being allowed to trespass on the line for a few vital moments.

'Your cold sounds worse, Mum. Are you sure you haven't got flu? Have you got a fever?' Flo told her it was highly likely. A fever of fear, with blessed moments of isolated stillness when she knew the glare of the day was moving slowly into evening and the gentle shadows were wrapping round the dunes and in the village, the children without toys were being called away from playing by night. She drank tea, she drank whisky and she smoked non-stop, not knowing if hope was a friend or enemy. She swept the garden clear of every leaf and tweaked out every tiny weed. She hosed the York paving and soaked the flowerbeds and climbing roses until the earth turned into mud and water cascaded down the sides of the stone pots.

Alex rang. 'Any news?'

'Nothing.' She tore down the curtains and shoved them in the washing machine, despising it because it was not a bucket on a kasbah roof. She turned the television on and switched it off again, sickened by obscenities perpetrated against children at home and round the world, then burned some toast and made a second cup of coffee then a third and spilled the milk. Kneeling on the kitchen floor, she dragged a cloth through the white puddle. The phone rang. Still on her knees, she answered it. There was a roaring sound.

'Florence?'

'Yes? Yes? Yes?'

'This is Biggles,' Bruno shouted above the engine, 'calling Florence. Mission accomplished! *A bientôt!* Roger, over and out!'

She stayed on her knees until her hands stopped shaking and her face eased of weariness, then, as if a match had sparked, a flame had taken, warmth began to spread through her rigid limbs. With great care, she wiped up the rest of the milk, rinsed the cloth and hung it on the side of the sink. She turned to a drawer to find her gardening gloves and secateurs. The roses were so bountiful this year, there were enough to plunder for the house, and the vine was getting out of hand again.

*   *   *

Alex's mother often said that eventually one bumped into everyone one knew. She was referring to Harrod's Banking Hall in the old days. Alex believed the same was true of Field's. Field's was one of the most exclusive hairdressers in London, Paris or New York and these days one almost had to have an audition to get taken on. Unlike his peers, Field didn't charge obscene amounts – enough to feed a Third World family for months – but, regardless of appointment times, he kept the women waiting for as long as he chose. But it was worth it. Safe in the knowledge that not a strand of hair had been insulted with a chemical, no client left his salon without feeling sleek and satisfied. As Alex's thick hair was parted, dabbed and parted, she noticed an almost blonde woman sitting next to her going through the same laborious but necessary process. There was something familiar about her. The woman's colourist asked her to turn her head slightly and Alex, who never forgot a face, even with hair scraped back and wet, recognised Cecille.

'Alex?' Cecille was brilliant at names and faces too. 'Flo's friend?' Alex admitted that she was.

'How is Bruno?' she asked. Cecille said that he was fine. Then that she was remarried and living now in Paris. Alex told her that she too was remarried and living in St Johns Wood. And that she had her own gallery. Unheeding the colourists dabbed on. They'd heard it all before, the triumphs and disasters of shopping and sad stories of treacherous husbands.

'And how is Flo?' asked Cecille.

'Do you ever go back to the desert?' Alex countered.

'The desert? Never! It was eating me alive.' This was a new one for the colourists, as were the desert stories and reminiscences that followed.

'Bruno was such a hero.'

'Wasn't he? He hasn't had so much fun since . . .' Cecille couldn't remember when. 'And he was only in the nick of time. Jalil was all but dead. The doctor said it was a matter of hours.' The colourists slowed down.

'He was very taken with Jalil, you know,' Cecille told Alex as she was wrapped up in bits of foil.

'Was he indeed?' Although Cecille's English was very good, the inference was lost on her.

'Oh yes, he took him on, I think, at the new hotel.'

'Oh yes, the new hotel.' Cecille told her all about it until they reached the backwash.

'Bruno always gets what he wants. I begged him to call it a day, he'll never do it, not with all that salt, but he is very wilful.' She smiled as an indulgent sister as they waited for Field and the manicurists to move in.

'And how is Flo?' Cecille asked again, examining her roots, smiling up at Field who had approached with his blow dryer. Alex concentrated on the varnishes in her manicurist's tray. 'Is she in town? I'd love to see her.'

Alex retrieved one of her hands from the bowl of soapy water on the manicurist's lap and rubbed her own head with a big, white towel. Flo was well and happy, she could have said. True, she sometimes looked a little wistful, true she'd pretended not to hear when Alex had mentioned there was a new Moroccan restaurant opening nearby, true she sometimes stared off into space, but then she always had. But she was OK. The job had turned out to be more high-powered than Damian had led her to believe: meetings, edit suites and viewings. Both her girls were home now. Polly was an angel and Flo was besotted by her. There was even talk of her parents coming home, and if they did, which both Flo and she greatly doubted, Flo would have her work cut out. Yes, she had a full life, as they called it. And then there was Robert. OK, he'd been a shit, but things did change. At least, Alex hoped they would, but when she'd questioned Flo about him, she just smiled and said, 'He's very sweet, very funny, very kind . . . but . . .'

From long experience, Alex knew that whenever anyone said 'but' like that, followed by a sigh, it was all over. Not that they weren't very good friends and that in itself was rare these days. By the time Alex emerged from the towel and gave her hand back to the manicurist, Field was hard at his blow drying, twisting Cecille's hair with a rounded, bristle brush.

'Flo?' she asked yet again. 'I'd love to see her but I'm only here until tomorrow.'

'She's in New York,' lied Alex. 'What a shame.'

Field's brush stopped in mid-air, his eyebrows flew almost to his hairline. He'd heard some porkies in his time, but this! Flo had been there, in the salon, only hours before, large as life, sitting in the same seat as Cecille. She'd chattered on about the party she was giving that evening. How, as it was midsummer and her granddaughter's birthday, they were celebrating both together. Without a doubt, he remembered she'd talked about candles floating in bowls of rose petals. New York indeed? He gave Alex a look in the mirror. Quite a look. Alex kept her head down. OK, it was a whopper, but so what? There'd been enough angst and anguish for anybody's lifetime, and she wasn't going to risk Flo being all stirred up again into Heaven knows what by some idle gossip from Cecille. After all, it was Flo herself who'd said that night, when there were snowflakes flying past the window, 'We'll talk of it no more.' At least that's what Alex thought she said.

EPILOGUE

SECURITY WAS HIGH but, without a glance, Jalil drove the prime minister, the name of whose country he'd forgotten, past the saluting guards and the police, out on to the runway and brought the blacked-out Range Rover to a smooth halt at the steps of the waiting private jet. The prime minister, a small man, got out and, looking up at Jalil, shook his hand. The guards stood to a stiff attention as the prime minister thanked him for reminding him about Bob Marley whom he'd liked as a young man. To the consternation of the bodyguards, Jalil, the tail end of his *shesh* flying like a banner in the breeze, reached back into the Range Rover for a cassette which he gave to the prime minister, who laughed, thanked him again, wished him a Happy Christmas and New Year, patted his arm and then was smartly up the steps, the bodyguards behind him. The door was shut, the steps wheeled away and within minutes the jet was taxiing along the runway. Air traffic control advised an incoming passenger plane on hold and circling to be prepared to land. As it began its final sweep around the mountains, Jalil drove the Range Rover back through the open barrier. His duties now fulfilled, he wound down the smoked window and grinned at the police.

'Salaam, Maleukum.' They knew him well at Ouar-zazate, as they did at all the airports in the country. Jalil commanded deep respect. He was from Le Jardin, which had risen in the desert, as unexpected and mysterious as a mirage. As Bruno had determined, his hotel was so luxurious there were not sufficient stars in the sky for it to have a category and, although it was said to be a hotel, it was so discreet, so exclusive, guests had to be invited. Bruno had appointed Jalil king of this little realm, to play host to other kings, princes, presidents, prime ministers and quiet men with briefcases and golf clubs. Sometimes they brought their wives and families to rest and play in the domed pavilions among the rose gardens and whispering fountains. Sometimes, but not often, a very famous film star might be permitted sanctuary.

'Salaam, Maleukum.' All charges against Jalil had long been dropped and forgotten. So what if he had beaten up Ahmed? He'd paid the price out in the desert and anyway, he'd only done what many people in the region had wanted to do themselves. Jalil gave the policeman a cigarette and lit one for himself, glancing up at the passenger plane which was making its final approach. The policeman told him it was coming in from Paris. Jalil drove on and parked in the car park to smoke a cigarette himself and wonder if it was a day for miracles.

It was a miracle the day Omar received the telegram. Zaide's brother-in-law worked at the Post Office and read it. No one but Zaide would know where to find Omar. The hotel had been demolished after Ahmed had sold all the camels, except Laassell who was too old to work now and the one with the blind eye who was useless. Then he scuttled back to Fes with all his millions. Omar nowadays was sometimes found, morose and melancholy, with old Muad in his shack or getting drunk in town. Zaide found him drinking beer at the back of a dark café. With a bound and a shout, Omar was on his feet and waiting for Bruno on the Zagora airstrip when he flew in. It was Omar who knew where the nomads might be. It was Omar who yelled and cursed and threatened until they admitted where they had abandoned Jalil. It was Omar, with Alex's binoculars (which he'd managed to prevent Ahmed from stealing) who had spotted a patch of blue, half hidden by a burning rock. It was Jalil. His eyes bulging through his gummed-up lids, his cracked lips and feet caked with long-dried blood and now too parched to sweat. The doctor said it had only been a matter of hours.

They took him to hospital and gave him injections to disperse the calcified stuff in his veins and stop his stomach hurting. When he'd recovered, Bruno took him to the site of Le Jardin. Great tankers full of water were arriving by the minute. Thousands of tons of sweet earth were dumped in piles all along the site. Everywhere there were tents with architects, engineers, water table experts and all manner of other experts trying to find a way to make a garden in the wasteland. Bruno asked Jalil if he'd like to take charge of the camels and the expeditions but he said no. The desert had given him a second chance and he was never going back. One must respect the desert for showing mercy. Jalil watched the experts for a moment as they scurried around like ants. Then he told Bruno where the water was. Bruno had saved his life. It was just a small spring, less than a kilometre from where the old hotel had been. A few people knew of it but had never found it necessary to tell anyone. But although the spring was small, it was enough to supplement the gallons being brought in for the man-made reservoir. They dug, they channelled and they bored. The gardens were laid out by a gardener from Spain who transported the tallest palms that could survive uprooting and imported English roses. Private pavilions sprang up around the main building, serene as the Alhambra, with one marble salon leading to another, draped with rainbow-coloured silks from Lyons. When the wind blew, not one grain of sand could infiltrate through the electronic windows that slid shut firm and tight, at the same time activating silent air-conditioning. Masons, carpenters, marble workers, tilers arrived from India, China, Rome and Essourira and the air was filled with the smell of juniper wood. A chef arrived from Paris and a pastry cook from Bruges. The vast freezers filled with strange foods from around the world. Guided by Jalil, Bruno engaged the local staff. Then it was time for the guests. Bruno asked Jalil if he would like the job of host. To be in charge. Because, as he said, one good turn deserves another and if Jalil hadn't told him where the water was, Le Jardin still might not exist. He offered him his own quarters at the far end of the gardens and a salary larger than he'd ever dreamed of. Jalil said yes. His family would never have to worry about shoes or education or his mother have to stoop to gather firewood again. And then Jalil suggested that Omar might be put in charge of the camels. As Bruno said, one good turn deserves another.

The guests arrived, those men who, it was whispered, made big decisions for the world around the crystal swimming pools and played gentle nine-hole golf on grass as green as anywhere in Ireland. Prince Charles came once and marvelled at the courage of the roses. Jalil liked him but felt sad for him as he painted pictures of the gardens, his brow furrowed and so serious. One day he said he'd like to go into the desert. With the camels fed and fit, he set off with Omar. The bodyguards were frantic as they sat around the camp fire, and Omar slapped the Prince on the back, called him 'mon ami' and tried to persuade him to smoke a joint. The Prince returned from the desert younger, lighter with fewer lines on his well-known face and declared the desert and Le Jardin paradise. He was so mellow. Jalil nearly asked him, that as he came from England, did he know Fatima? But he was there to serve and so kept silent.

He couldn't count how many times the moon had turned from sly and slender to a taunting silver disc in the dark sky. At first he wanted to throw stones at it but no one can argue with the moon and win. Men can rant and rave, live or die, but nothing happens until the moon is ready. Fatima had said she would always come back and one day she would. The Philosophe had offered to write a letter for him and Hamide urged him to telephone but Jalil believed, as he believed that she did, important things happen without words. But he listened carefully when the Philosophe explained that perhaps Fatima had found life in the kasbah hard. European women were not used to cooking with one pot, washing in a bucket and sleeping on the floor. Jalil watched the television adverts with a keen eye. With his first salary, he bought a washing machine. With the next one, a thing that burned the bread and sent it flying in the air when it was ready. And then a microwave although he wasn't sure it was correct for food to cook so fast, but the ladies on television were ecstatic about them. In Casablanca he found a carpet from England called Axminster, covered in flowers as were the cotton sheets and pillow cases. His mother washed and mended the mosquito net and he hung it over a bed he'd not yet slept in. Gradually, he found lamps with bases filled with coloured liquid and bubbles rising up and falling down, pictures of water birds and some of white horses galloping. Next he would buy a clock that played a tune when the hour struck, the same as the one Fatima had liked at his mother's house. He decided against curtains because the windows looked along an avenue of bushes covered in blue flowers, lit by lamps at night when he locked the door and made his way towards the servants' rooms behind the main part of the hotel. There, when they had served the guests, the cooks, the waiters and the gardeners withdrew and he and Omar ate tagine with their fingers as they had always done.

Jalil stubbed out his cigarette and looked at his watch. A few weeks ago Bruno had made a rare visit to his rooms, to talk about the next guests to arrive. As he'd done the first time that he'd seen it, he declared the place 'astonishing'.

'Ah, Tretchikoff,' he murmured, looking at the picture of the horses. Then he asked Jalil if he'd ever ridden horses. Would he like to? Jalil said he would have to learn to understand them as they were very different from camels. Bruno agreed, they were very different from camels. He then decided that Jalil should learn to play polo. And now Jalil had heard there was a stable somewhere in the foothills outside Ouarzazate where they had horses. He'd promised to visit them today. And also, the man who was looking for the musical clock had sent word that he'd found one. He searched his pockets for the ignition key and looked once more at the plane just touching down. As he had looked so often at planes coming in from London, at Casablanca, Marrakesh, Agadir and Tangier, searching for Fatima among the pale-faced passengers blinking in the bright light. Once or twice he thought he'd seen her and his heart had leaped. But it wasn't her. The way those women walked and held their heads was wrong and he'd turned away. Again he wondered if it was a day for miracles, but the policeman had said this plane was coming in from Paris.

It hit the tarmac with a light bump. The passengers sighed with relief. The last twenty minutes had been frightening, as if the tips of the wings might touch the dry mountainside at any minute. Flo, an unread book on her lap, her immigration card clutched in her hand, still had a thousand apprehensions. The card required that one should state where one was staying but she hadn't dared to think that far ahead. The kasbah? That would be tempting fate and she'd never known its address. Scheherezade? Where she would look for Jalil and learn if he was married to a young brown wife and now had brown-eyed babies. Or if he'd gone off at last to Timbuktu. Or if he'd turned into a sullen starer in a café. Or if he'd forgotten her. And then she'd have to write down La Fibule where she would stay a day and steal away again. The passengers were standing up, searching for their hand luggage. The musak played and they were rolling the steps towards the open door. Even from where she still was sitting, she could feel the air was warmer. Then she was at immigration, still unsure about her address. The man smiled and suggested she write down Zagora. He said he'd do it for her, then stamped her passport. She walked on to the baggage hall and waited for the carousel to bring her case.

Jalil saw her first. She was just the same. And it was a day for miracles. As he backed the Range Rover out of its place, a boy ran up to him and said his uncle in the coffee shop had a package for him. The clock man had left it, knowing he'd be unable to stop to pick up parcels if he had the prime minister with him. Jalil reparked the Range Rover, walked behind the boy and picked up his clock from the coffee shop. And the passengers, quite quick today, were already going through customs. She was just the same, a book under her arm and her grey shawl tangled in her trolley. The customs man waved her through. She heaved her case on to the trolley. And then she saw him. He was just the same. He was looking at her with a smile that could outshine the sun. She stood and blushed and walked towards him, looking as if she'd just been blown through a blizzard of rose petals.

They walked quietly to the car park, soft silence more potent than any protestations of surprise or passion. Jalil opened the door of the Range Rover for her and slipped the clock beneath the passenger seat. Fatima turned and asked him if they'd be back in time to see the sun set over Jebel Kissane and he told her he was sure they would. She settled down on top of the clock. Jalil helped her with her seat belt and then leaned over to make sure that all the doors were locked.

Warner Books now offers an exciting range of quality titles by both established and new authors. All of the books in this series are available from:

Little, Brown and Company (UK),
P.O. Box 11,
Falmouth,
Cornwall TR10 9EN.

Fax No: 01326 317444.
Telephone No: 01326 372400
E-mail: books@barni.avel.co.uk

Payments can be made as follows: cheque, postal order (payable to Little, Brown and Company) or by credit cards, Visa/Access. Do not send cash or currency. UK customers and B.F.P.O. please allow £1.00 for postage and packing for the first book, plus 50p for the second book, plus 30p for each additional book up to a maximum charge of £3.00 (7 books plus).

Overseas customers including Ireland, please allow £2.00 for the first book plus £1.00 for the second book, plus 50p for each additional book.

NAME (Block Letters) ....

....

ADDRESS ....

....

....

☐ I enclose my remittance for ....

☐ I wish to pay by Access/Visa Card

Number ☐☐☐☐☐☐☐☐☐☐☐☐☐☐☐☐

Card Expiry Date ☐☐☐☐

....